All Other Sins

by JK Ellem

ALSO AVAILABLE BY JK ELLEM

Stand Alone Novels
Mill Point Road
All Other Sins

The Killing Seasons
Book 1 A Winter's Kill
Book 2 A Spring Kill – coming soon

No Justice Series
Book 1 No Justice
Book 2 Cold Justice
Book 3 American Justice
Book 4 Hidden Justice
Book 5 Raw Justice

Deadly Touch Series
Fast Read Deadly Touch

Octagon Trilogy (DystopianThriller Series)
Prequel Soldiers Field
Book 1 Octagon
Book 2 Infernum
Book 3 Sky of Thorns – coming soon

All Other Sins

by JK Ellem

Chapter 1

The bad always came first.

It was better that way—for you, not for them.

Calmly and without emotion, tell them exactly the predicament they are in. Give them a moment for it to sink in, for their eyes to meet yours, for them to realize you're not joking. Finally, the expression on their face will sag, droop, and eventually fall. Their mask, broken.

Then you offer them an olive branch, just the tiniest slither of hope, of redemption—provided there was one to offer. Most times there wasn't. Only the cold, hard realization that they had seconds, not years, to live.

"I'll give you just thirty seconds to tell me the access codes, or I'll put a bullet in your head."

And there it was, all perfectly sequenced by Alex Romano, a master at delivering such a message. Not her message, but her father's. Luca Romano.

If it was her brother, Vincent, not herself, who had been sent as emissary to deliver such a message, then Alex was certain the man in front of her now would already be dead. That was Vincent's style: shoot first, ask questions later, even of a wordless corpse. However, when it came to the matter of retrieving access codes to an offshore bank account in the Dominican Republic, where two million dollars of Romano family money had been siphoned into during a three-year period, the task would have been made much more difficult if the man, who knew the codes, was dead before he was given a chance to disclose them.

Not impossible, just more cumbersome.

She already knew a few banking officials in Santo Domingo she could call on.

Alex looked around her.

It was a place of killing, where many had been brought before to die. The cold, dusty cement floor bore the dull red stains of that fact. No matter how hard you scrubbed, rubbed, and hosed blood, once it seeped in, it was almost impossible to remove.

After all these years, the electric chain hoist still worked, which was surprising. It was a testament to American workmanship and quality lubricating oil applied by a diligent operator. The hoist—while designed for lifting bodies—was never intended for the purpose it was being used for today.

For one, it had a load capacity of three tons…six thousand pounds. Joseph Durango weighed considerably less at one hundred sixty pounds. Secondly, the hoist was designed to lift deadweight, and Durango was very much alive—for the moment at least.

Durango tilted his chin down toward his chest, and glared defiantly at Alex Romano. "I don't know what you're talking about!" he snarled.

Alex cocked her head, let out a slow exhale. *Stubborn to the end.*

The conversation between them had started out cordially enough, with the two of them seated on chairs facing each other in the cold, cavernous space; old machinery, seized with rust and decay, hunkered in the shadows around them. But now it was just Alex sitting on her chair. Durango's chair sat toppled on its side, one leg broken when it was kicked out from under him.

Questions had been asked, the truth not forthcoming. So the meeting had escalated into an interrogation.

Alex leaned forward and looked at Durango's inverted face, his head where his ankles should be. His ankles were wrapped in thick chain as he hung from underneath the hoist like a carcass, his head a foot or so off the cement. Appropriate given the surroundings.

"I've done nothing wrong," Durango continued with his denials.

Raising one hand, Alex began counting off on her fingers Durango's betrayals. "I know you set up an offshore bank account. I know you have transferred close to two million into it. Money that was skimmed from the business my family entrusted you to run and manage for them. I know you intend to catch a plane to Miami in two days. From there you will leave the country...for good." Alex stood up, her patience wearing thin. Despite the long winter coat she wore, the air inside the abandoned slaughterhouse was frigid. "There is no point in denying any of it." Alex slid out her cell phone. "I have it all on here. It's only by the grace of God that my father sent me, and not someone else, to talk to you, to convince you to return the money."

Durango's body shifted, twisted slightly, but his look of contempt remained fixed in place. He knew full well whom Alex was referring to. That's why he had been so coy, so reluctant at first to admit to anything, especially to this woman. "It's my money. I deserve it. I've worked hard over the years. Made your family a lot of money—"

"For which you were handsomely paid," Alex cut in. There was no denying Durango had run the Midwestern trucking business in Wisconsin well for the last five years. Profits steadily grew each year, margins increased, costs were down. In reality, though, most of these improvements had come thanks to Alex

Romano's business acumen, direction, and guidance, which she had fed Durango over the years, since her father had first purchased the business, saving it and its sixty employees from the brink of bankruptcy. Durango was simply a tool, an employee, like the others who managed the various family business interests. Their efforts were monitored and they were held accountable by Alex Romano back at the family head office in New Jersey. A deep audit of the last two years' financial records for the trucking business had alerted Alex to a trail of bogus invoices to non-existent suppliers.

"You also seem to forget that we covered your medical bills when you were injured," Alex continued. "Then paid for full medical coverage for your family. Paid you bonuses as well. Set up a college fund for your three sons and also paid into it each year." Alex stepped closer, disbelief in her eyes. "And you still stole from us?"

"It wasn't enough!"

Alex knew for men like Durango, no amount of money would ever be enough. He had an incurable weakness for the horses and the slots. And, unlike his job over the years, neither had been profitable pursuits. Everything that he had earned, including the generous performance bonuses, and what was contributed into his kids' college fund, was now gone, bled dry. Alex doubted that the two million he had squirrelled away in the Dominican Republic would last long. Two years, three at most. Whoever coined the phrase "A fool and his money are soon parted" had Joe Durango in mind. It only further angered Alex knowing where the pilfered money would end up.

Costa, a fiercely loyal, quiet and unassuming foot soldier for the family stood behind the trussed up Durango, the control pad to the hoist in his hand.

They had plucked Durango from a warm bed an hour ago. Not his own bed, but the bed he shared one night a week with his considerably younger girlfriend. According to Durango's wife, her husband would pull an "all-nighter" at work once a week. That's how "committed" he was to the business. He would then stumble back home in the early hours of the next morning, too exhausted to talk to his wife, and slump into their marital bed.

The doe-eyed, naive, and waif-like girlfriend was almost half Durango's age. Her drowsy expression soon filled with fear when Costa materialized out of a dark corner in the bedroom of their love nest, pointed a gun at her head, and brought a finger to his lips. Alex remained in the warm comfort of the rented sedan parked at the curb outside the apartment building with the motor running. No doubt Durango intended to take the girl with him, not tell his wife or children, just leave like the thief in the night he was. New life, new wife. To hell with the consequences.

His wife would also inherit the huge mortgage and other debts he had racked up. Durango didn't want to pay off his mortgage with the stolen money, reasoning that it would draw too much suspicion from the bank as to where the funds had come from. No, he much preferred to maintain the illusion to his wife and kids and to the townsfolk that he was a devoted father and husband, a hard-working pillar of the community who always sat in the front pew of their local church on Sunday.

A trickle of red dripped from Durango's mouth. The cement floor of the abandoned slaughterhouse once again tasting blood.

"You think you're so much better, don't you?" Durango hissed, contempt in his eyes as he glared up at Alex. "With your Ivy-League upbringing and Harvard education. Beneath all your fancy clothes and finery, you're just a criminal like the rest of your family."

Alex didn't respond. She glanced at Costa, then raised an upturned palm.

Costa slid out his handgun from where he kept it tucked under his jacket and handed it to Alex.

Alex looked down at the gun in her hand, the feel and weight not unfamiliar. Her father had insisted that, at a very early age, she should become proficient at using one, despite being his only daughter.

Durango craned his neck, trying to see what she was doing with the gun, his groin in line with Alex's chest.

The time for talk was over. Alex pressed the barrel of the gun to Durango's groin. Immediately the man began to squirm and wriggle on the chain.

Good, Alex thought. She had guessed correctly. Despite all of his bravado, he was less fearful of dying, and more worried about going on living minus his functioning genitalia.

She pushed the barrel in harder, deeper until she felt it hit his pelvic bone.

"Wait! Wait!" Durango pleaded. His voice had gone up a few octaves, girl-like.

Alex ignored his protests and began to squeeze the trigger.

"Please!" Durango screamed. "I'll tell you! I'll tell you anything!"

Alex didn't relent. She pressed in harder, pushing Durango's body away using just the gun barrel. "The access codes," she said calmly.

Durango's lips suddenly spewed forth a babble of numbers, letters, and symbols, repeating the sequence twice.

Keeping the gun in place and pressure on the trigger, Alex

thumbed her cell phone with her other hand. Sixty seconds later she had accessed the offshore account, changed the access code to her own creation, and transferred the money back to the Romano main operating account, but not before making a separate deposit into another bank account.

Satisfied, Alex pocketed her cell phone but kept the gun barrel in place. "You will not return home. You will not contact your wife or children at all. You will leave town today and never return. If your feet so much as touch a single blade of grass on your wife's front lawn, my colleague here will cut them off and return them to you as bookends. Capisce?"

Durango nodded and breathed a visible sigh of relief.

Alex withdrew the gun and handed it back to Costa. She bent down so she was eye-level with Durango's face. "You will live for as long as we allow you to live. Do I make myself clear?"

Durango nodded profusely.

Alex stood up and nodded at Costa, who released the hook on the hoist, dropping the man not so delicately onto the cement floor.

Alex regarded the moaning Durango for a moment, his legs splayed, then promptly kicked him in the groin. If testicles were baseballs, Durango's would have cleared The Green Monster wall at Fenway Park.

Alex stood over Durango as he writhed and convulsed on the ground, his face contorted in pain, both hands clutching at what was most precious to him. "Your wife sends her regards."

Leaving the echoing sobs in her wake, Alex turned and walked toward the door, her high heels clicking on the cold cement as she went.

Standing outside next to the parked sedan, Alex placed a call and watched the dark sky slowly burn brighter in the east while four miles to the west, a cell phone on a table in a darkened kitchen rang just once before being answered.

"Mrs. Durango. It's done." Alex listened, then nodded. "Yes, I gave him your message." Mist swirled around Alex's legs as she spoke. She pictured the woman on the other end of the call sitting at the kitchen table, a pile of sodden tissues next to her. It was the same table Alex had sat at just two hours ago, watching the same woman contemplate the rest of her life. What she had—or thought she had—was no more, as Alex explained to her in full and clear detail about her husband, the double life he was leading, and the ultimate betrayal he was about to bring upon her and their two sons.

Then Alex offered Kim Durango an olive branch, hope, when the distraught wife and mother thought she had none.

"No. He's not dead. But he won't be bothering you or your sons anymore. He will vanish—that is unless you want him back?"

Kim Durango didn't want him back.

"Good, then everything is in place, as we discussed."

Then another question.

"It's been taken care of Mrs. Durango. You don't have to worry about your boys' education." Like so many mothers, all that mattered to Kim Durango was her children, their future. *Sacrifice* was the word that came to mind as Alex listened. "You don't have to thank me. Your loyalty now and in the future will be thanks enough. The operations manager is expecting you first thing Monday morning." Kim Durango was more than qualified to step into her husband's shoes. She had trained as a CPA. However at her husband's insistence, she had given up her promising career after he had taken the job at the trucking company. He didn't want her to work anymore, Kim Durango had explained to Alex. Alex had put it down to manipulation and control rather than husbandly consideration. Joe Durango didn't want his wife to have independence, something that usually came with earning a wage. Instead, he wanted her at home, dependent on him, vulnerable, subservient.

"Sorry, what was that?" The call cut out then returned. Alex frowned and looked up as Costa walked out of the building alone. The lights of the sedan blipped, and Alex slid into the leather back seat and shut the door, cutting off the world outside and the violence that was a necessary part of her job.

"Why do I think you'll do a good job, Mrs. Durango?" Alex said, repeating the question she had just been asked. Alex glanced out of the side window at the crumbling building as they slowly drove away, picturing Joe Durango squirming on the floor, clutching his groin. "Because you are a lot smarter than your husband, Mrs. Durango. That's why."

Chapter 2

"Is this Room 212?"

The woman holding the door open glanced at the three numbers on the door.

212.

"It says so on the door," the woman said, opening the door a little farther, welcoming the visitor inside.

Diane Miller hesitated, then subconsciously took a step back, as though the woman holding the door open, with the kind eyes and warm smile, was an ugly old witch standing at the entrance to her cottage deep in the woods, evil lurking in the periphery behind her, just out of frame.

"Mrs. Miller?" the woman asked, opening the door a little wider, revealing a little more of what lay beyond.

Diane Miller nodded, clutching her bag to her chest. The face behind the door was unfamiliar, so was the faint scent that drifted out from the room beyond. Sandalwood perhaps?

"You're my ten o'clock."

"Where's Dr. Farrell? My usual therapist?" Diane asked, her anxiety rising.

"He had to go away. An urgent personal matter. I'm covering for him for the next few weeks." Despite the smile, there was a hint of concern in her eyes. "I'm Dr. Amelia Redding." Dr. Redding had short black hair, severe straight bangs, brown attentive eyes, and a slight build…older than Diane, maybe mid-forties. Tastefully dressed. No wedding ring. Diane noticed such things.

Wedding rings were a sign for Diane: whether a person was bound and chained or free and unhindered. Diane had never thought about such inconsequential things before. Only in the last twelve months had such bitter thoughts begun to emerge in her mind. Diane subconsciously rubbed her thumb along the underside of the band of gold on her fourth finger as she appraised Dr. Redding.

Redding watched Diane's indecisiveness—a gazelle drinking at a waterhole, sensing danger, wondering whether to stay or flee—before quickly adding, "I have read your file. I'm completely up-to-date with everything you and Dr. Farrell have discussed, if that's what's concerning you." Redding was now a little more than curious about Diane Miller. Curious as to what had turned this once strong-minded, determined woman into the skittish, unsteady person who stood before her.

Diane thought for a moment. She had never had a female therapist before. Slowly her cautiousness gave way to the glimmer of new possibilities, of hope. A new perspective, a woman's empathy instead of a man's judgmental stare. Solace not pity. A different kind of understanding—perhaps.

Diane did feel the sessions with Dr. Farrell were useful. However, there was a certain black-and-whiteness to him. A removed, clinical style to his therapy. At times he could display understanding, nodding sympathetically at the right moments as Diane spilled forth her fears and paranoia to him. Other times, he was very matter-of-fact, like he was quoting, verbatim, passages from a textbook on psychology, rather than truly having a deep understanding of her. Then again, no one could have a deep understanding of her unless they had experienced what she had.

Time heals nothing. Only determination does—and a lot of medication.

Redding stood aside, beckoning Diane into the warmly lit room. "I thought it would be easier to use his room," she said. "Keep up the appearance of familiarity, the same environment and all that."

Diane stepped over the threshold, and the door closed promptly behind her. She found herself in the same scene repeated from the previous week, and the week before that, and every week for the last six months. The gentle hum of the air conditioning. The comfortable, low-slung, soft furnishings in passive colors. The reassuring, dark-framed qualifications of academic trust and credibility on the wall behind the desk. The tall potted plants, broad dark green leaves, waxy and glossy under the recessed subdued lighting. Sights and sounds that spoke of comfort and reassurance to Diane. The only difference was the essential oil diffuser, which sat on a small side table, a steady curl of smoke spiraling up into the processed air.

Definitely sandalwood. Better than the smell of lemon-scented cleaning wipes Dr. Farrell used to wipe a smudge or mark off his pristine desk while he listened intently to Diane.

Diane sat down in her usual chair, a plush oversized armchair with fat arms and a deep comfy cushioned seat.

Redding sat opposite, in a rigid chair, her posture upright. Correct lumbar support chosen over a sleepy, relaxed state. She opened a leather-bound notebook, placed it on her lap, unscrewed a fountain pen, then looked up expectantly at Diane. Taking her time, Redding observed her for a moment: Diane's posture, hand and arm placement…the subtle nuances: movement of her eyes, at the corners of her mouth, the tightness of the muscles in her jaw. Redding had been awake late last night reading Diane's file, preparing herself for this session, like she had done with all the other patients she was scheduled to see today.

Diane Miller, thirty-two years old, enlisted corporal in the U.S. Army, a drone operator, surveillance specialist, with three tours of Iraq under her belt. Diane Miller had an exemplary military record. While she wasn't high up in the chain of command, she was dedicated, confident, had leadership potential. The military brass looking down from lofty heights above had their eye on her.

However, that version of Diane Miller seemed like a far cry from the woman who sat opposite Redding, almost as if the woman's past achievements and stature had shrunken, withered, leaving a thin, gaunt shadow of her former self, wearing clothing that seemed oversized for her. Diane Miller's file sat on the desk behind Dr. Redding. Although Redding had briefly reviewed the file, she preferred to make her own notes, formulate her own assessment of the woman, rather than be swayed by someone else's diagnosis. However, Redding could understand how Diane Miller had fallen to where she now lay. The trauma she had experienced in the last twelve months would have broken anyone. This once-confident, self-assured, self-reliant and resourceful young woman was now filled with anxiety and self-doubt.

"How are you feeling, Diane?"

Diane gave a terse smile. "Fine—I guess."

Redding made a note in her journal. She knew Dr. Farrell was a fan of voice-recording these sessions, having them transcribed later for the file. Redding much preferred using ink on paper. It seemed more personal, less intimidating. She imagined how her own patients would react if she suddenly pulled out a digital recorder, thrust it down in front of them, as though they were giving a legal deposition, their words, comments, forever kept, maybe later twisted and used against them. No room for misinterpretation or misconstruing what they had said.

"How is the medication going?" Redding asked, her voice neutral. "I read that Dr. Farrell increased the dosage two weeks ago. How are you coping with that increase?" Redding made a note to look back at the file later, to locate the reason for increasing Diane's dosage. She couldn't find any documentation as to the reason for the increase when she had done the first pass through Diane Miller's file. According to what she had read so far, Diane Miller was already on a fairly high dosage of antidepressants, selective serotonin reuptake inhibitors, or SSRIs. In layman's terms, their role was to block the brain from telling you that you are sad.

Feeling a little more relaxed with Dr. Redding, Diane settled deeper into the armchair. It was her eyes, her voice. The way she looked at Diane, total concentration on her and nothing else. Her words held a genuine concern for Diane's wellbeing. She was different than Dr. Farrell. Dr. Farrell at times seemed as though he was just going through the motions, asking and recording, checking boxes off some questionnaire. His manner a little impersonal perhaps, Diane felt. And Dr. Farrell never came out from behind his desk during the sessions, preferring to instill a barrier between them—and also to fidget with straightening his pens and desk pad.

"It has helped," Diane said, her hands restless in her lap. "The medication, the higher dosage, has taken the edge off. I feel"— she searched for the right word—"better." Not happier, but better.

"And the mornings?" Redding asked, jotting in her journal. "When you first wake up. How do you feel then?" Redding knew the dosage had a tendency to leave the patient slightly doughy in the morning, almost lethargic. She scanned through the pages of file notes in her mind. Diane Miller was different, so Redding had taken the extra time to read the file last night, committing most of what she could to memory. It wasn't that Diane Miller's file was any thicker or thinner or different than the others. It had more to do with what Diane had said, what she had mentioned during her last session with Dr. Farrell a week ago. Something that Farrell noted in the file, then dismissed as just a case of "slight paranoia." Redding wanted to explore it further.

"I feel fine, like I said. The dosage is helping. Better than before."

Redding made another note.

Diane shifted in the armchair, her eyes watching as Redding's fountain pen scribbled across the page of her journal.

Redding looked up. "And are you eating?"

Diane frowned.

"You have lost a lot of weight over the months," Redding added, pointing at Diane with her fountain pen. Diane Miller's file contained her military stats, the results of her Army physicals, her annual fitness tests. From these, Redding had formed a mental picture of how Diane Miller would look. To say she was mildly shocked when Diane Miller knocked on the door a few minutes ago was an understatement. Redding guessed that Diane Miller was perhaps seventy percent her original weight and muscle mass compared to when she was in the Army. Clothes that once fit now hung loose and baggy from a frame that appeared to be all bone and sinew.

"I'm eating," Diane said unconvincingly. "I just don't have much of an appetite these days."

Redding nodded. "The increased dosage can have that effect." Redding made a note to order a new blood workup for

15

Diane, just to make sure. Redding placed her pen in the fold of her journal and looked up again. She needed to ask her. There was no point in skipping over it, even if Dr. Farrell casually dismissed it in his file notes. Redding wanted to hear from the woman's own mouth, in her own words, the full explanation why she had said what she said. There probably wasn't anything of concern in it. But Redding wanted to be thorough.

She smiled at Diane.

Diane moved uncomfortably in the armchair, almost as though she knew what was coming.

"Diane."

Diane nodded.

"In your last session with Dr. Farrell, you mentioned something."

Diane shifted her gaze to her hands in her lap. She wasn't crazy, and she didn't have a wild imagination either. It was just something she honestly felt at times. She couldn't explain it. Dr. Farrell had listened to her, then told her that it was perhaps her imagination, state of mind, or both.

"You said something to him. Do you remember?"

Diane finally looked up and nodded.

Redding stared directly into Diane Miller's eyes, and asked, "Can you tell why you believe your husband is trying to kill you?"

Chapter 3

The first mistake was stealing the cargo van.

But Anton Wheeler needed the cash. Had he actually known what was inside the van, he would have ditched it, taken what was hidden there, and flown directly to Vegas instead.

Everyone was running from something. In Anton Wheeler's case, he was running *toward* something. That "something" was a cocktail waitress named Mandy he had met online two months ago. Although he had only known her for a short time, their relationship had miraculously flourished, mainly due to the steady flow of cash Anton had poured into it. Instead of trading attention and affection for love, he was trading cash for it—his cash, and unfortunately, the relationship had drained most of his resources. As much as he didn't like to admit it, loneliness had also played a significant part in Anton's sudden brashness. For some reason, women weren't exactly falling over themselves to approach him, meet him, talk to him. His last girlfriend had left him six months ago, telling him as she walked out the door that he was the worst lay she had ever had. With his already low self-esteem suitably damaged, Anton had found solace in the online dating sites, where courage, confidence, and good looks could be easily exaggerated.

Then he met Mandy, who had promised him they would meet, eventually.

Their relationship started off innocently enough with what looked like a misdirected message from an attractive woman that had landed on Anton's cell phone during a shift at a not-for-profit commercial laundry where he worked as a delivery driver. Anton had ignored the message for a few days. Then, as the mundane days dragged on, he found himself a little more curious as to who the woman was. Then there was the photo she had attached to the next message, taken in her bikini, lying next to a swimming pool at what looked like a luxury resort, the sun glistening off her bronzed, oiled body. Finally, Anton gave in and messaged her back, explaining that she had mistaken him for someone else; he wasn't the person she was looking for. The woman replied almost immediately, saying how sorry she was for the error and asked Anton what he thought of the picture of her by the pool. If he thought she had a nice body. Did he have a girlfriend? What did he do for work?

Things quickly escalated from there.

First came selfies of the woman posing in skimpy underwear. Then selfies of her minus her skimpy underwear. And most recently, a live stream video of her performing an exploratory examination of herself while holding her cell phone at arm's length. Such footage would have had most gynecologists miffed as to how incredibly flexible the woman was. The video had been the clincher for Anton.

Then the videos and pictures suddenly stopped. A few days passed without word from Mandy despite a flurry of texts Anton had sent. After a week of silence, Mandy contacted Anton, told him she was sorry, that she had been fired from her job and had been too upset to text, and had spent her lonely days at home crying. She had tried to get another job, but no one was employing cocktail waitresses at the moment. She told Anton she had considered stripping, but Anton talked her out of it. He said she didn't need to resort to that kind of work. Instead, Anton wired her some money. Mandy was so appreciative, promising to repay him when she got back on her feet again.

Then, much to Anton's delight, the videos and pictures resumed. The bank transfers became more frequent, matching the frequency of her stories of financial distress. She was behind in her rent. Her car registration was due. She needed a new cell phone. Anton Wheeler didn't mind helping her out. He was now officially in cyber love, an affliction so many fall victim to. He didn't care how he would get the money—he would just get it. Their relationship blossomed. Commitments of love and devotion ensued along with Mandy's promise that Anton was the only man for her. She couldn't wait until they met up in Vegas, where she would repay him for his generosity with more than just money.

Anton had been a loyal employee for the not-for-profit for twelve months now, transporting laundry back-and-forth between hotels around town. However it was now time to move on, meet the woman, maybe settle down with her, swap the cold dark winters of Nebraska for the warmth, bright lights, and endless possibilities of Vegas.

Anton forwent the measly severance payment he would have received from his employer and decided to take the van instead and run. He reckoned he could get at least ten grand cash for it, maybe more. He knew people who knew people in the commercial vehicle dealing game who assured him it would be an easy sell. He just had to swap out the plates and deliver the van to them. He'd brought the stolen plates with him to work that morning and quickly swapped them out when he was out of the yard.

Ten miles out from Grand Island, heading west along the old highway toward the rendezvous point, Anton Wheeler made his second mistake. Pulling into a gas station to refuel, Anton didn't notice that other eyes were watching him and the stolen van. After paying cash for the gas and grabbing a takeout cup filled with strong black coffee, Anton climbed back into the van. All loved-up, as well as gassed up, he couldn't wait to sell the van, get his cash, board a plane, and head west to where his love was waiting for him. He just had to wire the cash to her, like he had done all the other times before.

To save money, Anton thought about getting a cheap rental, driving the twelve hundred miles to Colorado, then through Utah before dipping south into Nevada. But he was an impatient man, and being impatient meant you were prone to carelessness, being sloppy. With his head filled with thoughts of what he was going to do to Mandy when they finally met, Anton Wheeler didn't notice the security cameras discreetly watching him from above.

Chapter 4

At the drugstore, Diane dropped off the new prescription Dr. Redding had given her.

It was a new kind of medication, still effective but with fewer side effects. Redding had explained that, in her professional opinion, the dosage Dr. Farrell had prescribed was too strong and could explain the continued feelings of being lethargic, having no energy, and having the overall lack of awareness she had been experiencing lately. At times, these side effects would linger throughout Diane's entire day. Nervousness, agitation, insomnia, loss of appetite leading to weight loss. Diane Miller displayed all these but at a more pronounced level.

Redding wanted to get Diane off her current meds and on something new. She would take full responsibility and would advise Dr. Farrell of the change upon his return.

The young store assistant said it would take about ten minutes for the prescription to be filled, so Diane browsed the hair and beauty products aisle—an unfamiliar place for her in recent months—while she waited. Usually Greg would come to the drugstore to fill her prescription before she ran out, but Diane wanted to get started on the course of new meds right away.

Diane glanced in the small mirror at the top of a rotating sunglass display, noticing several loose strands of gray. A few more seemed to have sprouted since she last seriously took a look at herself. She avoided most reflective surfaces. The oven door. Windows at night. The rearview mirror. As she looked at herself, the woman in the reflection saddened her…but apparently not enough to do something about it. It hadn't always been that way, though. Maybe she should get a new hair color. She had never worn makeup in the Army, even during downtime. Not that there was really any downtime. Being in the armed forces meant being in an ever-present state of readiness.

Diane browsed the row of small cardboard boxes of hair dyes. Dozens of beautiful faces with glossy, shiny hair smiled back at her with perfect white teeth and the promise of salon-quality results for under ten bucks.

Ash blond perhaps?

"Diane?"

Diane looked up, slightly startled.

The voice came from over the top shelf in front of her. A woman stood on the other side, a smile on her unfamiliar face.

"Diane, it's me, Martha. Martha Hendricks."

Diane continued to stare at the woman, unsure if she was talking to her or someone else. But the aisle was empty except for Diane.

Diane tried to concentrate, place the woman's face. The woman started to look vaguely familiar now, as Diane began to brush away the dust and dirt covering her mind. But she couldn't exactly place the face or the name.

"You look great," Martha Hendricks lied. Martha, a kind soul, believed it was the right thing to do in the moment. Truth was, Martha was shocked, almost didn't recognize the emaciated, washed-out features of her friend who she was seeing for the first time in almost a year.

Diane continued to stare at the woman, trying her hardest to think back to whom she was. Slowly she remembered: Martha Hendricks, mother of three whose daughter was at the same school as Ella, Diane's daughter. Diane felt a slice of pain at the memory. Another ghost from the past, dragged up to remind her of Ella. Martha and Diane weren't good friends, just acquaintances. Over the years, however, they had grown to know each other more, swapped stories about the school, the town, their daughters.

Diane shook her head, sweeping away more dust and dirt in her mind. "I'm sorry, Martha. I didn't recognize you for a moment." And that was the truth.

Martha smiled. She could understand. "I haven't seen you in ages. Must be twelve months at least." Martha wanted to add, "since the funeral," because that would be factually correct. However, she kept the words buttoned up. "How are you coping?"

Diane gave a look that said, *average, just getting by.*

Martha leaned across the top of the shelf and lowered her voice. "Look, if you ever want to catch up over coffee, or just talk, then let me know. Anytime."

For the last twelve months, Diane had lived like a hermit, only coming out for therapy sessions and occasional runs to the grocery, if she was up to it. In that time no one, including her friends, had really contacted her. Maybe they felt Diane didn't want the company, wanted to be alone. Maybe it would be a good idea to talk to Martha. "I would like that very much," Diane finally said, her voice unsure, hesitant. "No, let's do that," she affirmed, feeling more confident after her session with Dr. Redding.

"Good. Let's do that." Martha pulled out her cell phone. "The odd thing is that I did try calling you over the last few months—not to pry or anything," she added hastily. "But just to check on you. See how you were doing. See if I could help."

Diane frowned. She couldn't recall receiving a phone call

from Martha. Come to think of it, she hadn't received any phone calls in the last few months at all. Diane pulled out her cell phone and thumbed the screen. There were no notifications, missed calls, or text messages. Her inbox was completely empty. Nothing. She had no reason to use her cell phone, though, or check it constantly like she used to. Twice a day Greg would call her—once in the morning and then again in the afternoon—to see how she was. Apart from that, the phone lay idle. Dormant. Inert. Almost like how Diane felt at times.

"When did you call?" Diane asked, now puzzled.

"A few times in the last couple of months. But I just got the same disconnection message. So I didn't bother anymore."

Disconnection?

Diane glanced at her phone again. "Try my number now," she said, holding it up for Martha to see the screen.

Martha opened up her *Contacts* page, found Diane's number, and called it. She switched the phone to speaker and held it up to Diane.

Moments later Diane could hear a hollow robotic message through the speaker of Martha's phone, telling her that her own cell phone was disconnected. Diane looked at the cell phone in her hand. Nothing. The screen was lit and the little icon said she had full signal strength.

"I didn't know you changed your number," Martha said, ending the call. "I really thought you might have gone away, moved to another state, started a new life."

"I haven't. I didn't." Diane felt confused. "I've always had the same cell phone number. I've been here, around, the whole time." Just then Diane's pager buzzer vibrated in her hand. Her prescription was ready. "Look Martha, I've got to go. Give me your cell number."

Martha read out the number, and Diane entered it into her phone.

"Give me a call when you can," Martha said. "Don't leave it too long. Let's catch up this week."

Diane nodded before heading off to the counter.

Chapter 5

The truth was, Anton Wheeler had no idea what was really in the back of the van.

All he saw were piles of bed linen and towels, freshly laundered and neatly folded into crisp stacks tied with recycled plastic strapping. He didn't care about the cargo. It was the problem of the person who was going to buy the van—not his.

He had a few miles to go before he reached the rendezvous point, so he pressed the gas pedal some more, ignoring the speed limit. He didn't want to be late just in case the buyer got cold feet. He had a gun stashed between the armrest and the seat. Just in case the deal went sideways. He wasn't going to lose the van or be cheated out of a fair price. It was his ticket west to where all the pleasures he had been fantasizing about for so long waited for him.

Flat barren fields of dull yellow and gray sped past, and the narrow ribbon of blacktop stretched away in front of him, all the way to the base of a band of mountain ridges in the hazy distance. There were no houses, settlements of any kind, just a wide, empty landscape.

Anton checked his rearview mirror, saw an infinitesimally small shimmering speck in the distance. Ignoring the dark speck, he focused on the road ahead and pressed the gas some more. The van groaned then lurched forward even faster. A creeping unease fell over Anton, the kind of feeling you get that something is sneaking up behind you. Anton's eyes narrowed as he glanced in the rearview mirror again. The speck had now grown into a blob, getting steadily larger as he watched. He forced himself to remain calm. It was nothing, just another car, but it was closing rapidly on him, too rapidly for his liking. He touched the brakes and bled off some speed, slowing the van back under the limit. He would let them pass. Probably just someone like him running late for an appointment.

"Damn it." To Anton's horror, the blob morphed into an unmistakable shape, with a distinctive light-bar mounted on its roof. Moments later the lights and siren came on. Dread gripped Anton as he saw all his plans slowly collapse into dust around him. Maybe he could apologize for speeding, just get a warning, then move on. He eased back on the gas and coasted over to the shoulder of the highway, the van streaming a dusty funnel of dirt and grit behind it. He glanced down to where the gun lay, hidden from the view from the driver's side window. He grabbed the side mirror, swiveled it until he could see a woman in uniform in the sheriff's cruiser behind him.

Sheriff Meredith Charmers eased out of the driver's seat and adjusted her duty belt. Someone was definitely in a hurry, she thought as she regarded the cargo van pulled over twenty yards ahead of her. She could see large blue lettering plastered across the hinged cargo doors at the rear of the van. Charmers headed toward the driver's side window, unbuttoning the strap on her holster as she went.

The window was down, a young and nervous face glanced at her as she stepped alongside. The man's eyes were darting back-and-forth, as he forced a smile at her.

"Did I do anything wrong, sheriff?" Wheeler asked, glad it was a woman not a man. Maybe she would cut him some slack if he acted dumb.

"Where are you going in such a hurry?" Charmers asked.

"I'm making a delivery, clean laundry." Anton flashed a smile and thumbed behind him.

Charmers leaned back and looked along the length of the van. She turned back to the nervous young man. "I know what you're carrying but what the hell are you doing all the way out here? There isn't a hotel or motel around here for miles."

Anton's best smile froze into a guilty grimace. The unanticipated question threw him. He fumbled then found an unconvincing answer. "Special delivery." His hands came off the steering wheel and into his lap.

Charmers glanced down, the movement not lost on her. Something didn't seem right to her. The guy was jittery, nervous. Not telling the truth.

Anton slid one hand down between the armrest, his fingers feeling the cold steel of his gun.

Charmers's hand went to her gun, the webbing of her right hand sliding firm under the beavertail, her fingers curling around the grip, ready to draw. "Keep your hands where I can see them, sir."

Anton thrust his hands up. "Okay, lady. Stay cool."

"Can I see some identification please: driver's license and vehicle registration?"

Anton reached for the glove box while keeping one hand still raised. "Registration is in the glove box."

Charmers nodded and stepped back, opening up her angle better. She knew the glove box was where most people kept the vehicle papers. And—if they were stupid enough—where they kept a gun.

Anton had no choice. He pulled out the registration papers and together with his driver's license handed them both to Charmers, then watched her in the side mirror as she walked back to her cruiser. If the van had already been reported stolen, it would only take a simple check for his dreams to vanish. Anton shifted uneasily in his seat, his mind racing. He needed to act, do something. Ahead the highway was deserted, but the sheriff's cruiser would easily haul him in, as it had done moments before. Anton wasn't going to go back inside, no matter what. He'd done his time.

There was no way he was going back.

With his eyes glued to the side mirror, he slowly slid the van into gear but held the brake, feeling the restrained torque of the engine beneath him build. The woman was still in her car, tapping away on the dash-mounted computer as far as he could tell, his license held up in her hand.

There was no way he was going back.

Through the windshield, he watched her, her chin down, her eyes focused on the computer screen. Any moment now he imagined her head would suddenly bob up. Her eyes would fix on the van, on him. Alarm bells instantly went off inside Anton's head, knowing what Charmers was reading off the screen, then picturing the next two miserable years of his life: The van was stolen. Apprehend the driver. Handcuff him, twenty-four hours in county jail followed by another two-year stint back inside a federal prison.

Anton revved the engine.

There was no way he was going back.

He pulled his foot off the brake and smashed the gas pedal. The rear wheels spun up dirt and gravel as the van lurched forward, the rear end fishtailing off the shoulder, back-and-forth, the chassis groaning, until all four wheels found the black top again and the van accelerated away.

At the sound of the revving engine, Charmers's brain went into overdrive.

Looking up, she saw a dirty, billowing haze where the van had been parked moments ago, followed by the shape of it roaring away in the distance.

"Son of a—" She slammed the door shut, put the cruiser into gear, and roared off the shoulder back onto the highway in pursuit.

Anton gripped the steering wheel, his face scrunched, teeth gritted. Self-preservation was the only thing on his mind.

The van was sluggish, though, too slow with the weight of the cargo onboard. The needle on the speedometer crept slowly forward. Anton's foot was pressed all the way to the floor. If only he could reach the rendezvous point. Maybe he should go off the highway, cut across the dirt and scrub, then he could still make it there. The van had a high clearance; it would cover the rough ground better and faster than the low-slung cruiser that was chasing him. If worse came to worst, he could jump out of the van, abandon it, take his chances.

He wasn't going back to jail for anyone, not even for Mandy.

He glanced in the rearview mirror, saw the cruiser swell in size.

Bitch was gaining on him. It would be only a matter of seconds before he would be overtaken.

Anton smiled. He had a better idea. The speedometer hit eighty miles per hour.

The cruiser slid up alongside him. He glanced across at the woman in the driver's seat, couldn't make out what she was yelling, but her threats were obvious.

Anton wrenched the wheel hard to the left.

The van loomed toward Charmers.

She had anticipated the move. She touched the brakes, angling away, then watched as the van hurtled diagonally clear across the hood of the cruiser, across both lanes, before swaying back violently as the driver tried to compensate for the over-steer. The laws of physics and gravity took over. The van toppled onto one side, slid briefly in a shower of sparks and screeching metal until the one corner of the box framework dug-in. Then the entire van flipped, two, three, four times, shedding metal, glass, rubber, aluminum, towels, and linen, leaving a corkscrewing debris field in its wake as it rolled off the blacktop, then onto the shoulder before disappearing down the slope, smashing and compacting in size with each tumbling impact. The twisted ball of wreckage finally came to rest at the bottom of a gorge in the dirt and scrub.

What was left of the van would eventually be loaded onto a flatbed truck and taken to the junkyard. Anton Wheeler would be rushed to the nearest ER, which wasn't near at all. Over the next few hours, the site would be cleared up by a gang of county road workers. Which meant that the job would be haphazard, with minimal care taken for the minimum wages paid. That also meant not everything from the van would be gathered up. None of the road crew would venture more than a few yards away from the resting place of the van, assuming that none of the wreckage was thrown any farther away.

But something had landed farther away. Not far, but far enough and out of sight for lazy feet and careless eyes to reach. And if any of the road crew had been more thorough, more diligent in their duties, it would've been a life-changing moment for them.

Chapter 6

"Can you spare a dollar?"

Greg Miller looked down at the grubby, outstretched hand. "Get a job like the rest of us," he sneered. Greg had parked his car at the rear of the block, preferring to cut through the alleyway to get to the bank and not be seen approaching from the main street. Just in case. He angled around the homeless man who had crept out like a trapdoor spider from between a steel dumpster and a pile of wooden crates.

Inside the bank Greg waited in line, letting other customers go in front him so he would get the teller he wanted. Sharon was her name. *Sweet, sexy Sharon.*

Greg had flirted with her on several occasions. Stupid bitch didn't know better. Christ, women were so easy to manipulate. Just tell them they look good or have lost a little weight or that they have a nice smile and then boom! They're eating out of the palm of your hand.

Finally Sharon was free. She looked up, saw Greg was next in line, and smiled.

Sweet, sexy Sharon. Greg swaggered over.

"Hi, Greg," Sharon said through the Plexiglas window.

"Hey, babe," Greg replied. Young women, girls like Sharon, liked being called "babe." They all did. He'd seen her photos on Facebook too. Posing in front of a bathroom mirror, all dressed up to hit the town at night, a nice firm curvaceous cleavage on display. *Teasing slut.*

"What's this?" Sharon asked as Greg slid a sheaf of paper through the slide tray.

"The account form you wanted," Greg said. "From last week. Remember? Diane wants to be removed as a signatory on our account."

Sharon scrutinized the form. She could vaguely recall Greg coming in last week, saying his wife, Diane, wanted to be removed as a signatory from the joint checking account. Greg had mentioned Diane's problems many times over the past months. How she now spent most of the time on medication, not going out much in public, lying around the house all day not fully lucid.

"She's finding it more difficult to carry out certain functions as you can imagine, Sharon."

Sharon nodded, checking both sides of the form to make sure it had been filled out correctly. Sharon liked Diane, had gotten to know her quite well when she used to come into the bank herself. The woman was headstrong, articulate, and in control…knew what she wanted. It was hard to believe twelve months later that same woman had been reduced to a suffering mess with mental issues—according to Greg. Then again, Sharon couldn't begin to imagine what the poor woman had gone through. No one could. Simply horrible. Greg, though, seemed to be coping well.

Diane had written her signature on the bottom of the form, giving authority to remove herself as a signatory of the account. Greg had countersigned the form as well.

"Everything looks in order," Sharon said. It looked like Diane's signature on the form. Sharon had seen it numerous times when Diane had come in. But that was more than a year ago. Sharon tapped away on her keyboard, bringing up two bank account details. She noticed the balance of Greg Miller's separate account, the one she had opened for him a few months back.

"You've got quite a bit of money built up in your separate checking account, Greg. You should really talk to one of our wealth advisors. See if they can get you a better return on your money."

Greg gave a slight smile. "I'm fine at the moment, Sharon. I'm just happy to leave it there, let it build up."

"Did you get your bonus this month?" Sharon asked, looking up.

"Sure did." Greg gave Sharon a wink. "Never missed a month yet, babe."

"You should buy something for yourself, Greg. Maybe a new car," Sharon said. There was more than enough in his separate account to buy several cars. "Maybe take an overseas holiday too," Sharon added.

Greg looked thoughtfully at Sharon. "You know I might just do that." The truth was, what Greg really wanted to do was to take Sharon on an overseas trip, tie her to a large bed in some exotic resort, and beat the living crap out of her until she begged him to stop. That's what he really wanted to do.

Sharon scanned the form Greg had given her for the third time.

Greg drummed his fingers impatiently on the counter, watching Sharon closely. "You look nice today, Sharon." He threw out the compliment, trying to distract the stupid bitch so she would just process the damn form.

Sharon looked up and smiled. "Thanks." She turned the form over one more time, her mind undecided. She had a new supervisor who was a stickler for following due process. The signatures on this particular form had to be witnessed by an independent third-party. Previously, Sharon had just accepted the forms Greg had brought in to her without actually citing

Diane signing the form or it being properly witnessed. She just trusted Greg and had been persuaded by him that his wife had signed the previous forms.

"Is there a problem, Sharon?" Greg stopped drumming his fingers on the counter, his face now almost pressed up against the glass.

Sharon glanced over her shoulder, then leaned toward the speaking holes. "Greg, I'm sorry," she said in a hushed voice. "But I'll need to verify that this is actually Diane's signature."

Greg made a choking sound. "But you know it's hers. You've seen her signature plenty of times before."

Sharon grimaced. Thinking about it now, she had been pretty casual in the past with the bank's policies when it came to Greg Miller. He'd always been so cheerful, so nice toward her despite what dramas he had shared with her about what was going on at home. Poor man.

But then again, Sharon didn't want to lose her job if it was subsequently discovered that she had been verifying Diane's signature on official forms as though Diane herself had come into the branch and had signed them in front of her.

"Look, I'm sorry. But with this type of form, I really need to verify your wife's signature. It needs to be witnessed or is it possible that she can come in to the bank herself?"

Greg gave a sympathetic look, as though talking to a delinquent child. "You know she's not well, Sharon, don't you?" The smile on Greg's face then morphed into a grimace, a hint of anger in his voice. "She has mental issues. I don't want to put her through the drive to come in here to sign the form again that she has already signed."

Sharon nodded. "Look, I know what you're saying Greg. But it's just that they have really tightened up on procedures here. I really need this witnessed properly."

Greg stared at Sharon, and for a moment she was taken aback by the cold and callous look on his face, something she hadn't seen before in him. She slid the form back through the tray. "Can I give Diane a call perhaps?" Sharon offered. "Get confirmation over the phone from her?"

Greg didn't touch the form, just stared down at it in the tray. "I don't think she's at home at the moment."

"I thought you said she wasn't well, that she spends most of her time at home?"

Clever, little bitch.

"Doctor's appointment," Greg hurriedly replied, snatching back the form. "I'll get it witnessed and then I'll bring it back."

"I'm sorry Greg but—"

Greg turned his back on Sharon and stormed out of the bank, pushing the swinging doors a little too hard, almost knocking over an elderly lady on the other side but not bothering to apologize to her.

Outside in the blazing sunlight, Greg glanced back at the bank and swore under his breath, then balled up the form in his fist and threw it into a trash bin. He could feel the right side of his head throb. He took a few deep breaths to calm himself as people strolled past him on the sidewalk. Still simmering with anger, he cut back down the alleyway, his mind elsewhere, trying to formulate another plan to get Diane off the checking account.

His thoughts were suddenly interrupted.

"Sir, can you spare a dollar?"

Greg stopped in his tracks and glared down at the homeless man who had scuttled out again from behind the dumpster. The proffered hand was filthy, coated with street grime, the nails chewed right back, knuckles grazed and misshapen.

Greg took another step past to walk on, then he stopped.

He glanced up at the walls of the alleyway, scouring both sides. Then looked left and right to each open end. They were alone, just the two of them.

Greg gave a thin smile, revealing a row of sharp little teeth. He bunched both his fists, then moved toward the homeless man.

Chapter 7

It was dark by the time they had completed everything they needed to do for the day.

They were staying at a modest hotel on the outskirts of town, separate rooms, but Costa was nearby just in case Alex needed him for whatever reason.

Apart from being the physical enforcer of Alex's wishes, her father liked to think of Costa as her bodyguard, despite Alex believing she didn't need one. She much preferred to use her own skills as a seasoned negotiator to defuse any difficult situation she found herself in.

After a quick bite to eat at a local restaurant, Alex returned to her hotel room. No sooner had she turned the key and pushed open the door than she realized the atmosphere in her room had changed since she had departed this morning. She felt a presence that was hostile, menacing, like a caged animal was lying in wait for her. As her eyes adjusted to the darkness, Alex made out the vague outline of a man sitting in a chair next to a lamp.

Alex remained standing in the doorway. She knew Costa was only three rooms down. In her pocket was a small transmitter, military-spec quality, similar to what the Secret Service protection details used. A simple press and Costa would come running with lethal intent.

Before she could summon Costa, the man reached across and turned the lamp on, throwing dull yellow light around the room. "Hello, Sis."

Stepping into the room and closing the door behind her, Alex could see a gun sitting on the small table next to her brother. She had no idea how he'd gotten into her hotel room. But that was Vincent's method, his signature. He had an uncanny ability to get into anything. A room, a car, a house, your mind, under your skin, despite what countermeasures you had erected to keep him out.

"Why are you here, Vincent?" Alex asked as she took off her coat and threw it onto the bed.

Vincent gave a slight smile and cocked his head. The fifty bucks he'd used to bribe the night manager, together with the threat of violence if his request to get access to the room was turned down, was money well spent. The look on his sister's face right now was priceless. She was more than mildly surprised by his presence. "I thought I would come and see how everything is progressing."

The temperature in the room seemed a few degrees colder to Alex. She knew why her brother was there, who had sent him, and for what purpose. He was there to check up on her. It was rare for Vincent to go into the field anymore. He much preferred to use his army of foot soldiers, his minions, sending them forth to do his dirty work while he remained ensconced in his leather and mahogany office in New Jersey, plotting and scheming as the next in line for the family throne. Despite the logistics of distance, different time zones, and geography, Vincent Romano could touch anyone, anywhere; such was the limitless reach of his web of influence and violence.

"I'm doing just fine," Alex replied. Did her father not trust her with this assignment he had specifically assigned to her? "I don't need a babysitter," Alex said. She couldn't believe Vincent would have been sent by her father to check up on her, to make sure everything went smoothly. Maybe this visit was of Vincent's own making. Given her father's ailing health, it was only a matter of time before Vincent, who was older than she was, would assume the mantle as the head of the family. In Alex's mind, there were dark days coming when that happened.

"There's been a change of plan," Vincent said, his fingers stroking the gun absentmindedly as he kept his eyes fixed on his sister. Silent threats and provocation were all staples in Vincent's armory. The same manipulations and mind games he played with people outside the family group also extended to his own blood. He made no distinction as to whom his threats could fall upon.

"I didn't know there was a 'plan' as you say," Alex said as she sat down on the edge of the bed, taking her shoes off. It had been a long day, and she didn't need her brother there. Obviously, Costa had been a party to her brother's new travel itinerary. The fact that she had not been told in advance, given any warning that her brother had been dispatched, annoyed Alex. Despite being counselor for the family, having her father's ear, giving him sage and wise advice over the years, Vincent had a way of intertwining himself into all of her father's decisions. Deep down Vincent despised the fact that his younger sister seemed to exert more influence over their father than he ever could. Even though Alex and Vincent moved in different orbits around the same sun, their paths rarely crossed. Alex preferred to live in the family home in New Jersey to be close on hand to her father. Vincent preferred to live in his apartment in Brooklyn, where his machinations for power would go undetected.

Sons and daughters had different dynamics in the eyes of their parents, especially their fathers. Not that Luca Romano had extended any special privileges or favorable treatment to his only daughter during her upbringing. But he did have a certain softness toward her that didn't extend to Vincent.

"I'm not here to spy on you, Sis, if that's what you're thinking. An issue has arisen in Nebraska. Family business that I personally would like to take care of."

Alex looked across at her brother as she began massaging her sore feet. She glanced down at one of her discarded high heels, wondering if she could use it as a weapon. "Then you don't need me. I have plenty to do back home. I have a flight out of here first thing tomorrow."

Vincent never shrugged. To him shrugging was an outward sign of ignorance, of being uninformed. And Vincent liked to be informed—about *everything*. He presided over his side of the family business, making sure he knew everything about everyone. "You can ask father if you like. I was more than happy to do this alone but he insisted that you"—Vincent paused for effect—"tag along."

It annoyed Alex to no end how Vincent always managed to belittle her, like it always had to be a game, a competition between them, not for their father's affection but for his attention. Vincent craved attention, even more so in his adult life than Alex could remember in her childhood. The patronizing, condescending manner he had toward her would surface at every opportunity he could find. In front of other family members. In front of employees and business associates. But never in front of their father. Vincent had once belittled her in front of their father, and Luca Romano promptly put Vincent in his place, reprimanding him viciously. Yet, in private, Vincent constantly reminded her that in the family pecking order, she was firmly at her brother's feet.

"Costa will be sent home. He is not needed anymore," Vincent continued. "It will just be the two of us." Vincent seemed to be relishing the prospect of it but for all the wrong reasons.

"You're kidding me, right?" Alex had never worked with Vincent in the last five years. Now they were going to be together on family business in Nebraska, joined at the hip? This didn't seem right.

As if reading her thoughts, Vincent spoke. "Call him if you like. He'll still be awake."

"I prefer Costa to stay."

Vincent stood up and made a show of spreading his arms in false affection. "If I can't protect my little sister, then who can?"

Alex glared at her brother. The thought that she shared the same DNA as he had made her skin crawl. Maybe he had been adopted. And he knew exactly how to get under her skin and deep into her flesh. Like the way he always referred to her as his "little sister." It was demeaning, putting her in her place, so she knew, in the whole scheme of things in his devious mind, where she belonged. Below him, beneath him, subservient to him. Yet, she was more accomplished than him, more conducive to the subtle art of family politics and diplomacy. Then again, there was nothing diplomatic about how she had treated Joseph Durango. But he deserved it.

Alex slid her cell phone out of her pocket, shut the room door behind her, and stood on the outside walkway for privacy. If her brother was her protector, as he claimed to be, who was going to protect her from him? Alex placed a hand on the cold metal railing, dialed her father's private direct line, and stared out into the night. Tires hissed on the wet streets below as street lamps glowed orange under a light drizzle. In the distance she could see the luminescent ribbon of highway. The night air was cold and heavy with dampness. She looked at the desolate outskirts surrounding her: a few industrial buildings, the neon outlines of a few cheap stores that remained open at this late hour. She was a long way from home, in an unfamiliar place, with an unfamiliar backdrop.

She hated being there.

But her father had thought it would be a good idea for her to get out of the heaving metropolis, get out of her office, be on the ground, to touch, feel, and smell what the family business was about rather than seeing it from the comfort of a desk as only figures on a spreadsheet.

Her father's private number answered on the fifth ring. Before she could get a word out, Luca Romano spoke. "Before you get started, Alex, I wanted Vincent to be there with you. It's important to me."

"I don't need Vincent with me." She could hear her father give a sigh on the other end of the line.

"I won't be around forever, Alex," he said, his voice husky from a lifetime of explaining. "You are my only two children, my successors. I need you and Vincent to put aside your differences. I will not be swayed by you, Alex. Grant me this one wish as a dying man."

"You are not dying." Alex knew it was a lie. He was dying. But in his eighty-five years, Luca Romano had heard plenty of lies. One more wouldn't make a difference.

"We are all dying one way or another, Alex. Every day we die a little."

Alex hung her head in defeat. She knew her father's choice was deliberate, to force them together. She had no choice but to work side-by-side with Vincent.

"There's a problem in Nebraska. Some money has gone missing. A delivery driver has vanished. I wasn't going to bother you with it, but since you were in the vicinity, I thought I would send Vincent along and both of you can deal with it." Luca Romano went on to explain the details of the assignment. As she listened, Alex knew it was a test. Vincent always had a different approach, a reputation, a different way of "dealing" with problems. She had never seen it firsthand, just read about it in the headlines in the newspapers the next day. Without really saying it, her father wanted Alex to tone-down her brother, bevel some of the sharp edges.

"I was impressed with what you did with Durango," Luca added, almost as an afterthought. "And his poor wife."

"I am *Consigliere*," Alex insisted, ignoring the compliment. She did what she had done with Kim Durango because she had wanted to. It was her choice. "I have your sole authority, not Vincent."

"I know that, Alex. But please get along. I am dispatching the two of you to work together on resolving this matter in Nebraska." Her father finished explaining the situation. "Just try not to kill each other. No parent should outlive their own children," Luca Romano said jokingly before ending the call.

Alex turned around and leaned against the railing. She looked back at the closed hotel room door, thinking that perhaps her father's last comment wasn't a joke.

But, rather, a distinct possibility.

Chapter 8

"Don't you remember, honey?" Greg Miller said.

Diane thought she could sense a touch of sarcasm in her husband's voice, the endearment, *honey,* drawn out longer than it should have been. Sourness not sweetness.

"You were getting too many calls. People pestering you, asking all sorts of questions. I didn't want you to get more upset."

Greg had just arrived home from working late—again. He was moving about the kitchen, looking for something to eat, banging cupboards and pulling out drawers almost in frustration.

Diane stood with her arms folded on the other side of the counter.

"We spoke about it. Decided it would be best for you to get a new number." Greg gave her that look he always did, making her feel tiny, insignificant.

Diane wanted to know what had happened to her previous number, why it had been disconnected. She had already gone back through her cell phone contacts folder. It was completely empty—except for the new addition of Martha Hendricks. Her cell phone looked like her old cell phone, the same one she'd always had. But she didn't quite know when the change of number had occurred.

Diane watched as Greg poured himself a glass of milk, his own cell phone in his hand. Somehow Greg had mastered the art of doing many things around the home one-handed with his cell phone practically attached to him.

"You agreed, Diane. Don't you remember? People still called

me and I ran interference for you. With everything that was happening, and how you were ill, I wanted people to leave you alone. I was more than happy to field the phone calls. After a few months, they pretty much died down anyway."

Ill?

Greg seemed to use the term more often to describe her. It was almost second nature to him. The word had woven its way into his everyday vocabulary whenever he would describe her. Past and present tense. Like a permanent feature. Not that she had brown hair or gray eyes or was this or that.

Just…ill.

Diane let the comment slide, preferring to focus on her cell phone number. She couldn't recall agreeing to canceling the number and replacing it with a new number. She understood the logic. But didn't understand ever agreeing to it. Now she knew why Martha Hendricks couldn't get hold of her. Nor anyone else, come to think of it. How many of her friends had tried in the past? Work colleagues from the Army too. Up until now, Diane had thought they had just lost interest, that she had dropped off their radar.

"I can't honestly remember telling you that, Greg."

Greg watched Diane carefully over the rim of his glass. "Well you did. Maybe it's the medication you've been taking."

That was another thing Diane disliked. If there was a problem with her understanding something or not remembering something, Greg would always put it down to the meds.

"Is there a problem?" Greg asked, seeing the puzzled look on Diane's face.

Diane began to feel uncomfortable with the coldness in Greg's voice, like he was challenging her. Wanting to start an argument. Maybe she had told him to change her number.

Maybe Greg was right, maybe he had stepped in, out of compassion, and had taken away trivial day-to-day interruptions, the tasks that perhaps she couldn't cope with in the aftermath.

"I just can't remember, that's all." Diane stared at the cell phone in her hand. And that was the truth. She couldn't remember—if what Greg was saying was true.

Greg drained the milk, placed the glass on the counter, walked around to his wife, and held her by the shoulders, an exaggerated look of concern on his face. "It was for the best, honey." He rubbed her shoulders. "I didn't want people hassling you, asking you difficult questions, making you feel worse than what you already did."

Diane thought about this for a moment. "Maybe my friends had good intentions. Just wanted to make sure I was okay."

Greg smiled. "I'm sure they did. But you needed time, Diane. We both did. We'd just lost our daughter. We needed time to grieve."

Diane would never stop grieving. It was something no parent would ever recover from. Ella was everything to her, the only thing that had kept her in this marriage.

Greg kissed his wife on the forehead, then went to pick up his empty glass. "What's this?" he asked, noticing for the first time the small screw cap plastic bottle on the counter.

"Some new medication," Diane replied, scooping up the bottle before Greg could. "The doctor thought she would try something different for me, a new type of medication. Something not as strong as what I had been taking."

Greg frowned. "She?" Greg sat down on a stool at the counter.

Diane said nothing.

Greg watched her carefully as she went to the cupboard and pulled out a glass. She unscrewed the top of the pill bottle, swallowed two tablets, and washed them down with some water.

"Let me have a look at them." Greg held out his upturned hand. A command, not a question.

Diane slid the pill bottle quickly into her pocket. "It's nothing, really."

Greg's expression tightened. He regarded his wife for a moment, confounded by her newfound defiance. He glanced at Diane's side pocket and could see the slight bulge where the pill bottle was pressed. "I thought Dr. Farrell was a *he* not a *she*?" Greg gave Diane a disapproving look that always reminded her of a teacher in high school whom she never liked. "Don't you remember, honey? Or are you getting forgetful?"

Again that sarcastic tone. Diane shook her head. "Dr. Farrell is away. His replacement is a female doctor. She suggested the new medication."

Greg's eyes narrowed. "Is she allowed to do that? It's not as though you're her regular patient and she's your regular therapist." Greg was annoyed by this new piece of news. The fabric of his carefully laid plans had developed a fray.

Diane just shrugged. "I guess she can. She said she had gone through my file, knew my history. I don't know when Dr. Farrell will be back. She said he had to attend to a personal matter."

Greg got up, pushing the stool back with a grating sound, in two minds whether or not to ask his wife again to look at these new pills. "But you've been feeling better lately, haven't you?" he asked. "Because of the new dosage, that Dr. Farrell recommended a while back?"

Diane looked at the floor. "I have been feeling better. But I think the increased dosage has been making me sleepy during the day. Giving me insomnia at night. Dr. Redding said it could be too strong for me, dull my senses."

"Dr. Redding," Greg said slowly, saying the name like it meant something distasteful. He gave a grunt and placed his glass in the sink. "Perhaps this Dr. Redding," he said in a mimicking tone, "should just stick to the course of medication prescribed by your proper doctor and not interfere."

"Dr. Redding is a proper doctor," Diane insisted.

Greg turned back to his wife, irritation in his eyes. Then his cell phone buzzed, saving what could have been an outburst from him. Greg gave Diane one final look before turning back to his cell phone, preoccupying himself with another text message.

Chapter 9

The next day Costa boarded an early flight back east to New Jersey, while Alex and Vincent boarded another flight heading west to Omaha, Nebraska.

Touching down, Vincent hired a black Suburban SUV at the rental desk. Alex preferred something less conspicuous but was overruled, leaving her wondering why her brother needed such a large vehicle.

After two hours heading west along Highway 80, they approached the town limits of Grand Island from the south. On the outskirts they pulled up in a semi-industrial area that was a scatter of open lots, broken concrete sidewalks, and buckled wire fences netted with trash and debris. Every town had a decaying, neglected side to it, where the past was left to deteriorate among the weeds and foreclosure signs. Such a location provided a certain level of invisibility for particular business ventures.

The not-for-profit commercial laundry was situated on a large, flat corner block. The building, the business, and the land were owned by a subsidiary company registered in Delaware. The subsidiary company was owned by a holding company controlled by the Romano family. It was registered in an unremarkable office, in a nondescript building on a small island just a short ninety-minute flight south of Miami. It was an island where thousands of other companies just like it were also discreetly registered.

The commercial laundry mainly handled the work of a number of small motels and larger chain hotels within a twenty-mile radius of the city. Its workforce was comprised mainly of ex-convicts on integration programs, transient tourist backpackers who had drifted too far west of Omaha and couldn't find their way home, and down-and-outers who shuffled in from the surrounding domestic population. And there were plenty of down-and-outers in the local area.

The general manager, Tyson Banks, showed them to his small but functional office at the rear of the laundry where Alex and Vincent sat down. Straight away, Vincent was all business, no formalities, handshakes, or discussions about the weather or local economy. With a few clicks and scrolls of the computer mouse, Banks brought up what Vincent wanted to see. On the drive over, Alex had reviewed the employment file, emailed to her by Banks, of the particular employee in question.

"What exactly am I looking at here?" Vincent asked impatiently.

Banks had been in his office since six that morning, checking and making sure everything was in order. "This is the van here," Banks said, pointing at the computer screen smudged with greasy fingerprints. The video footage was of one of the laundry's delivery vans that was backed into the loading dock, ready for its daily six a.m. run around town, dropping off clean linen and collecting the soiled.

Alex watched the grainy footage as the ghostly shape of the van's driver materialized from the left of the screen. The man loitered in view for a few minutes, talking to another person, making small talk it seemed.

"His name is Anton Wheeler," Banks explained. "Been employed here for nearly twelve months now. Did time a few years back for petty theft. But he's always reliable, always turns up for his shift on time, gets along with his fellow co-workers.

No complaints about him at all from his shift supervisor. He seemed like an honest hard worker."

Seemed? In Vincent's mind there was no such thing, just liars biding their time, waiting for the right opportunity to steal from you. Vincent squinted at the screen, his fingers drumming impatiently on the desk. "How much was on the van?" he asked, without taking his eyes from the screen, committing to memory the shape of Anton Wheeler. How he looked, how he walked, how his shoulders and arms moved. Picturing the young man as a moving target. Details that would be important when they caught him. And Vincent Romano was going to catch him. After that nothing else would matter, especially not for Anton Wheeler.

Banks's eyes darted nervously left and right, his mouth twitching. "The usual. One million in cash," he finally said, staring at the ground, not wanting to meet the glare of Vincent's eyes.

In the video, Anton Wheeler jumped down off the raised concrete apron of the dock and climbed into the van before pulling away.

Vincent said nothing for a moment, just stared at the screen, his silence making the atmosphere in the small, cramped office seem even more ominous.

Alex could feel her brother bristle with contained anger. It was shimmering off him in waves, like a radioactive decay.

Despite the not-for-profit being called *Helpful Hands Mission*, the only mission the organization conducted was laundering as much money as possible for the Romano family. The business was a front, a midwestern hub through which dirty funds from various illegitimate family business activities poured in and then channeled out clean to an array of legitimate businesses that the family owned.

"And you are certain he was working alone?" Alex asked Banks.

Banks finally looked up, feeling not so threatened by Alex. She seemed to have a calm, rational demeanor to her. Unlike her brother, who oozed menace. "I can't be certain of that. But what I can be certain of is that he missed his first drop off and neither he or the van has been seen since."

"Has Wheeler been acting—"

"What about the tracking system onboard the van?" Vincent cut in over his sister.

Alex glared at her brother for a moment, biting her tongue, not appreciating him verbally pushing her aside.

"You can track him, can't you?" Vincent demanded. "You know where he's gone."

The business had a fleet of twelve vans of various sizes, all equipped with GPS tracking devices that transmitted real-time telemetry back to the office. While the business used typical GPS tracking for their fleet of vans to reduce fuel costs, improve efficient route scheduling, and increase driver productivity, there was an underlying, more important reason to track the whereabouts of each of the vans. The vans transported something the drivers were totally unaware of and more valuable than just piles of laundry.

Banks shuffled awkwardly in his seat, considering not the question, but how to best answer it without being beaten to a pulp.

"Ten minutes after he pulled out of the yard, we lost the van's signal."

Vincent rounded on Banks, a look of pure disbelief in his eyes. Vincent's glare cut to Alex, who just sat there, also perplexed by this new revelation.

"Are you kidding me?" If Vincent had a gun on him, he would have used it. Smacked Banks in the head with it, taken him out the back into the alley, and put him down like a rabid dog.

Banks said nothing, just looked at everything else in the office but Vincent Romano.

Vincent turned and gave Alex the questioning look, silent permission from her to do what he wanted to do to Banks right here, right now.

Alex gave a slight shake of her head.

Banks began to sweat, his lips began to quiver. He knew the moment would come when he would have to tell Vincent Romano that they couldn't track the van Anton Wheeler had stolen with the million in cash onboard.

"Like I was going to ask," Alex said, "had Anton Wheeler been acting strangely lately?"

Banks looked up, his face saggy with defeat. "Like how?"

"Late to work. On his phone a lot. Walking outside to take and make calls. Being in places inside the business where he shouldn't be. Looking over the vans more than usual."

Banks shook his head. "Nothing that I've noticed."

"And you're certain none of the drivers know about the money onboard the vans?" Alex asked.

Banks shook his head. "I don't think so."

It was such a pitiful response from Banks, lacking any conviction. It even made Alex angry.

Vincent postured, bunched his fists, hunched his shoulders, ready to uncoil his fury on the withering man who sat within arms' reach of him. Tyson Banks was an imbecile and should never have been placed in charge of this operation.

Alex touched Vincent's knee, temporarily restraining him.

Vincent glared at her. He looked about to burst at the seams, ready to unleash on the man who seemed to have shrunken inside his clothing.

"You get paid to notice," Alex said, trying to remain calm. "To watch everything. To notice things. You are our eyes and ears here, Mr. Banks. You should have paid more attention."

Banks hung his head. What could he say? His failure was absolute.

This was no impromptu theft. Anton Wheeler had planned it all along. The two-bit, convicted felon driver who served time for petty theft had just driven off with a million dollars in cash and no one knew where he was.

Alex got up and went to the door, opened it, then paused and looked back at her brother.

Their eyes met.

She gave a slight nod, then left the room, closing the door securely behind her.

Chapter 10

In the past, Diane had contemplated the idea of leaving Greg.

To move on, leave the past behind her, especially during the last twelve months.

How Greg had behaved last night only compounded how suffocating and inert the relationship had become. Diane never would have entertained the idea of leaving while Ella was alive. Ella was much too important to her. She had loved Greg—once, in the past, when he was kind, caring, and considerate. He used to make an effort for her. As the years went on and five years of marriage grew into ten, then sixteen, she felt things change. Then her world fell off its axis.

Diane hated being away from Ella when she was deployed to the Middle East. It felt like part of her heart had died, stopped beating. A young daughter needs her mother more than ever during those formative, adolescent years. She believed Greg was up to the task, and he had been. He doted on Ella. Dropped her off at school each day, helped her with homework when he could. During satellite video calls to her daughter, while Diane sat in an Army tent surrounded by heat, dust, and sand, and Ella sat in the family kitchen thousands of miles away, Ella would tell her mother how much she missed her. Would ask her when was she coming home. Diane could tell, despite the reassurances from her daughter that everything was fine, things weren't. It made it all the more heartbreaking for Diane when she had to leave home again to return to her job.

When she came home after her last tour, a six-month stint in

Iraq, something had changed with Ella. She had taken on a remoteness toward Diane, distancing herself from her. Ella spent more time in her room, withdrawn and reclusive, surrounded by distractions that seemed to build up around her like a wall. Maybe she was growing up, shedding her adolescence, a precocious twelve-year-old becoming a woman.

Diane had tried to broach the subject with Ella, give her daughter motherly advice that perhaps was long overdue. But Diane was silenced, told there was no need. Driven by a deep sense of guilt, Diane promptly resigned from the Army. Cut short a promising career so she could spend more time with her daughter, try to fill the gaps that only a mother could, gaps she felt she had created through neglect.

But it had been too late.

Diane walked into the kitchen, fully awake, showered and dressed, having slept right through the night for the first time in ages. The new medication seemed to be working. She was feeling a lot better. Better than she had felt in the last twelve months. Dr. Redding said the new medication would be fast-acting, that Diane would start to see results in a few days rather than a few weeks like most of the other common antidepressants on the market. What she had prescribed was relatively new, almost experimental. Diane had to sign a few forms at first, medical waivers. She gladly did. Anything to pull herself out of the doughy haze she had felt for so long.

Greg sat at the breakfast bar, drinking coffee and scrolling through his cell phone. He had been up before her. He usually was. "Hey, honey," he said, looking up from his phone. "You're up early. How are you feeling?"

He said the same hollow words to her each day. To which she usually responded with the same lie each day. But today was different. "I feel good," she replied, lifting a coffee cup down from the cupboard. "I really do." And she meant it.

Greg promptly pocketed his cell phone and watched his wife.

Diane couldn't understand why a man who had a desk job in an office got so many emails and text messages on his cell phone day and night that required his immediate and urgent attention. It wasn't like they had a huge circle of friends.

"Have you paid the bills this month?" Diane asked, indicating a pile of bills sitting on the counter, untouched from where they had been for the last two weeks.

Greg's face hardened slightly. "I will, honey, when I get a chance to get to them. Money is just a bit tight this month, as you know." He gave a forced smile, then added, "With you not working and everything."

And there it was, that daily snipe, a barb of subtle contempt that Greg couldn't resist throwing at her. Comments about how she doesn't work anymore. How she doesn't "contribute" financially or otherwise to the relationship. Greg couldn't let a day go by without making a niggling, snide comment.

Yet, Diane wanted to work. She had told him numerous times in the last few months. Said that it would do her good, get her mind off other things. And each time Diane raised the subject, Greg shot her down, arguing that she needed to stay at home until she was better. Diane believed, however, it suited Greg to have her at home, so he knew where she was. A job meant her earning her own money again—and independence, the one thing Greg feared the most, she thought. Diane had been the strong, independent one in the relationship, earning more than him, and that riled him to no end. Now the tables were turned, and Greg wanted to keep it that way.

"A warning light also came up in my car yesterday, while I

was in town," Diane said. "I think it's well past its service date."

Greg's eyes narrowed.

Diane could feel him slowly quiver with annoyance.

"I'll add that to the list, honey. I've been flat out with work lately. You know that. Things would've been better if I had gotten my bonus last month. But like I told you, I missed out on getting it. I was short by a couple of sales that I thought I had. I'm trying to make it up this month."

Diane nodded. Greg seemed to say the same thing each month. How he just missed out on his sales bonus again at work. How he thought he'd done enough but failed just short of his monthly quota. She wished she could contribute more. Maybe she would get a part-time job. Ignore Greg's protests and surprise him one day by bringing home a paycheck. And yet, for some strange reason Diane knew Greg wouldn't be happy for her.

She had received a healthy payout from the Army, but that had been used up on typical household expenditures, utility bills, and medical costs, including the funeral. Greg had assumed the role of taking care of all the family finances, telling Diane she shouldn't bother herself with such trivial things.

"I'm sorry," Diane said. "I know you're trying to do your best." Even as the words came out, Diane didn't believe them. Despite every opportunity to remind her of how hard he worked, she couldn't really see the fruits of all that hard work during the last twelve months. He told her they were just coping, just managing to keep their heads above water. That's why Diane wanted to get a job, no matter how mundane. Surely the skills she had learned in the Army could be put to good use in one form or another in a nine-to-five job.

Greg kissed Diane on the cheek. "I promise, I'll take care of everything this week. You stay at home and get well. I've got to get to work for a meeting." Greg thumbed his cell phone as he walked away.

"I'm going out today," Diane said quickly after him.

Greg stopped and turned around. "Sorry, what was that?"

"I'm going out today. I have another session with Dr. Redding," Diane lied.

Greg's smile suddenly vanished. "Again? So soon? You just saw her yesterday."

"She said she wanted to see me again. We ran out of time yesterday to cover everything. Plus, she wanted to see how the new medication is going."

"It's only been—what? A day? It takes weeks for medication like that to work."

Diane's eyes narrowed. All of a sudden, Greg knew a hell of a lot about how antidepressants worked.

Seeing the suspicious look on his wife's face, Greg stuttered, "I imagine."

"I can only go on what the doctor said. She wants to see me again."

Greg nodded. He certainly wasn't happy with this new, meddling doctor Diane was seeing and how she had taken a sudden interest in his wife's condition. Maybe he would pay this new doctor a visit. Like how he had done with Dr. Farrell.

After Greg had gone, Diane walked into Ella's bedroom and sat down on the bed. She touched the sheets, ran her fingers along the perfectly tucked in sides and folded corners. She needed to change the bed linen. An unused bed still accumulated dust and dirt just like everything else.

As she sat there, like she did most mornings after Greg had left for work, alone with just her thoughts, Diane couldn't help feeling like a huge part of her was empty. Not just missing—but gone, never to return or be replaced while she remained in this house. There was no going back, no matter how hard she had wished she could. There was only going forward, one grinding step at a time.

Diane didn't know how long she could go on like this. She hoped the new medication would work. And it was working. Yet as she sat there, with a familiar feeling of despair creeping slowly over her, she knew no amount of medication could alter the scenery, her surroundings, the daily reminder of the horrors of the past.

For Diane to break free, she needed to move on like everyone had told her.

Leave all this behind.

Chapter 11

"You're pregnant?"

Monica Styles nodded ruefully. "So the two pink lines say."

"Definitely?"

Monica nodded again.

"You did the test properly?"

Monica's eyes went theatrically wide. "Yep."

"Are you sure?"

Styles gave her boss, Sheriff Meredith Charmers, an *I'm not totally stupid* glare. There were three test kits in the box, and Monica had used all three. Just to be certain.

"Fuck," Charmers said, looking off into the distance, imagining what the next five years would hold for the most dedicated and brightest deputy she had ever known. An unsightly mirage of dirty diapers, baby poop, no sex, sleepless nights, and bad-hair days.

"That tends to do it," Styles replied introspectively. *Fuck*.

They were sitting at a picnic bench outside Charlie's Cafe, the only place in Hazard that sold decent coffee.

Charmers looked at her deputy again and sighed. *My God, she's just a child*. Twenty-two years old. A baby. Her whole life ahead of her. She'll make sheriff someday. No doubt about it. Not here, though. Sherman County wasn't big enough and Hazard was just a one-sheriff, one-deputy town. Some place bigger more likely. Grand Island maybe, or Lincoln. Hell, the young woman was bright enough to find her way to Omaha. That was if she could navigate through all the male testosterone that tended to exist in the larger sheriff's departments.

Charmers reached across the bench and squeezed Monica's hand.

Monica smiled but turned away, not wanting her boss to see tears begin to form in her eyes. That was a sign of weakness, a lack of self-control. Internal strength and self-control were the two characteristics Styles prided herself on—those and her unbridled dedication to the job she loved so much. "I'm fine," Styles insisted, suddenly taking a keen interest in the overhead traffic lights at the nearby intersection. The problem was a lack of self-control—of another person, not her.

For a moment neither of them said anything, content to sit and drink coffee under the warm rays of the morning sun. Two women, face-to-face, at opposite ends of their lives. One, whose loving husband of more than thirty years worshipped the ground she trod on, with three adult children of her own, with lives of their own. The other, a young woman, with no immediate family, who had spent all her life in Hazard. Born and bred. Who had never turned her back on the town while most her age had moved to the bright lights of the big city. Monica was loyal to the end. With so much potential. Potential that would have to be placed on hold for the time being.

"What happened with that stolen van yesterday?" Styles asked, wanting to change the subject.

Charmers shrugged. "Not certain. I ran the plates and they don't belong to the van. At this stage it looks like some idiot with priors just stealing a laundry van. My guess is he thought he could sell it and make a quick buck. He's pretty banged up in the hospital, though. Hasn't regained consciousness. When he does, I'll know more. It was a miracle he survived the crash. The van was totaled. It's been hauled to a holding yard. It belongs to some laundry business in Grand Island. I'm going to pay them a visit today. Tell them the bad news."

"You haven't notified them yet?" Styles asked.

Charmers shook her head. "The van wasn't reported stolen. Plus, it was a real mess yesterday out on the highway. I just wanted to get that sorted first before I go looking for the owner."

Styles just nodded.

"I can't understand people these days," Charmers said. "You steal a van to make a couple of bucks and nearly end up killing yourself." Charmers looked at Styles. "Then there's that homeless man who was bashed in the alleyway near the bank in town." Charmers just shook her head as she drank some more coffee. "The world has gone to crap."

"I'm going back to the alley today to take another look," Styles said. "He's in the hospital too. The doctor says it is touch and go. It looks like someone stomped on his head as well. He may never come out of a coma, or if he does, he might end up a vegetable for the rest of his life."

They sat in silence for a while, contemplating the recent ugliness of the world they had witnessed. It was unusual for the small town of Hazard, even for the county. Normally the highlight of their day was busting kids for drinking in public or an odd traffic violation, maybe a DUI. But nothing like they had seen in the last twenty-four hours.

Charmers reached out again and touched Styles's hand. "Does he know?" she asked as gently as possible. She didn't want to pry. It was none of her business. But Styles had no one else she could talk to.

Monica wiped her eyes on her sleeve. "He doesn't want it. Told me to get rid of it."

Charmers face turned to granite. "Really?"

Grabbing a napkin, Monica blew her nose. "Yep."

Charmers leaned back. "Typical." Then she glanced up again and saw fire in Monica's eyes. She had seen that look only once before—last year. A drunk driver had run a red light on Wilson Street, T-boned an SUV, killing the female driver instantly. The drunk driver had a six-year-old strapped in a child seat in the back. Charmers almost had to restrain Monica from beating the crap out of him with her baton.

Monica saw the look Charmers was giving her. "It's not negotiable," Monica whispered.

Charmers nodded. "Your body, your choice. This is Nebraska."

"So I got rid of him instead."

Charmers smiled. "Good for you."

Monica looked away again, more tears building. "I want kids. I really do. I just never planned on having any this early."

Charmers frowned. "Weren't you—?"

Monica glanced back. "I was. But I missed one. I don't know how. So I wanted to wait a few days, let my system catch up again. But Carl insisted, said it would be fine. I said no. Then one thing led to another…" Monica's voice tailed off. She took a deep breath, then let it out slowly. Her expression shifted and she became all business. She stood up, drained the rest of her coffee. "I'm fine, honestly."

Charmers could see that her deputy wasn't. But she knew better not to push. "If you need anything. Anything. Just ask me. Okay?"

Monica nodded, adjusting her duty belt, subconsciously touching the grip of her holstered handgun, checking it was where it should be. "Thanks."

Charmers watched as Monica walked down to the sidewalk where her own cruiser hugged the curb. "Hey!" Charmers called out.

Monica turned.

"Be safe," Charmers said, forcing a smile.

Monica pointed back at Charmers and smiled for the first time today.

Charmers watched as Monica climbed in and pulled away, accelerating a little too quickly up the street. Anger and frustration coming through loud and clear in the fading whine of the engine.

A gust of wind spun across the street and up to where Charmers now sat alone at the picnic bench, blowing her hair across her face. The sun ducked momentarily behind a cloud, taking all the warmth of the day with it.

Chapter 12

The irony was, they couldn't exactly report the van as stolen.

Technically one of their employees was still driving it. But Alex and Vincent weren't willing just to sit by until the van turned up torched, left as a smoldering wreck, abandoned on the side of the road or dumped in a field somewhere out in the open plains. They had to find the van and Anton Wheeler, discreetly, without drawing the unwanted attention of the local authorities. Otherwise, questions would be asked: Why steal a load full of clean laundry? What was the motive? Was there more involved? Who owns the laundry business? What other activities do they do? The only unwanted attention Vincent had in mind was what he was going to rain down on Anton Wheeler when they caught up with him. You simply do not take a million in cash from the Romano family and expect to get a slap on the wrist.

Vincent had killed people for a lot less. The shallow marshes and swamps of the Meadowlands in New Jersey stand testament to those who had crossed Vincent Romano's path, only to then take up permanent residence there—at his insistence. Pelham Bay Park in the Bronx, a vast twenty-seven hundred-acre forlorn place of haunting woods and unsettling silence was another favorite where Vincent had sent many of the now forgotten.

"So what now?" Alex was driving.

Vincent sat in the passenger seat, staring out the window, his face creased with gruesome plans of retribution folding like origami in his mind. "I need to visit a library."

Alex glanced at him for a moment, knowing what the term

meant. Vincent traveled light, had to, especially when flying. But Vincent wasn't into reading books. It wasn't the kind of library he had in mind. The only similarity was that, unlike books, certain "items" could still be checked-out by the borrower and returned later, even to a different location.

"Do you know any here?"

Vincent nodded as a sly smile slowly spread across his face. "Plenty." Vincent glanced at the GPS, then plugged in an address from memory. His network of colleagues, alliances, and helpers stretched far and wide across the Midwest, built up fortuitously over the years. All of their locations were stored and catalogued in Vincent's head, a plethora of criminal resources to be accessed by him when needed.

"Five miles," Vincent said as the GPS fixed in the location, then drew up the fastest route in a pink, crooked line.

Alex nodded, an unsettling feeling coming over her. The assumption of violence wasn't her method of dealing with things. Joseph Durango was more of a theatrical demonstration than anything else. However, it had yielded the same result. It was amazing how self-preservation kicked in and loyalty went out the nearest open window when a gun was pointed at your head—or your groin. Yet somehow as she drove on, Alex got the feeling that Vincent wouldn't be that patient. He had a reputation for plunging into bouts of extreme violence. No warning. No questions. It was all black and white to him.

Over the years Alex had mastered the subtle art of finding out what made people tick. Then getting them to do what she wanted them to do. In her mind there were only two primal motivations in the human skull: greed and lust. The greed to live a little longer. The lust for pleasure, in whatever form your persuasion took. When people saw Alex, they saw a supremely focused businesswoman sheathed in the tailored suits she wore like armor. However, under the seemingly unwavering poise, subtle elegance, and business acumen was a deliberately deceptive, seriously driven, smiling assassin—minus the violence. The threat of violence was always present, though. To be wielded by another if required, never by her. An indiscriminate nod here, a subtle look there. Then someone like Costa, a foot soldier, the hammer to smash her nail, would step in, and do unto others what she couldn't do to them herself.

Ten minutes later Alex found herself outside a small strip mall with an Italian restaurant on the corner. She drove around and parked at the back, remaining in the car while Vincent went into the restaurant via the kitchen backdoor. He emerged five minutes later, carrying a small duffel bag, which he promptly threw on the backseat.

"So where to?" Alex asked.

"There's no point in going to where Anton lives or finding his girlfriend, if in fact he has one," Vincent replied, looking around through the windshield.

"Because a million in cash gives you better options. Discard the old and embrace the new," Alex replied, thinking about what "books" Vincent had "borrowed" in the duffle bag on the backseat.

Vincent turned and looked at his sister and nodded. "He's making a run for it. They all do. He isn't going back to his old life. That amount of money makes for a new life."

"You think the police will catch up with him before we do?"

"I hope not," Vincent replied. "I gave instructions for the van not to be reported to the police." Vincent checked his cell phone, then gave it a frustrating glare.

"What's wrong?" Alex asked, pulling away from the curb.

"Nothing. Just get to the highway," Vincent said, noticing Alex was watching him with his cell phone. He held it up. "I put the word out last night to my contacts around here. I'm expecting an update from them any time now."

"And you think they will find him?"

Vincent gave a knowing smile. "Wheeler is a thief. And like all thieves, they eventually slip up, make a mistake."

"What happens if he doesn't know he's got the money," Alex asked. "Maybe he just stole the van to sell and has no idea about the cash on board."

"I doubt that," Vincent replied as he looked at his sister. She was too soft. Always had been. Her being on this trip meant that as *Consigliere,* she, not he, represented their father in voice, mouth, and ear. That meant it was her authority that would dictate the course of events over the coming days. She could seek advice from their father if she so chose. However, in their father's absence or through his incapacity, Alex Romano wielded the scepter of family sovereignty. Any significant decision that would impact the family was hers and hers alone to make, not Vincent's. Knowing this gave Vincent no reprieve from the envy he felt. His role was to get them to the end, to find the money, to retrieve what was stolen from them. Alex's role was then to decide how that end ultimately played out.

"Anton Wheeler knows exactly about the money in the van," Vincent continued. Vincent had dismissed the possibility his sister was suggesting. It was not in his nature to choose a softer alternative. Pick the worst-case scenario, and from there you can have all bases covered. "I'm not going to take the risk. Either way we find him, the van, and everyone involved."

"I don't want anyone killed, Vincent." Alex looked at her brother sternly.

Vincent avoided his sister's glare.

"Vincent?"

Vincent just nodded, anger simmering under his skin. For Vincent, Anton Wheeler had made his choice. His fate was already sealed. He was going to suffer the consequences. So was anyone else who came in contact with the money.

Chapter 13

The alleyway reeked of decaying food and excrement, the lifecycle of human inputs and outputs that filled the narrow channel between the buildings.

Monica Styles stood in front of the dumpster, a dark stain of dried blood at her feet. They had yet to identify the homeless man. He had just come out of surgery again this morning, she had been told. Bleeding on the brain this time. More complications.

Monica had walked the length of the alleyway, twice, from opposite ends. But the perspective remained the same. The same angles, the same shapes, just in reverse. Apart from trash cans, crates of rotting vegetables, and the steel dumpster, there was nothing else of significance that indicated the unprovoked violence that had occurred. The victim had some loose change in his pockets and a crumpled dollar bill. So theft was ruled out as a motive. They found no drugs and no ID.

So it was—in Monica's mind—unprovoked, and that angered Monica. You don't beat up on a homeless person. They already have nothing to give, yet you want to take more? What little self-respect and hope do they have left in the world? Or even their life? Styles shook her head as she watched a trickle of oily water run down the center groove of the alleyway and through a steel grate.

She walked south and emerged on the sidewalk of the main street, the bank on her right, and a spread of low-key stores on either side and across the street. Turning around, she walked back along the full length of the alleyway again and found herself in an open parking lot at the rear of a strip of stores, two on the left were empty, vacant; For Lease signs hung skewed in their windows. The three stores on the right were almost devoid of life as well. One was a small electronics store, offering cheap repairs and secondhand refurbished computers. Another was a hairdresser with sun-faded pictures in the window, depicting hairstyles that were last in fashion when Truman sat in the White House. The end store sold common, everyday household items at discount prices.

It made no sense to Monica for someone to attack the homeless man. It was either another homeless person, in an act of desperation, or an act of total cowardice, with no motive other than pure malice by a passerby.

Monica walked toward the three stores on the right, stood under the exterior awning that ran the length of the building's facade, then glanced up.

She smiled. Her hunch paid off.

What she was hoping for was concealed under the slanted ceiling, almost deliberate in its placement, smudged with grime, and wrapped in dirty cobwebs.

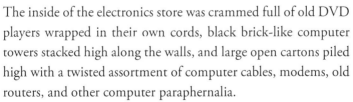

The inside of the electronics store was crammed full of old DVD players wrapped in their own cords, black brick-like computer towers stacked high along the walls, and large open cartons piled high with a twisted assortment of computer cables, modems, old routers, and other computer paraphernalia.

The kid behind the counter looked no older than eighteen. He glanced at Monica when she walked in. His eyes quickly slid down to her breasts, lingered there for a moment, before sliding back up to the embroidered badge on her uniform and lastly to her face. Judging from the kid's reaction, she guessed not too many females walked into this establishment.

"Does that thing work?" Monica asked, pointing through the window to a spot under the awning outside the store.

The kid's face went from a smirk to a lopsided grin. He snuck another quick look at Monica's chest, just for good measure. She allowed him the moment. She was proud of what she had, despite only being five six.

The kid finally spoke. "It should." He slid off his stool and eagerly rattled off something about megapixels, frames-per-second, aperture range, night filters, and progressive scanning CMOS—whatever that meant.

"I take it that's a yes," Monica replied dryly.

The kid nodded.

"How about we go out back then?"

The kid's jaw nearly hit the floor at Monica's request.

The back-office was crammed with even more computer castoffs. A small laminate desk hugged one wall, a computer and widescreen monitor sat on it, the keyboard lost under a layer of packing slips, bills, and burger wrappers. The computer screen was displaying some online, shoot'em up, military-style game where apparently America was invading North Korea. Another online player called "teabagyamom88" was single-handedly wiping out the Korean People's Army.

The kid, who, much to Monica's shock and dismay, turned out to be the storeowner, swept the food wrappers aside and looked up at her. "We're talking yesterday correct?"

"That's right. A homeless man was attacked in the alleyway next door to this building. I'm surprised you didn't hear about it."

The kid shrugged, sat down at the keyboard, and began tapping, scrolling, and clicking, his fingers a blur. He obviously was a hermit, content to bury himself in his own little world. Looking around the cave-like existence, Monica imagined the kid probably didn't even know World War II was over.

It only took him a few moments to bring up footage from yesterday morning. Styles told him the timeframe she was interested in looking at, and he began scrolling through the video footage from the camera he'd installed under the awning outside his store.

A clear, wide view of the parking lot appeared on the screen. "Hi-res," the kid said proudly. "No one really knows the camera is there." He turned and smiled at Monica. "Made it look old, like it doesn't work too well if anyone does notice it."

Clever, Monica thought. Most surveillance cameras were not discrete, more of a deterrent than anything else. But this camera was well-concealed and looked inert. Most people would have ignored it, gone about their business, thinking they were safe, unseen, hidden. Unfortunately, the camera didn't capture the entrance of the alleyway itself. It was in a black spot, out of the frame of the camera, which was understandable.

"I don't know exactly what I'm looking for," the kid said.

Monica leaned in and stared at the screen. "Anything unusual."

The kid leaned slightly toward her and inhaled.

"You get any closer and I'm going to arrest you," she said flatly as she focused on the video footage.

The kid leaned away. "Plenty of unusual things happen around here. Especially in that alleyway. Mainly kids hanging around, doing deals. A few drunks and the like." He hadn't seen anything out of the ordinary yesterday morning, he explained.

Spent the entire day inside the store, except for closing at lunchtime for half an hour when he ducked out to grab something to eat.

"Do many people use the alleyway to get to the main street?" Monica asked. "Bank customers parking in the lot back there, then cutting through the alley to the main street?"

"I don't really notice. Don't really keep track of the goings and comings in the parking lot. I installed the camera just to see if anyone was loitering outside my store at night when it's closed. It runs twenty-four seven, all backed up on disk." He pointed to a black brick on the desk with a winking blue light.

On the screen a few cars sped in and out of the parking lot at triple speed. People getting out of their cars, either dropping off computers to be fixed or picking up other items. But foot traffic was sparse, and no one seemed to have been heading in the direction of the alleyway. The time clock on the video footage sped on toward 10:00 a.m. Then just past that, a dark sedan pulled into the parking lot, away from the electronics store, and parked next to one of the lampposts. A man slid out and started walking to the right of the screen. Monica leaned, her eyes narrowed. The man had his head down, and as far as she could tell, he was wearing business attire, not a suit, but a shirt and tie at least. Moments later he disappeared, out of frame.

"Back up and run that man again."

They watched the video several times more, re-running it again and again; the car arriving, the man getting out in a shirt and tie, and heading to what seemed to be the entrance of the alleyway. The kid froze the screen just before the man disappeared from the frame.

Monica stared at the image. From the direction he was walking, he couldn't have been going to the other stores on the other side of the entrance of the alleyway. They were both empty.

"I need a copy of this footage."

The kid grabbed a thumb drive, backed up the video footage for yesterday, but held the thumb drive out of her reach. "What do I get in return?" he asked.

Monica raised an eyebrow. "In return?"

The kid nodded. "How about a date?"

Monica did a double take. The kid must have been sixteen. She was twenty-two. A six-year age difference would not be an issue if they were in their thirties and beyond—that's if she was interested, which she wasn't.

"What? Like I take you out for an ice cream?" she said sarcastically, reaching for the thumb drive.

But the kid pulled it away. "No. Like a real date," he said, smiling, getting his hopes up.

Monica stepped back and let out a sigh of exasperation. She didn't want to do this. Not today. "I have a partner," she said.

"So?" the kid replied. "Don't tell him."

He had balls, she had to admit. She stepped toward the kid. "I don't keep secrets," Monica replied, "from her."

And with that, the twinkle of excitement faded from the kid's eyes. "Oh," he said, long and slow.

"Oh, indeed," Monica said, snatching the thumb drive out of his hand.

She didn't like lying to the kid. But it was better than saying she was knocked up and had recently kicked out her boyfriend.

Chapter 14

As much as Diane hated the thought of doing it, the urge to pee was simply too much.

She thought she could hold on until she reached home. It was only another five miles or so.

But no matter how hard she squeezed her thighs together and gritted her teeth, it was no use. It was either pull over and do it on the side of the road or keep driving and risk having an accident inside the car.

So Diane decided to pull over.

She found a stretch of lonely, flat highway she knew where the ground dipped down, falling away from the edge before flattening out across the plains. There, she would be concealed from passing traffic. It was well away from the last gas station she had passed two miles back. Thankfully there was no one around, and she pulled over.

Getting out, Diane hastily scanned the horizon in both directions.

Good.

No one in sight as far as she could see, and it would only take a moment.

She locked the car and quickly went down the dirt slope, the urge to urinate increasing with each sliding step she took toward pure, sweet relief.

At the bottom of the slope, the ground was flat, scattered with small rocks but nothing substantial like a boulder she could crouch behind. To her relief, thirty yards ahead she spied a small thorny-looking bush. In the distance she could see a cluster of small trees, but knew she wouldn't make it that far. The small bush would have to do. It wasn't perfect but it was better than nothing.

Reaching the bush, Diane glanced back toward her car perched at the top of the shoulder of the highway and listened. The air was still, just a slight breeze but no sound of approaching traffic. She was below the line of the highway. Someone a mile away along the highway, if they happened to glance in the right direction, might see her as a dark blob against the barren landscape, that's all.

Almost bursting and unable to wait any longer, she hurried around the other side of the bush, turned her back to the highway, and just managed to rip down her panties and squat in the dirt before the combined result of three coffees she had drunk at the coffee shop with Martha Hendricks and a twelve ounce bottle of spring water came gushing out in one endless, steamy stream.

Holding on to her panties around her ankles, Diane closed her eyes for a moment and sighed in pure ecstasy.

When she opened them again, she took in the flat landscape in front of her. To her left the ground seemed churned up. A short, wide furrow cut a sway through the dirt like someone had plowed the ground. Then she saw something a few feet away, something white, a small washcloth. It looked pristine, like it was new, clean, out of place amongst the weeds, scrub, rocks, and dirt.

Finishing, Diane crouched up, and with her panties still around her ankles hobbled to where the cloth lay. She couldn't believe her luck.

The washcloth felt soft to the touch, freshly laundered.

She gave a smirk, wiped herself down with the cloth, and

pulled her panties back up. Maybe the washcloth had been thrown out of the window of a passing car. But it wasn't soiled. She shrugged, folded it in her hand, deciding to dispose of it properly when she returned home.

Diane took a moment to admire the landscape. It was a beautiful, wide expanse of earthy hues, deep blue sky and a scatter of high clouds.

Then she spotted something. Something glinted, farther away. Another shape, an object that stood out among the natural backdrop. Diane walked toward the strange object. It lay partially hidden among a clump of weeds, metallic-looking, the high sun reflecting off one shiny edge.

Stooping down, she looked at the object. Instinctively, Diane looked up, straight up into the sky, thinking that it had fallen out of an airplane cargo hold. How could it? There'd be wreckage everywhere. That's what the object looked like. Luggage.

She studied it some more. It was a small case, polished aluminum, shiny sides, the kind carried by stockbrokers, bankers, businessmen, she guessed. It looked solid, well-constructed, machine finished, commercial quality. It was scuffed, damaged, and dusty.

It took two hands to turn the attaché case over; it had a heaviness about it, full not empty, a large dent on the other side, one metal clasp torn free, the other still intact, the lid closed but skewed at an angle, a slight gap along the seam where the two halves of the case should have closed seamlessly together.

Feeling like she was being watched, Diane glanced around but saw no one. Her car still sat parked where she'd left it, the highway empty, the landscape empty, the sky empty. God and her conscience were her only companions in this lonely place.

She examined the case again. Before she knew it, her fingers had flipped the undamaged clasp and she had lifted the lid.

Diane's heart stumbled, her eyes went wide. She stared at the contents of the case for a full minute, couldn't tear her eyes away.

Seeing what Diane saw, most people would become devious, take on an alternate personality that they never knew was always hiding within them, just under their skin. Hyde would appear, and Jekyll would vanish into the periphery. Plans would start to formulate, calculating minds would suddenly spring into action. A life beyond reach suddenly within reach. Options now where there were none before. Happiness born out of despair.

Some people would smile. Others might even dance in the dirt in celebration.

Diane Miller felt none of these emotions. Only one emotion slowly crept over her as she gazed, almost in awe, at what lay inside the case.

Fear.

Rows of tightly stacked hundred dollar bills were layered end to end inside the aluminum case. A rectangular wallpaper of stoic-faced Benjamin Franklins stared up at her, taunting her. Diane's fingertips touched the many faces, feeling each one, expecting them to vanish in a wispy puff at any moment.

But it wasn't a mirage, an optical illusion. Diane wasn't hallucinating. The money was real, seemed real at least to her.

She slowly got to her feet, left the case where it was, and looked around.

The wind suddenly picked up, ruffling the corners of the bills in the case. The landscape around her felt empty, hollow, limitless. At that moment Diane felt like the only person standing on the earth.

She glanced back again over her shoulder to where her car was parked.

She glanced back down at the open attaché case, the blocks of money inside.

Quickly, she bent down, closed the lid, latched it, tucked the case under her arm and walked quickly up the slope toward her car.

The highway was clear in both directions. She opened the trunk, placed the case carefully inside, covered it with an old blanket, then slammed the lid, her heart racing.

The fear she had felt was now exacerbated. She couldn't shut it off. Was it fear she felt or adrenaline-fueled excitement? Her adrenal glands and neurons were going into overdrive at the possibilities that flooded her head.

Leaning against the trunk, Diane closed her eyes and took a few deep breaths, forcing her chest, her heart to slow down. She steadied herself and waited a few moments for her breathing to relax.

Opening her eyes again, she glanced back down the slope to where she had just come from, saw the bush she had peed behind, and farther in the distance, the spot where she had found the case, thinking it was still all a dream. But it wasn't. The case was in her trunk. She could feel it under her buttocks, pulsing, radiating through the sheet metal like she had found a piece of kryptonite in the sand hills.

It was there. A pile of money. Her ass, literally resting on top of it.

Suddenly Diane had the compulsion to move, to get in her car and drive away as fast as she could from this place.

So she did.

Chapter 15

After the third knock, the door finally opened.

Greg Miller stood on the other side, his face obscured, crosshatched by the screen door. He had come home early for the day, expecting Diane to be home, but she wasn't.

Monica Styles stood on the porch. "Greg Miller?"

Greg's eyes drifted over her uniform, badge, and then to the gun on her hip. "Yes. What's the problem?"

Monica took a step forward, expecting the screen door to open—but it remained firmly closed.

"No problem, Mr. Miller. I would just like to ask you a few questions about your visit to the bank in town yesterday."

Greg Miller looked over his shoulder, then opened the screen door and stepped outside, closing it behind him. He seemed slightly unsettled by the question.

"A homeless man was attacked yesterday morning in the alleyway next to the bank. I'm making some routine inquiries of everyone who may have visited the bank yesterday morning around the same time the man was attacked." Monica fixed him with her neutral gaze, one she had practiced many times in the mirror. She had it down pat by now. No smile. No frown. Deadpan with just a hint of glib.

Greg Miller shook his head. "I just had to take care of some banking business, that's all."

"That's okay, Mr. Miller." She slid her notebook from her top pocket in one deft motion. Another practiced move, like drawing her weapon from its holster. Smooth, effortless, muscle memory in action, her gaze not breaking with Greg Miller's eyes. The action spoke volumes: I'm going to write down what you say next, commit your words to ink on paper, public record. To some, the action was more intimidating, more threatening than a hand being placed on a holstered gun. It made you think twice, to come clean and tell the truth. Policing was ninety percent psychology, ten percent use of force.

Greg Miller's eyes narrowed as he watched Monica look at him expectantly, pen poised over the notebook.

Monica raised an eyebrow. "Can I ask you what time you visited the bank, exactly?"

"How do you know I visited the bank?"

Styles just smiled. *Defensive right away.* "Sorry. I forgot to explain. The bank provided us with a list of customers who they believed came in between nine and midday. There weren't that many. I'm just contacting each of them to see if they saw anything or heard of anything in the alleyway next to the bank."

Greg nodded but remained tight-lipped.

The silence dragged on.

"What time?" Monica persisted.

"Around ten," Greg finally spoke.

"And did you see anything, Mr. Miller?"

"No, I parked in the street across from the bank."

Styles turned and pointed to the sleek, black sedan in the driveway. "And that's your car, Mr. Miller?"

"That's correct," Greg replied, somehow thinking the young deputy already knew the answer to that question. "Like I said, I drove there and parked across the street."

Monica scribbled something in her notebook. More psychology. "Have you ever used the alleyway at all next to the bank?" She didn't look up as she wrote. "Maybe parked in the lot at the rear of the building? Or visited any of the other stores at the rear of the block?" Monica finally looked up, a cordial smile on her face.

Greg made a show of thinking, then shook his head vehemently. "No."

Monica held his gaze, and he reflected it back, more defiantly, though.

She went back to her notes. *Greg Miller denies parking in the lot and using the alleyway. Suspect is lying.* She underlined the last three words—twice.

Greg Miller's car was definitely the car she had seen on the security footage, the car that had pulled into the parking lot at the rear of the bank just after 10:00 a.m. Seeing him in person only confirmed her suspicions that he was in fact the driver of the car. It was he who had gotten out, walked across the parking lot toward the entrance to the alleyway. She had pulled an image of the license plate from the security footage she had sent to the tech guys in Grand Island to enhance. DMV records then brought her to Greg Miller's doorstep.

"Perhaps, Mrs. Miller, on occasion may have parked and visited the bank herself, maybe used the alleyway as a shortcut?"

Greg shook his head again, like it was an absurd suggestion. "I can't imagine why she would do that. That parking lot—the adjacent stores, she wouldn't go there. I take care of all the family finances, not her."

Styles made another note in her book. *Denies wife goes to bank. Greg Miller is a control freak.*

"Maybe she has in the past, and she just didn't mention it to you?" It was a pointless question, designed to further unsettle Greg Miller. Monica was giving him an out, a life-line to admit that he was in the parking lot and had ducked through alleyway to get to the entrance of the bank. She could place him at the scene around the window of opportunity when the attack happened. But there was no evidence that he had actually been in the alleyway. Just his word that he hadn't.

"Is Mrs. Miller home today?"

Greg started to feel his irritation rise. "No. She's out at the moment. She hasn't been feeling well, and I really don't want her being bothered about something as trivial as this."

"Oh, I'm sorry to hear that. I hope she gets better." More scribbling in the notebook. *Suspect seems unsettled. Doesn't want me to talk to his wife.*

"Is there anything else I can help you with Officer…Styles?" Greg asked after reading the name on Monica's tag.

Styles continued to smile. Then she tapped the gold star pinned to her uniform with her pen. "I'm not a police officer. I'm a sheriff's deputy."

Smart, little bitch.

Monica gave Greg a cold stare. "And this isn't something trivial. A man is in hospital with life-threatening injuries."

Greg Miller wiggled his jaw side-to-side, niggling pain creeping up one side of his face He looked down at Styles, appraising her with contempt. Maybe if they had met under different circumstances, things could have been so much better. What was she? Five six, maybe a hundred fifty pounds max? So much better, he thought as he studied Styles, his mind drifting toward more tantalizing possibilities. He would have pulled her into a dark space where no one would hear her scream. Slapped her around a few times. Made her lips bleed. Pulled her hair too. Maybe wrench it hard enough for some of it to come away in a tuft in his hand.

"No. That will be all today, Mr. Miller."

Greg snapped back from his cruel fantasy.

"Thank you for your time and your co-operation." Monica Styles slid her notebook back into her top pocket, turned, and walked back down the porch steps.

Greg Miller watched her closely as she slid into the sheriff's cruiser and pulled away, eventually disappearing down the street.

He stood there for a long time, staring down the street, slowly grinding his teeth, the pain in his jaw growing steadily worse.

Alex and Vincent spent the rest of the day following up on what few leads they had in and around Grand Island. Information was slowly being drip-fed to Vincent via his network of contacts, nothing significant, though. There was still no sign of Anton Wheeler or the van.

That was until late afternoon. Vincent received a call from the shift supervisor whom he had swiftly promoted to the temporary general manager position to replace Tyson Banks at the laundry. The supervisor knew nothing other than a company van had been stolen by an employee, and if law enforcement made contact, he was to provide as little information as possible to them, and call Vincent immediately.

Alex drove while Vincent took the call.

"Any news?" Alex asked, when her brother ended the call, almost throwing his cell phone into the windshield in frustration.

"Sheriff turned up at the laundry," Vincent hissed, his face tight, jaw clenched, like he had trouble forming the words. "The van ran off the highway and crashed some place out of town yesterday."

"Yesterday?"

Vincent nodded in disbelief. "Things move slow out here apparently."

"And Anton Wheeler?"

"In the hospital, unconscious. But alive. Under police guard, I imagine."

Alex knew better than to ask about Tyson Banks. He was either in the hospital as well or at home, taking a few days off to recuperate from his injuries. She knew law enforcement would come knocking eventually. Both she and Vincent didn't want someone as weak and as hesitant as Banks accidentally saying something that he shouldn't. Just like Joe Durango, Tyson Banks was another employee who had let them down. He was expendable. "And where is the van now? There must be wreckage."

Vincent twisted his neck up and down, joints popping and cracking as he did. "Some damn towing yard. Not much left of it, so the sheriff claims. The sheriff was pretty tight-lipped as well. Would not reveal the location."

"And the money? Does the sheriff know?"

Vincent twisted his neck some more, trying to abate the tension he felt. "Didn't mention it. I'm guessing they don't have a clue or they would have said something."

They drove in silence for a while, contemplating what to do next. They both knew their options were limited. They couldn't exactly walk into the sheriff's office, identify themselves as the owners of the laundry business and demand to see the wreckage and also to talk to Anton Wheeler.

Vincent glanced at his cell phone again. "Pull over."

Alex checked her mirrors, then pulled off the road and onto the shoulder. This time of day traffic was minimal.

Vincent rubbed the back of his neck, while imagining leaning over Wheeler's hospital bed and slowly choking the man, all the time watching with delight as the pulsing blip on his heart rate monitor gradually slowed and eventually flatlined. It was like they were being taunted. They had found the van or what had happened to it, and Wheeler, only to discover both were painstakingly out of reach.

"There couldn't be that many towing places around here," Alex said.

Vincent was already thumbing on his cell phone. "Three," he finally replied, squinting at the screen. "They would have used a local contractor, someone in the county. Grand Island is too far." On the cell phone screen, Vincent could see three red pin drops. One south of Hazard. Another twenty-two miles west of Loup City heading toward Ansley. The last location was just outside the small village of Rockville, fifteen miles south. It would be a simple method of elimination.

"They're all closed at this time of day," Vincent said, reading off his phone.

"It's not a good idea to break-in to them, even at night," Alex suggested, hoping her brother wouldn't be so stupid.

"Let's call it a day," Vincent finally said, exasperated. "Make a fresh start tomorrow." Truth was Vincent needed a drink. He always thought better with some alcohol inside him. He wasn't about to give up, to accept failure. Especially as their father was watching.

Alex nodded. It had been a long, almost fruitless day. With this new piece of news, they needed to go back to the motel, regroup, and formulate a new plan for tomorrow.

Chapter 16

Impulse took over.

A sudden burst of selfish clarity demanded decisive action from Diane. And before she knew it, Diane Miller was turning into the twenty-four-hour self-storage facility, her instincts and her heart, navigating the steering wheel, not cold pragmatic logic.

She didn't intend to turn into the facility. She intended to drive right past, as she had done on countless occasions before following the route home. However, there was something about the large black sign, perched high on a steel pole on the edge of the east highway, that caught her attention and set in motion the first stages of a plan. On the sign was the image of a spaceman tethered on an umbilical cord, big, bold white letters emblazoned underneath: *You Need Space, Man*! with the promise of twenty-four-hour safe and secure storage.

The drive back home had given Diane plenty of time to think. Just her, alone, no radio, and the sound of the wind bristling off the leading edges of the car, her side window down, the breeze in her face, and endless possibilities flowing through her head. It felt like she was driving with radioactive material in the trunk. In the wrong hands, it could do so much harm, be destructive, ruin lives. In the right hands—her hands, she could finally do some good for herself. She didn't know what to do with the money—for the moment. She couldn't just leave it in her car. She knew however what she wasn't going to do about it—tell Greg.

Diane had a deep-seated feeling of not trusting him. Lately, his words of concern, of care for her seemed unconvincing, not genuine. Maybe it was the new medication, awakening her to him. She didn't know. All she knew was she could not tell him. In the back of her mind, images of what she could do with the money—the freedom, the choices, a new life, leaving this town, this place that was slowly strangling her—were also swirling around, complicating matters further. The frontal lobe of her brain was telling her a different story, though, trying to modify what she thought were selfish emotions that seemed to be engulfing her. Trying to shape possible outcomes into what was more socially acceptable: Go to the police. Hand in the money. Tell Greg. Do the right thing. However, for Diane, the idea of keeping the money wasn't her being selfish or dishonest at all. She wasn't a bad person; bad things had happened to her. For just once, she wanted some good to happen to her, to experience something joyful and uplifting. She saw the money in the trunk as a means of creating a better future for herself.

So when she pulled into the parking lot of the storage facility and up to the front of the small office, desperation, hope, and self-interest had won the battle over cold logic and "socially acceptable" behavior. For once in a long time, Diane Miller thought of herself only—what was right for her. No one else.

There were thirty storage units in total, three different sizes to choose from, a sign outside the office announced. Reinforced aluminum construction, heavy-duty roller door with commercial quality locks.

A buzzer sounded as Diane stepped inside the cool office.

Behind the fake wood laminate counter, a man in his fifties with fading dark hair, and faster fading hope of finding a better paying job at his age, glanced up.

A plastic sign holder on the counter displayed the various unit rental prices.

"Can I help you, ma'am?"

An old water cooler dispenser sat in one corner, with an inverted empty water bottle perched on top, dusty and yellow with neglect. Next to it sat the brittle remains of what had once been a tall rubber plant that seemed to have died of thirst and heat exhaustion.

"I'd like to rent one of your storage units," Diane said with purpose.

The man quickly retrieved a clipboard from under the counter, thumbed through a few pages, found the page he was looking for, and placed it on the counter. "We have twenty-five units available. Take your pick."

Diane stepped forward and looked down at the small map of the complex. The units that were taken were all at the front of the complex, saving the renter time and effort to drive or walk. There was a row of unoccupied units along the back, farthest from the office and the entrance gate. Diane chose the unit in the far eastern corner of property, right on the end of the empty row. It was the most isolated, and that suited her just fine.

"I'll take number thirty," Diane said, tapping her finger on the map. The particular unit was ten feet by twenty feet and eighty dollars a month to rent.

The man looked down to where she was pointing and shrugged. "Suit yourself." He took back the clipboard, conjured up almost out of thin air another clipboard and handed it to Diane to fill out a one-page form. "For how long?"

Diane glanced at the form fastened to the clipboard. She was making this up on the fly. But it was the right decision, to hide the money, to buy her some time until she decided exactly what she was going to do next. "Three months."

The man nodded, went to a steel floor safe, and retrieved a set of keys.

Diane filled out the paperwork, all except the spot where a name and address had to be inserted. She stared down at the form, indecisive. She gave a little smile, then wrote a name, together with a street address in town that didn't exist and handed back the clipboard. "I'd like to pay all upfront, in cash."

The man behind the counter raised an eyebrow. Cash was good. Rare, but much appreciated. He handed over a set of keys together with a swipe card and explained to Diane there was a fifty-dollar replacement charge for both if lost. The swipe card was for the security access pedestrian gate next to the main gate, the keys were for the lock on her particular storage unit. Then he gave her the access code to open and close the main entrance electric gate when she drove in and out.

There was twenty-four-hour access, and automatic security lighting came on at dusk and switched off at dawn. He also gave her a small printed brochure, with a smaller version of the map of the complex on one side, an emergency contact number, and a list of rules.

Diane opened her purse and stared at two ten-dollar bills and some change and panicked, momentarily forgetting the present and still living in the past. She glanced at the man, slightly embarrassed. "I'll just need to go to my car to get the cash."

"No problem." The man watched her as she went outside and around to the rear of her car, then lifted the trunk, effectively blocking the view of what she was doing on the other side.

Who kept cash in the trunk of their car?

Diane returned and handed over three hundred-dollar bills.

The man behind the counter rang up the sale, handed back

sixty dollars, and told Diane to have a nice day.

After Diane had left the office, he opened the cash register again, withdrew eighty dollars in cash, and slipped it into his pocket before sliding the cash drawer shut. For some inexplicable reason, he had forgotten to mention to Diane that with a three-month rental, the first month was free, an oversight he had used on previous occasions with other customers.

Diane climbed back into her car and drove along the double lane that ran down the center of the complex, past storage units that were grouped like barracks on each side, a row completing the U-shape at the back. Each unit was gray aluminum sided with white aluminum roof sheeting. An eight-foot chain-link fence topped with barbed wire encircled the entire complex, completing the simple but secure look. Her unit was at the far right-hand corner. She pulled up outside and got out. The place was empty, no one else around. She unlocked the hardened steel industrial padlock, and lifted the door upward. Inside, the space was a simple slab design. Poured gray concrete floor, with a smooth troweled finish, two fluorescent fixtures in the ceiling, with a light switch near the door. Glancing over her shoulder one more time, Diane looked around before she popped the trunk and lifted out the attaché case, placing it squarely in the middle of the floor inside the bare unit. The case looked so lonely in the empty space; however, Diane had other plans on how to fill it. She pulled the roller door down behind her and flipped on the lights. Crouching down, she opened the case and stared at the contents in awe. She closed her eyes and took a deep breath, thinking that at any moment she would snap out of the dream she was having and slide comfortably back into the nightmare that was her life.

But it wasn't a dream, and the nightmare was fading a little more every time she looked at the money.

The money was stolen she guessed. It looked like it. But then her life had been stolen from her, along with her daughter's life too. The money was some form of recompense toward that.

She reached out and touched the money again. Each brick of notes was secured by a paper wrapper, the bills in one brick, the one she had taken the money from to pay for the storage unit, not as tightly bound as the others. From that same brick, Diane quickly peeled back five bills, slid them out, and tucked them into her pocket. She needed to break down some of the money into smaller denominations, otherwise it would attract suspicion, store cashiers holding every bill up to the light to make sure it wasn't counterfeit. Like the drones Diane used to pilot, she needed to fly below the radar from now on.

Closing the case, Diane exited the unit, secured the padlock around the latch, wobbling it in place a couple of times to make sure it was secure, then drove out of the complex.

At the bank there were two other customers in front of Diane as she stood in line. When it was her turn, a young woman beckoned her over.

"Hi, Mrs. Miller."

It had been such a long time since Diane had been in the bank, she didn't recognize the young woman smiling at her through the Plexiglas. She looked vaguely familiar, like everyone else in Diane's life, ghosts who flitted in and out. Diane's recollection of faces was getting better lately. She looked down at the nametag on the woman's chest. *Sharon.*

"Hi, Sharon, how are you?" Diane still had no idea who the young woman was or how she knew her name.

"I'm good. I haven't seen you in here for ages."

"I've been busy, that's all." Diane played along with the small talk.

Sharon nodded sympathetically. She wanted to tell Diane that she was sorry to hear about her daughter, Ella. Then thought better of it. Best not to dig up the past, not remind people of something they probably spent every waking hour trying to forget.

Diane slid the five one hundred dollar bills through the transfer tray. "I'd like you to break this down, easier for me to use."

"Sure," Sharon said, taking the bills.

Panic hit Diane, and she felt like grabbing the money back.

But it was too late. Sharon expertly thumbed through the bills, holding each one up to check they weren't counterfeit.

"Tens and twenties okay?"

"Great," Diane replied, trying to hide her relief.

Sharon pulled out her cash drawer and counted out the smaller bills in front of her. "Did you bring in that form by the way?"

Diane watched as each bill was expertly counted out like a casino dealer. "What form?"

Sharon kept counting out the money, small neat little piles, perfect edges, no overlap. When she was finished, she fixed a rubber band around the entire bundle, placed it into an envelope and passed it back through the transfer tray. "I told Greg yesterday that I needed to verify your signature on that form. The form you signed."

Diane took the envelope, placed it quickly in her bag, and zipped it shut "What form was that?"

Sharon gave a puzzled look. "To remove you as authority on your joint checking account."

Diane just stared blankly at the young woman.

Chapter 17

The Sheriff's Department was located in the Loup City courthouse, the county seat of Sherman County.

With a population of just over one thousand, Loup City was a fifty-mile drive northwest of Grand Island. To call it a "department" would be to conjure up images of multiple desk pods, phones ringing, and an army of sheriff deputies and admin support staff hustling around, solving numerous crimes and misdemeanors.

But there was no army of helpers. Just two desks in a small room; one of which Monica Styles was now seated at.

Charmers walked in shortly after 6:00 p.m. to see her young deputy deeply engrossed with whatever she was looking at on her computer screen.

Monica had spent the last hour going through her day, fact-checking, clarifying, and expanding on the notes she had taken from investigating the alleyway where the homeless man had been assaulted, the subsequent conversations she'd had with the eager kid from the electronics store, and then her conversation with Greg Miller.

In the corner of the cramped office, a bar refrigerator hummed away. Charmers went immediately to it, pulled two beers out, popped the caps, then placed one on the desk in front of Monica before collapsing with a heavy sigh onto the chair opposite her.

Monica glanced suspiciously at the beer bottle in front of her.

Charmers drained almost half her own beer before she spoke.

"One beer isn't going to kill you."

Monica pushed the bottle toward her boss. "I'm fine, thanks."

Charmers gave a shrug. "Your loss. More for me."

When they could, the two of them would meet back at the office for a wrap up of the day's events, compare ideas, and plan for the next day. Monica had already checked-in with Charmers several times during the day, keeping her up-to-date with matters she was handling. But it was always good to catch up, face to face, and shoot the breeze.

"How's Anton Wheeler?" Monica asked, her eyes never leaving the computer screen. She had just started a search on Greg and Diane Miller, wanting to find out more about the couple. She had been allocated the follow-up on the homeless man assault while Charmers was working on the stolen van and Anton Wheeler.

Charmers leaned back and rested her boots on the corner of the desk, billowed her cheeks, then let out a slow breath, the culmination of a twelve-hour shift full of frustration, dead ends, and zipped-up mouths. "He's still in an induced coma at the hospital. Doctors reckon he's lucky to be alive. I paid a visit to the towing yard this morning. The van's totaled. Can't tell which is the front and which is the ass. Just a twisted mess. I might go out to the crash site tomorrow, double-check. I think the road crew grabbed everything. Simple auto theft. Wheeler has priors. So if he ever wakes up, he'll be going back inside. I back-tracked from the crash scene and caught him on security footage filling the van at a gas station a few miles back. Plain as day."

"And the business that he stole the van from?"

"Here's the strange thing," Charmers said, taking her boots off the desk and leaning forward, cradling her beer bottle in her hands. "It's a laundry business in Grand Island, like a charity. I paid them a visit this afternoon. They were very tightlipped."

"How so?" Monica glanced sideways from her screen.

"They weren't really forthcoming about Wheeler. The guy running the place was more concerned about the wreckage, wanting to know when they could get it back. I told him it had been totaled. Showed him some photos I took with my cell phone. He wasn't convinced. He said that once we're done with it, he'll send a truck to collect it. Said it was for insurance purposes and the like. I told him he could have a copy of my report for the insurance company. But he was insistent on getting the actual wreckage back." Charmers shook her head. "It's a worthless piece of junk now."

Monica just nodded and went back to typing away on her keyboard.

"The homeless man has been identified as Miles Burke," Monica said, "no fixed address. No next of kin as far as I can tell." Monica had visited the hospital again after talking to Greg Miller. Like Anton Wheeler, Burke was also still unconscious. The doctor had given her an update, saying that Burke had to be wheeled back into surgery again because of more bleeding on the brain, head trauma suffered from someone kicking him repeatedly in the skull. Styles had already relayed this to Charmers during an earlier phone call.

"So no solid leads on the scumbag who attacked him?"

"Here's the deal," Monica said. "I went and saw Greg Miller after I ran the plates through the system, got his address out of the DMV. His car does match the one I saw on the security footage in the parking lot behind the bank. But I can't clearly see him entering the alleyway, and I don't know where he was walking to."

They sat in silence for a few moments, Monica engrossed in her search on the computer, Charmers contemplating what her deputy had just told her.

"So he's lying to you," Charmers finally said.

Styles glanced away from the screen. "I haven't told you yet what he said when I interviewed him."

Charmers just smiled. "That's why I'm sheriff, Mons." She drained her beer, tossed the bottle into the wastebasket, and reached for Monica's. "I can tell from the look on your face. You look irritated, puzzled, smacking those keys like it's an ATM that just swallowed your card. You're not convinced about what he told you." Charmers nodded at the coffee cup on the desk next to Monica's right elbow. When Charmers walked in before, she could smell the raw, bitter scent of cooked coffee, saw the old residue simmering in the glass carafe on the hotplate in the small kitchenette. At least an hour old, not freshly brewed. "That's probably your third cup. My guess is you've been sitting here for an hour, maybe two, going through the databases, checking up on him."

Monica smiled at her boss. While she thought of herself as smart, observant, a good judge of character—except for her last boyfriend—she still had a lot to learn. "You know you should be a detective, Meredith."

Charmers nearly gagged on a mouthful of beer. "It doesn't take a detective to solve most of the problems in this town," she said, wiping her chin. She pointed her beer bottle at the back of the computer screen. "So what can you tell me about Greg Miller?"

Styles spent the next ten minutes describing her informal interview with Greg Miller. How he had lied about not parking in the lot at the rear of the bank, saying instead he had parked in the street out front.

Charmers sat quietly, slowly drinking Monica's unwanted beer, listening as her deputy went through her notes.

Greg Miller worked as a sales rep for a large medical supply company in Grand Island. Forty years old. Married to Diane Miller. No previous criminal record, just a few parking and speeding violations. No social media accounts. Not much else to go on.

"And his wife, Diane?"

Monica closed her notebook. "I haven't looked into her yet or gone into them in-depth as a couple. But I will."

Charmers nodded and finished her beer, the empty bottle joining the other one in the wastebasket. "Maybe go by there tomorrow. See if you can catch her at home when her husband isn't there. Talk to her alone." With a grumble, Charmers rose off her chair, stretched, and cracked her tired muscles and sore joints. "Not getting any younger," she complained. "Guess I better head off and do the family thing. Husband and all that." She looked down and noticed Monica wince slightly at her comment. "Hey, I'm sorry," she said softly. "I didn't mean to—"

"No problem," Monica waved her off. "I'm fine. Really."

Charmers held her deputy's gaze for a moment, her heart going out to her. So young. So talented. And then this.

"I'm going to stay back for a while," Monica nodded at her computer screen. "Keep going. See what else I can find about Greg and Diane Miller."

"Are you sure? Do you want me to bring you something? You're eating for—" Charmers stopped herself, then hung her head in mock shame. "Sorry. Just my motherly instinct putting my big foot in my big mouth again."

Monica smiled. Charmers was like a mother to her, like the mother she never had, or had but had never really gotten close to. "Really, I'm fine. I'll grab some takeout if I get hungry."

Charmers gave a look of concern. "Don't work too late."

Monica nodded and went back to her computer search.

Charmers gathered up her gear, gave a final farewell wave, then was gone.

Chapter 18

"Where have you been?"

Diane could tell Greg was angry. She had just arrived home. It was dark and after the bank, she had decided to run a few more errands around town.

She thought it was best not to mention what Sharon had told her at the bank, about some form Greg apparently went in with to remove her from their checking account. Diane had no intention of removing herself from anything at the moment. In the past she may have conceded to Greg, relinquished some of her responsibilities, just for the sake of ease. Now, however, as she regarded Greg as he stood in the kitchen, a scowl wrapped across his face, she saw him in an even more suspicious light.

"I had a longer than usual session with Dr. Redding," Diane said, dumping down a bag of groceries on the counter.

Greg looked at her skeptically, searching her face before offering a smile, his initial suspicion appeased.

"Steak and salad okay for dinner?" Diane asked, unpacking the groceries without waiting for a response.

"I didn't mean it that way, Diane," Greg replied, still watching his wife carefully, almost like she was a stranger in their house, bewildered by this recent change in her behavior. Diane hadn't cooked in ages, and here she was, navigating around the kitchen, opening the cupboards and drawers, pulling out utensils, like a chef starting a meal service at a restaurant. "I was just worried where you were."

Diane turned to face him, a large chef's knife suddenly in her hand, the tip pointed at his spleen, a smile on her face that made Greg slightly uneasy. "No problem. Just give me twenty minutes and dinner will be ready."

Greg nodded, glanced at the knife in his wife's hand, and grabbed a beer from the fridge. "I'll just catch up with some work in the study."

Diane placed the knife down on the counter then did something that she hadn't done in ages. She reached up and gave Greg a kiss on the cheek. "I just want things to go back to how they were, Greg." She gazed into his stupefied eyes. "I want to contribute more. Ease back into the domesticated things I used to do when I was home. Cooking, cleaning, making dinner. Dr. Redding suggested that it would be a good idea. To keep my mind occupied with normality. Take some of the pressure off you."

Greg searched his wife's eyes again, baffled by her words. In her absence, he had searched the kitchen, their bedroom— everywhere, looking for the pill bottle, the new medication Dr. Redding had prescribed his wife. But he couldn't find it anywhere. Then it dawned on him that Diane must have kept the bottle of pills on her at all times. Greg nodded, not quite knowing what to say, then scuttled down the hallway to the study.

Diane's smile of domesticated bliss soon vanished, replaced with a cold look of loathing on her face as she turned back to the counter, pulled out a cutting board, and began slicing and dicing carrots, picturing them as Greg's fingers with each determined stroke of the blade she took.

Later, they ate at the dining room table, no candles but real napkins. It felt good to Diane to make something, to prepare a meal. She wanted to get back into the full swing of things, or at least give that impression.

While preparing dinner, Diane could feel herself starting to crash, coming down off the medicated high she had been feeling. Her confidence started to wane. She could feel herself slipping back into the listless state she was so used to. So she carefully retrieved the bottle of pills from her pocket, making sure Greg didn't see, and swallowed another two.

"So what did Dr. Redding say?" Greg asked.

"Not much." Diane was deliberately vague. "Just that my progress was good. This new medication has really helped me, cleared my head." Diane watched his reaction carefully.

Greg gave a smirk, not bothering to even look up from his steak as he cut into it. He chewed gleefully on a piece of the tender meat. "This steak tastes wonderful, honey," he said, looking up. "What did you marinate it in?"

"A little bit of this and a little bit of that." Diane gave a loving smile, thinking back to what she had done to Greg's steak before cooking it in a separate frying pan than her own.

"And did she say when Dr. Farrell would be back?"

Diane gave a breezy look, "Oh, not really. But I like Dr. Redding a lot more than Dr. Farrell. I find him too stuffy, too old school, not willing to try new things."

Greg looked up on hearing this. "Try new things?"

Their eyes met across the table as Diana took a sip from her wine glass.

"Should you really be drinking if you're taking medication?"

Diane hadn't touched a drop of alcohol in over twelve months. She wasn't really a drinker, maybe one or two glasses of wine a week with a meal in the past. But this was certainly a new development, Greg thought as he observed his wife.

"Dr. Redding said it was fine to drink alcohol with this medication. It's one of the new ones." Another lie. Redding had actually cautioned Diane against consuming any alcohol while taking the pills. It could augment the effect of the medication. "She also said I need to get back into how I was—daily habits, diet, and everything else. Do all the things I used to do."

Greg gave Diane a perplexed look, then went back to slicing off another piece of his steak, chewing on the meat, grinding it down with his teeth, savoring the gritty, spicy rub Diane had obviously coated it with. *Dr. Redding this, Dr. Redding that,* a little voice inside his head mocked as he chewed. Diane couldn't shut up about the damn woman, singing her praises at every opportunity she could. It was really beginning to irritate Greg to no end. "That's nice, dear," he said mechanically, in a tone that hinted he really didn't care about Diane's opinion or what she had just said and hadn't really been listening to her, anyway. It was a ruse, though. He had been listening, and watching, very carefully. Subtly noting everything, storing it away in one of the many filing cabinets inside his scheming mind.

Diane smiled and topped up her wine glass under Greg's watchful eye. "And how was your day?"

"The usual. I'm working on a major sales proposal for a big corporate client. If I can pull it off, I'll finally get that bonus I've been telling you about."

Diane raised an eyebrow. "The one you missed out on the last month?"

"That's right."

Diane gave a sly smile and returned Greg's previous compliment. "That's nice, dear."

Greg frowned, looking at Diane. "Is everything okay?"

Diane mocked puzzlement. "Everything is fine. Why do you ask?"

"I don't know. You just seem…"

Diane waited for Greg's response.

Greg shrugged. "I don't know. You just seem…different."

"How so?"

Greg thought for a moment. "I don't know. Just different. You seem more relaxed. More like your old self." *Decisive. Self-assured. Certain. Even slightly arrogant,* Greg felt like saying but didn't. Diane's recent behavior gave Greg some concern. Not alarm, just concern. He didn't want Diane to return to her old self. It meant he would be losing control over her—something he wanted to avoid at all costs.

Diane reached for her glass. "Well, that's a good thing, isn't it?"

So many questions, Greg thought. Diane has definitely changed in the last few days—and he knew who was to blame.

"I agree," he said happily, his expression not matching the words that came out of his mouth. "I want you to be how you were. Before everything changed."

Diane nodded. "So do I." Diane went back to her meal, then spoke again without looking up. "That reminds me, Greg. I was in the bank today."

Greg coughed, almost choking on a piece of meat. "The bank?" he asked, struggling to keep his voice civil, unwavering. "You know I do all the banking. Why were you in there today?" Greg quickly swallowed some wine to clear his throat.

"Like I said, I want to resume my responsibilities. Go back to keeping an eye on things financially." Diane looked at Greg lovingly. "You've been such a big help over the last twelve months, and I agree with what you said before, that I needed to contribute more. Do more to help around here."

Greg began to slowly grind his teeth.

"I was thinking of getting a part-time job as well. I just

wanted to see how much money we had in the bank, check on our finances."

The side of Greg's head started to throb.

"The man behind the counter was very helpful. He didn't know me, but after I showed him my driver's license, he printed off a statement of our joint checking account."

Greg nodded slowly. *Good.* Diane hadn't been served by Sharon. Muffling a sigh of relief, Greg went back to his meal, slicing his steak a little less vigorously this time.

"And you were right," Diane continued. "We're just living from day-to-day. I feel like such a burden on you, on us."

Greg shook his head, the throbbing he initially felt subsiding slightly. "I disagree. You're not a burden. I told you, I would take care of everything while you were recuperating. That's what husbands are for."

Diane placed her cutlery down and wiped her mouth with her napkin. "Well, things are going to be different from now on. I need to have more control."

Control? Greg thought incredulously. The throbbing had returned with a vengeance. *You mean fucking dominate!*

"I want to start earning some money for us. The man at the bank said we should make an appointment with a financial advisor. You know, do a financial plan, a plan for our future together. Take a look at everything, all our expenses, maybe even do a budget."

Under the table, one of Greg's legs started to involuntarily spasm, jitter up and down, a subconscious trigger. He was losing control of the situation. It took every ounce of restraint for him to calmly resume eating and stifle the urge to take his fork, reach across the table, and stab his wife repeatedly in the head with it. Inside, Greg was screaming. On the outside, he was a picture of peace and composure.

It was the old Diane coming back to haunt him as she had done for so many years before. To control him, to dominate the relationship, to take the lead. He wasn't happy about suddenly being questioned about the home finances, the sudden interest Diane had in wanting to work, or questioning what he was doing at work. The last thing he wanted was some squid-faced financial advisor from the bank poking around. It would only take a matter of minutes for them—or Diane—to discover the real story as to why it appeared like they were living paycheck to paycheck each week.

Greg's cell phoned buzzed. He glanced at the screen, then almost looked relieved.

"What is it?" Diane asked, not happy that even at the dinner table Greg felt the need to have his phone by his side.

Greg gave a long, drawn-out sigh. "Just something for work." He turned the phone over, screen-side down, then smiled up at Diane. "I might have to go out later, that's all."

Chapter 19

The truth was Monica Styles really had nothing else to do that evening.

It was either work, eat takeout, and delve into the lives of the Millers or go home to her empty, one-bedroom apartment with a bare refrigerator and the aftershave scent of her ex-boyfriend, the father of her unborn child, still lingering in the air. Too many hurtful memories that Monica didn't want to deal with at the moment. She would go home—eventually—when she was too tired to notice the remnants of a failed relationship and just crash out on the bed, then get up in the morning to do it all again.

At her fingertips, Monica had access to the various law enforcement databases, state and national level. She combined this with common knowledge searches on the Internet and began to look for any information about Diane Abigail Miller. Half an hour later, she had curated a brief biography of the woman. She had already done a DMV search on Greg Miller, Diane's husband, and noted that both vehicles owned by the Millers were registered in Diane's name only.

Some of the basic background information about Diane Miller came from a local newspaper article two years ago. It was a feature piece on women in the military, about how older women, mothers in particular, could return to the workforce and have a rewarding career. Diane Miller, thirty-eight years old, Drone operator, surveillance specialist, three tours of Iraq under her belt. Married to Greg Miller. Together they had a young daughter, Ella Louise Miller.

Drone operator? That was certainly an interesting career choice, Monica thought. She wondered if Diane Miller had operated any of the predator drones. That information would be classified. While she could not access military records for Diane Miller, she did find another Department of Defense promotional piece dated eighteen months ago on military families and service women. There was a press photo of Diane, in full military uniform, stoic-faced. While Diane Miller wasn't exactly the typical poster girl for the US Army, there was certainly a family-orientated, motherly theme that Monica knew would resonate with a lot of older women and would also inspire young women to consider a career in the armed forces while juggling a family life too. There were no recent mentions in the news or with the DOD about Diane Miller. She simply dropped off the radar. Diane Miller had no social media footprint either.

A deeper search on Greg Miller didn't bring up any information that hadn't already been discovered. It was Ella Miller, though, their daughter, that caught Monica's attention. However, a search on Ella Louise Miller drew a blank. There was no mention about the daughter in any of the DOD information about Diane, other than her name and that she was twelve years old. No social media footprint either. This was strange given Ella's age.

Returning to the DMV database, Monica pulled up Diane Miller's driver's license and quickly printed off her photo in full color. She folded the page and slid it into her notebook.

It was 8:00 p.m., and Monica couldn't ignore her hunger pains anymore. Locking up the office, she cut across O Street to the diner on the corner, where she grabbed a soup and sandwich special to go. Returning to the office, she sat down again in front of her computer, began eating, and continued her search. She wanted to know more about Ella Miller and why Diane would have left her young daughter at home and gone to serve in Iraq. After meeting Greg Miller, Monica was more than just a little curious. Greg Miller hadn't come across as the fatherly type. Not that she knew him well at all. It was just the vibe she felt when she first met him face to face. Arrogant, condescending, smug even. Even how he looked at her, where his eyes spent most of the time. Not that there was anything wrong with that. It just felt slightly unnerving for Monica, like he was contemplating vile things.

Monica rubbed her eyes and sat back in her chair, feeling a little more than frustrated. There had to be something more about the family than what was in the public domain. Her mind kept going back to Diane's twelve-year-old daughter, Ella. There certainly would be no publicly available records of the child from the middle school she was attending.

On a whim, she decided to change her approach, give it one last shot before she called it a night and went home to her empty apartment. She went back into the law enforcement databases and typed in Ella Louise Miller, expecting nothing to come up. While the search engine crawled through the databases, she finished her half-eaten dinner, wrapped everything up, and tossed it into the trash can in the kitchenette. Returning to her desk, she was surprised to see a local police report on the screen. She quickly scanned it. Words like "the deceased" sprang out. A feeling of shock and horror crept over Monica as she read the report. Ella Miller, the twelve-year-old daughter of Diane and Greg Miller, had died just over twelve months ago.

Monica sat back in her chair, staring at the computer screen, her heart full of sorrow for the couple. She couldn't believe it. Perhaps, now she understood why Diane Miller was such a recluse and was feeling ill, as Greg Miller had mentioned the other day. It was too horrible to imagine the death of a son or a daughter. She glanced down at her tummy and placed her hand on it, a protective yet unsettling feeling. Was it worthwhile to bring another precious life into the world? How would she cope if such a gut-wrenching tragedy happened to her? The simple answer was she wouldn't cope.

For the first time since finding out she was pregnant, Monica felt different within herself. She was a different kind of person now. She was a mother, part of an exclusive, privileged club. She hadn't really thought about it before. Whom she was carrying suddenly made everything different. Everything was so precious, so important. There was another person depending on her, someone she needed to protect—no matter the cost. With her life even. She had never felt this way before—ever.

Monica dug further into the police database and soon found what she was looking for: the county coroner's report on the death of Ella Louise Miller. She slowly scrolled down the screen past the medical terminology, some of which she could understand, until she finally found the section entitled "Cause of Death." Just one word had been typed into the space.

Monica Styles brought her hand to her mouth as she read the single word, then gasped in horror. "Oh, my God!"

Chapter 20

It was late; all the clinic support staff had long since gone home for the day, including the receptionist.

The rest of the floor seemed deserted.

Amelia Redding sat at her desk, Diane Miller's file open in front of her. Redding wanted to go back over the file, cover the areas she may have skipped over when she had first reviewed the file. Also, she was a little curious about what Diane had said about Greg, her husband, and what she had told Amelia as to why she thought he was plotting to kill her.

Maybe the increased dosage had made Diane Miller somewhat paranoid. Whichever way Amelia analyzed it, she could not justify why Diane Miller's dosage had been increased so dramatically by Dr. Farrell. Amelia wanted to find the clinical reasons, the escalation in symptoms that would warrant such an increase.

After only ten minutes of reading through the file, Amelia's concentration began to waver. It had been a full day with Dr. Farrell's other patients. Amelia slid her glasses up onto the top of her head, leaned back, and rubbed her eyes. Maybe she should just go home. Call it a day. But then again, there was no one at home for her. No husband, partner, not even a pet. She lived alone and she preferred it that way. She could be excused for putting too much time and effort into her work. Amelia was passionate about her patients, even the ones who weren't hers, as was the case with Diane Miller. Of all the patients she had seen so far, and the case files she had read, Diane Miller's was the most intriguing.

Getting up, Amelia went out into the corridor. It was silent. All the other office suites she passed were dark, their blinds drawn. The communal kitchen was located at the end of the corridor, near the bank of elevators. A large laminate sign was stuck to the cupboard over the sink that screamed that people must wash up their own plates and cups or place them in the dishwasher. Amelia smiled as she saw a stack of dirty coffee cups and plates piled high, tilting precariously in the sink. The psychology of communal kitchen laziness was an area of study that often amused Amelia. She suffered none of these baffling quandaries. She ran her own practice from a dedicated office she had specially built on the ground floor of her home. It had off-street parking and separate side access with a discrete, private entrance. She enjoyed working from home and certainly didn't miss the days when she used to work in a high-rise office block similar to this one, as a consulting psychiatrist.

She filled the water reservoir of the coffee machine, turned it back on, then leaned against the counter waiting for it to brew, her thoughts drifting back to Diane Miller again.

Just then the elevator chimed.

Amelia stuck her head through the kitchen doorway and glanced to her left.

An elevator had stopped on the floor. Amelia stepped back into the corridor, and watched the doors slide open, expecting someone to step out.

But it was empty. The elevator sat open for a moment before the doors silently slid shut again.

Strange.

It was as though someone on this floor had summoned it. But she couldn't remember if she had seen the elevator button on the wall illuminated or not when she approached the kitchen.

Amelia turned and glanced back down the corridor to where her office was.

Had she closed the office door? She couldn't remember.

No one else was on the floor at this late hour. She watched the elevator lights count back down as it descended through the lower floors, then past the ground floor before settling on the basement parking garage level. She had been told that the elevators automatically locked off at 6:00 p.m., and that she needed to use her swipe card to access the ground floor and basement where her own car was parked in Dr. Farrell's slot. She couldn't access any other floors with the swipe card, only the third floor, the ground floor, and the parking garage level.

The coffee machine gave a loud, final splutter, making Amelia jump. Returning to the kitchen, she took a cup, filled it, then made her way back down the corridor to her office, glancing over her shoulder every few steps with the distinct feeling that someone was behind her. Ahead, a fluorescent tube in the ceiling began to flicker and jolt, strobing the section of the corridor near her office.

Amelia slowed, then stopped completely. She watched as the light flickered a few feet in front of her, alternating between dull light and intermittent darkness. She berated herself for being so stupid. She continued on, walking under the flickering tube and stopping at her office door, noticing it was ajar.

She glanced one more time toward the bank of elevators in the distance, but there was no one there.

Amelia shrugged, certain she was the only person on the floor. The other offices all had their blinds drawn and the lights off, she was certain.

She was alone.

Amelia pushed open the office door.

Back behind her desk, Amelia began leafing through Diane Miller's file once again, adding to the notes in her journal.

Bright orange sticky tags protruded from the file, marking particular pages that Amelia thought were important and kept referring back to. As she turned the page, she discovered a loose sheet, folded once, jammed in between the other pages. The page hadn't been hole-punched and looked like it had been hastily thrust in like an afterthought.

It was a meeting note, dated two months ago, written in Dr. Farrell's untidy scrawl. This was unusual given he preferred to dictate everything and then have it transcribed. It must have been something last minute, hastily written down, less important.

As far as Amelia could decipher from the messy handwriting, Diane's husband, Greg Miller, had dropped by the office unexpectedly. Dr. Farrell only met with him for a few minutes, the note said. Apparently he was concerned that his wife was not improving. Her bouts of crying and sleeplessness were escalating. Dr. Farrell had recorded these observations on the note as well as Greg's concerns for his wife. The words, *Diane mentioned nothing,* had been ringed several times in pen, the surface of the paper furrowed around the statement.

Reading further, it seemed that Greg Miller had asked Dr. Farrell if there was anything he could do—different medication, perhaps something stronger, even a stronger dose of the current medication—to help his wife.

Amelia leaned back in the chair and looked at the note in front of her. It did seem unusual that a spouse would approach their partner's psychiatrist, voicing their concerns and almost suggesting that the doctor alter the course of medication they had originally prescribed. Had Diane been consulted on this? There was no doubt Diane Miller had a trauma-related disorder. However the strength of her increased dosage would indicate her condition was at an extreme level, almost requiring hospitalization.

For her own patients, Amelia sometimes did talk to both parties involved: the patient and their spouse or partner. However, it was always at the consent of the patient first. It wasn't her policy, nor did she think it professional, to ever discuss a patient's file, medication or any other matters with another party…spouse, family member, relative, or otherwise.

Amelia looked up from the file and stared at the office door.

A sound had come from outside, on the other side of the door—in the corridor, like someone had just walked past the door.

Had she locked the door? She was certain she had.

Amelia got up, walked to the door, rested her hand against the surface, and listened. It seemed quiet outside. But she had distinctly heard something, like footsteps, walk right past her door.

She turned the handle; the door was unlocked.

Sticking her head out, Amelia glanced left then right.

The corridor was empty, the only sound came from the faulty fluorescent tube hissing and flickering, the mercury vapor inside struggling to ionize.

Maybe it was the office cleaners or the security patrol doing their rounds. Yet, she could see no cleaning cart, nothing at all. Amelia closed and locked the door, then went back to her desk.

It was getting late. Maybe she needed to pack up, go home, pour herself a long glass of wine, and take a hot bath.

She slid Diane Miller's file into her leather bag, switched off everything on the desk, and moved to the office door. She paused again and listened intently.

Nothing.

Amelia wasn't prone to a vivid imagination. However, she had definitely heard something.

She turned the door handle and looked outside again.

There was no cleaner, no one.

Locking the door firmly behind her, she walked quickly to the elevators, thinking that at any moment one of the doors of the other suites would burst open and hands would reach out and snatch her inside.

Both elevators were on the parking garage level. She pressed the button and watched the numbers blink along the display panel as the elevator rose with excruciating slowness.

Looking back toward her office, through the strobing section of corridor, *past* her office door, Amelia saw something. A shadow moving, a distortion in the darkness at the end of the corridor where the overhead lights didn't reach. Someone was near the fire escape. She could see them.

The elevator chimed and the doors parted.

Amelia rushed inside, hit *B* and thumped repeatedly the *Close Doors* button.

The doors began to slowly close.

"Come on, come on!" Amelia thumped the button harder, not caring if she broke it.

She glanced through the narrowing vertical gap between the door panels and saw the shape again, this time much clearer, the outline of someone advancing down the corridor toward the elevator—toward her.

The doors closed with a clunk. Amelia was overcome with a rush of relief as she felt the familiar sensation through the soles of her feet of the elevator descending.

Moments later, the elevator slowed then came to a stop.

Ground Floor—But Amelia hadn't pressed *G*. She had pressed *B*—Basement.

The doors parted slowly, a vertical frame of widening darkness beyond. Instinctively, Amelia sank back into the interior and felt the rear wall of the elevator press against her back. She fumbled a bunch of keys out of her pocket. Somewhere she had read how you can use the blade of a key like the blade of a knife. She quickly selected her house key. It was the longest with the most teeth along one side. Clutching it in a tight fist, the tip of the key protruding between her fingers, she brought up the only weapon she had. This had never happened to her before. A smothering sensation of fear slithered down her back, her mouth dry, her heart beating faster as the elevator doors finally receded completely into the sides.

The ground floor to the building was in semi-darkness, just a shimmer of the streetlights from outside coming through the closed glass front doors. She waited a few seconds. There was no one there, yet the elevator had stopped on the ground floor, like someone had called it.

Shadows danced and flickered across the lobby as the branches of the trees outside buffeted in the wind. The glass lobby doors rattled but held firm.

The fire escape. The person had taken the fire escape stairs down to the ground floor, beating her here, then pressing the elevator button to stop her descent.

Amelia's mind raced.

She punched the *Close Doors* button repeatedly. Like torture, the elevator doors took an eternity to close.

Reaching the parking garage level, she already had her remote in her hand, pointing in the direction of where her Audi sat in the semi-darkness twenty yards to her right. Amelia ran directly to it, not looking left or right, just making a beeline for it, knowing she would be safe inside by locking the doors, a panic room on four wheels.

She wrenched the door open, didn't care where her bag landed inside, jumped in, slammed the door, and activated the door locks.

It wasn't until she was speeding up the exit ramp and out onto the street, doing ten miles per hour above the speed limit, that Amelia finally breathed a sigh of relief and eased back on the gas pedal.

Then a gloved hand slithered out from behind her headrest and latched around her throat.

Chapter 21

The rest of dinner had been rushed, Greg apologizing that he had to go in to work for a few hours and for Diane not to wait up for him.

After Greg left, Diane stood at the study door.

The door was locked.

That wasn't surprising. Greg often locked the door to the study. It was a spare bedroom they had converted a few years back into something more functional, separate from the rest of the house. In the past, Diane had no compulsion to go looking in there, content that Greg was looking after the utility bills, property taxes, everything financial and household-related. She lacked the mindset, the motivation to care about such things.

She felt differently about it now.

Diane had a change of heart, a change of mindset. She wanted to know what was in there, behind the seemingly always locked door. The visit to the bank and what Sharon had told her spurred Diane into action. The new pills were allowing her to regain some semblance of control, of awareness of the things that were happening around her.

Before leaving the Army, Diane couldn't recall Greg ever locking the study door. It was a shared space. She used to wander in and out, door wide open, rummage through the files, make sure things were in order, bills paid on time, nothing missed.

Now it was Greg's domain and his alone. A place he would often retreat to in the evenings. That is if he wasn't working late at the office. When he was in there, he would keep the door open with the back of the screen facing the doorway, the front of the screen hidden, the mouse in his hand swirling and banging in sync with his facial expression. Diane would walk by but not take much notice. There were occasions, however, thinking back now, when she would pause, stand in the doorway, and wonder what Greg was doing. He would see her approaching in his periphery and with a quick shift and a click, close down something he was looking at before smiling sweetly at her. These little snippets of memory were coming back to Diane, fueling her urge to locate the key and explore what lay behind the locked door. It was probably nothing, just her imagination. Yet, her intuition was telling her something different.

She remembered she had kept a spare key on a ring with a bunch of household spare keys in the closet in the side pocket of an old Army jacket. She'd hidden them in case she lost her main set of keys.

Taking a small stepladder, Diane went into the closet, climbed up, and began rifling through a pile of old clothing. The jacket wasn't there. She searched again, this time pulling everything out and dumping it on the bed.

No jacket.

Diane searched through her drawers and hanging garments.

Still nothing.

She sat back on the bed, trying to remember what she had done with the old jacket.

She walked out of the bedroom and into the garage. Pushed into the bottom of a set of storage shelves she found a large plastic trash bag. A few months after the funeral, Diane had gone through her clothes. Trance-like, she had sorted and separated anything that related to her time in the Army, wanting nothing more than to purge the house of anything physical that would remind of what had taken her away from Ella. She had forgotten the bag was there, assuming Greg had taken it to a thrift store.

The jacket was in the bag, and her fingers soon found the bulge in a side pocket. She reached in and retrieved the spare bunch of keys, tarnished with a metallic smell to them.

She went back to the locked study door but couldn't remember which key it was. So she tried the keys that looked like they might work, cycling through them. She was successful on the fourth attempt. The locked knob clicked open; she twisted and pushed the door back against the doorstop, pocketing the bunch of spare keys for later, making a mental note of the one that opened the study door.

The room was small, as she had remembered, perhaps twelve feet by nine feet, with a single window covered by blinds. Two filing cabinets, a small desk and computer, a swivel chair, and a small desk fan filled the room. Greg had been here recently; she could smell him, the cologne he wore. Something she had never purchased for him as a gift or otherwise, something he had bought for himself.

Like her, Greg was neat and orderly. The desktop was clean, uncluttered, not a sheet of paper in sight other than a small pile in a plastic filing tray with some unopened mail on top. Diane turned on the light, walked around the desk, and sat on the swivel chair. The hinges creaked and the casters slid slightly under her. The computer screen was blank, a dull opaque rectangle. The ghostly blur of a featureless face stared back at her.

Under the desk, the boxy shape of the computer was cold and silent. Reaching down, she switched it on. While it whirled and beeped to life, Diane went through the three desk drawers on the right. The first drawer contained loose stationery, pens, pencils, clips. She pushed and lifted the items aside.

Nothing magical here—

Another cell phone? Diane picked it up out of the drawer and stared at the locked screen. She turned it over in her hand. Thin aluminum case, miniature camera lens, sleek design, smooth beveled edges, expensive. How could Greg afford this? Work already provided him with a cell phone. Diane swiped the screen and a face ID request appeared. Her own cell phone could be locked and unlocked with just a simple PIN code. This phone was more sophisticated, requiring the facial image of the owner to unlock it. Diane weighed the phone thoughtfully in her hand, contemplating what to do with this new discovery. If she took it, Greg would know instantly. But she knew it existed and where he kept it. That information was invaluable. She carefully placed the phone back in the drawer, positioning it as she had found it under some loose stationery.

The second drawer was crammed full of small notepads and a variety of colorful post-it notes and tags.

The third drawer, the bottom drawer, the deepest drawer, contained a row of hanging file folders. Dull standard green, neat DYMO labels on the clear plastic tabs, which Diane remembered printing and organizing what felt like a lifetime ago. She shuffled the files back, and selected one labeled *Utilities*. She pulled the hanging file out, laying it flat on the desk.

The computer screen came alive in front of her, a password box in the center.

Diane thought for a moment, struggling to recall her old password. Then it came to her. She typed it in and—as expected, it failed. She tried again.

Incorrect.

He was too clever. Greg had changed everything—but why?

Diane switched her attention to the folder of household bills in front of her. The first tab was labeled *Power*. The first sheet behind was a bill dated six months ago She noticed her name as the addressee, the account holder. No other name, just hers. The account used to be in joint names.

Diane thumbed to the next page underneath. An older bill, nine months ago. Again she was listed as the sole account holder. Diane thumbed farther back until she found a bill more than twelve months old. On that bill both hers and Greg's names appeared at the top, joint names on the account.

Diane sat back in the swivel chair. Greg had told her that, for the last twelve months, he had assumed responsibility for all the utilities, the bills, everything to do with the house. Said it would be better if he looked after such matters, not burden her. Yet only her name was on all of the power bills for the last twelve months, as the sole account holder, solely responsible.

Diane flipped to the next tab in the file.

It was the same there as well. Her name was listed as the sole account holder for gas, telephone, and property taxes.

She glanced at the papers in the filing tray, the unopened mail, and began rummaging through the small pile. She found an unopened power bill, the power company logo printed on the outside of the envelope.

She went to rip the envelope open, then stopped herself.

Sliding the top drawer open, she found a letter opener.

She placed the unopened envelope face down, flat on the surface of the desk. Instead of slitting open the top with the blade, she carefully pried apart one corner of the sticky flap, then worked the blade under and along, careful not to damage the flap or tear the paper.

She slid it out, and unfolded the single page that was inside.

There again, at the top of the page was her name as the sole account holder. Big red warning letters glared back at her, threatening legal action. It wasn't a bill, but a warning notice. Greg had told her he had paid the bills, had brought everything up to date. The power company was threatening legal action against her, Diane Abigail Miller, not Greg Miller. His name was nowhere to be seen on anything.

Diane rifled through the rest of the files in the bottom drawer.

Five minutes later the entire surface of the desk was covered with a tablecloth of bills, overdue account notices, and threatening letters. Every one addressed to her. Even both car loans were now in her name. Any loan, any financial commitment, for the last twelve months had been transferred into Diane's own name. Total financial and personal responsibility had been shifted to her. But over the last twelve months, she may have been mentally incapable of assuming such responsibility or financial capacity! Greg had not told any of the utility companies or financial institutions about her condition, her state of mind.

Diane sat bolt upright.

Frantically, she started searching again through the files on the desk, but couldn't locate the most important one, the one she hadn't thought about.

Surely not.

She pulled the bottom drawer open again. There at the bottom, half-buried under a pile of empty unused folders, she found another file. It was hidden, deliberately placed there. Feeling ill at the thought, Diane pulled out the thick file and placed it on the desk squarely in front of her. She looked at the label.

Home Mortgage.

She didn't want to open the file, didn't want to confirm the horrible thought that had entered her head moments ago. Her mind was already filled with enough dismay and shock for one day.

But she had to. She had to look inside.

She swallowed hard, then willed herself to turn the cardboard front of the file and reveal what she feared.

Her eyes scanned down the first page of the statement, over transactions dated just a few weeks ago. She thumbed farther back in disbelief, first going back just a few months, then years. Three years to be exact. Three years of treachery, lies, and betrayal. She could clearly see the pattern of the home loan balance reducing, her Army pay together with Greg's pay going in, using the home loan as a line of equity if needed, keeping the balance low for as long as possible, minimizing the loan interest over the years. Hard work and sacrifice—all for nothing.

Diane could remember vividly when she was home, stateside, not buying the things she wanted or needed. New shoes. A new dress perhaps. Forgoing her own needs for the sake of Ella—and for the sake of paying off the home loan sooner, as Greg had suggested. Better to pay it down faster when they were both working. So everything went into it. All her base pay from the Army as well as her combat pay for being in a danger zone. Her Family Separation Allowance, and a host of other allowances she had been paid, all went into reducing the home mortgage account. Money, her money, hard-earned under the ever-present risk of being injured or killed. Building a life for them. Short-term pain for long-term financial gain.

Now the financial bombshell. The monetary earthquake that had commenced twelve months ago when the home loan balance had suddenly reversed. Diane checked the statements again just to make sure. The loan balance increasing not decreasing. Climbing up, not edging down. More debt, not less debt. Withdrawals, not deposits. The loan statement balances for the last twelve months that Diane thumbed through showed the loan balance steadily growing. Sometimes daily. Then nothing for a few weeks, then large lumps of cash being withdrawn suddenly, huge leaps backward in their financial security and safety. *Her* financial security. All safety gone.

Then, on the last statement, the most recent that Diane clutched in her hand, there was a fee for a recent property revaluation. More equity had subsequently been freed-up only to be sucked out again by Greg.

Gone. All of it.

The home loan fully drawn. Maxed-out. Everything now owned by the bank. And just like every other financial debt, commitment, undertaking, she had just discovered: Diane Miller was the sole person on the mortgage statement. She was indebted to everyone. Not Greg.

Diane closed her eyes, needing a moment to compose herself. When she opened them again she had regained some of her calm. Saw things slightly clearer. In her mind she saw the case full of cash sitting alone in the cold darkness of the storage unit. It was her only salvation. Not for Greg—but for her. He had done this to her. Financially ruined her. Diane knew exactly what she was going to do with the money she had found. Her husband had made the decision easier for her.

She lifted the file to return it to the drawer when a small piece of loose paper slid out and fell to the floor. Diane reached down and scooped it up. It was an itemized motel statement. The Red Coach Inn & Suites, Grand Island.

Why would Greg stay at a motel in town?

Her eyes scanned down the page. *Room Charge. Minibar. Restaurant. Gratuity.*

Diane's face turned ashen.

"Bastard!"

Chapter 22

The place was nothing special.

Maybe that was a good thing, a sign that the relationship was nothing special. Cheap. Trashy. Just like the motel. The big red and black sign read, *Red Coach Inn & Suites* and was located on the aptly named *South Locust St*, two miles south of downtown.

Greg was indeed a locust, an insect, a bug to be squashed. He had consumed everything Diane had worked so hard for over the years. Gorged himself, then lied and cheated. Lived a lifestyle, a double-life, at her expense. He had skillfully created the illusion that they were broke, living from paycheck to paycheck. Technically Diane was broke, destitute, according to what she had found in the study. However, the money must have gone somewhere.

All the more reason to keep what she had discovered about Greg's treachery to herself.

Diane had left the study as she had found it. Her reasoning was simple. During a stop in Hawaii, refueling for a final leg back from Iraq, Diane had discovered a battered copy of *The Art of War* by Sun Tzu that someone had left behind on the transport plane. By the time she had touched down at Edwards AFB, she had read it cover-to-cover. Twice.

She recalled a quote from the famous book on military tactics and warfare: *Let your plans be dark and impenetrable.* As she was returning everything to its place in the study, Diane began formulating her own dark plans, the decision made so much easier by what she had lost…and what she had now found.

Diane sat in her car, in a shadowy corner of the motel parking lot, and watched one particular room intently. And just like a locust, Greg was moving on to his next crop to harvest, to strip bare, not a blade of green to be left behind.

The MainStay Suites behind Diane were nicer. So was the Best Western Plus a quarter mile farther north, on the main road heading back toward town. She hadn't been to any of those places. She had never really been to this part of town. Yet she could tell from the low ambience of her surroundings, that Greg saw nothing in this new relationship other than the low economics of sex. Transactional. Pleasure for the least cost.

While she sat patiently watching and waiting, Diane laid out in her head a likely pattern of matrimonial deceit perpetrated by her husband. A little money spent on intimate dinners at mid-range restaurants with his new liaison. Maybe a two-for-one coupon quickly produced at the cash register, out of sight so as not to break Greg's delicate facade of being a caring, sharing, generous man. A small gift perhaps, an insignificant trinket of affection. High-shine silver, not gold. A hollow commitment accompanied by carefully chosen compliments. And sexual rendezvous in motels like this one, under the guise of going back to work.

How romantic.

The woman was probably a client or a co-worker. Greg probably had leered at her at some sales presentation or product launch. Been chivalrous and opened the door for her once, or got her a drink from the open bar paid for by his work at a conference.

Diane glanced at the green digits on the dash and drummed the steering wheel. She had been watching the room for almost two hours now. God knows what they were doing in there. Greg hadn't taken that much time with her since the first year of their marriage. After that, foreplay gave way to perfunctory, cursory, and spiritless intercourse, all predicated on satisfying Greg's rudimentary need for stress-relieving sex. Rutting followed immediately by a hot shower.

Diane called up the satellite map of the area on her cell phone and zoomed down until she guessed she was hovering at about three hundred feet overhead. The view was all straight lines and buildings and sheds placed at right angles. Pivoting the map with her thumb, she imagined guiding a drone there, placing the target reticle directly over the L-shaped outline of the motel, right on top of the room they were in, and sending a Hellfire missile right through the front door. Then watching the screen blur brilliant white at the moment of impact.

But there would be collateral damage. There always was—in the past.

However now, Diane didn't seem to think so. What else could be damaged? Ella was gone. There were no relatives to harm, no immediate family. Diane was already damaged by Greg. The loss of her daughter had done the most damage, more than anything or anyone could possibly do.

So Diane viewed Greg's indiscretions as pure betrayal, nothing more. Their marriage was damaged and in her mind—over. Nothing could be salvaged. He couldn't be trusted ever again.

Now was the time for her to mend, to recover, to build and grow, to get stronger. Not to weep about the past, even though Ella would never be out of Diane's thoughts nor her heart. Now was the time for action.

There would be blame. Greg would blame everyone else, especially Diane. He would never take responsibility, admit he was at fault. He would blame her for everything: a failed marriage, failed family, failed life. He would say that was why he strayed, became adulterous on a regular basis…or so it seemed to Diane.

There were other women. Diane didn't know for certain, but she could now smell it on him. See it in him. Her senses were gradually becoming more receptive, a woman's intuition steadily returning to her, the curtain of illusion had been drawn back.

It was irrelevant in Diane's mind as to where the money had gone. Though after observing him today, she had a fair idea. But what was done was done. Her mind was made up. It was time to move on.

Unscrewing the top of the pill bottle, Diane tapped out two more pills and washed them down with a small bottle of water she kept in the center console. She didn't know what it was, but every day she seemed to feel better, her mind clearer, the cobwebs of the past dissipating. It wasn't that she was changing. It was more like she was getting back to how she used to be, when Ella was alive, when Diane was in the Army, surrounded by friends and colleagues, people who would put their lives on the line for her. She was going back to how she was before the nightmare began.

Diane looked up to the second floor where the external walkway was lit by dull orbs of yellow light equally spaced outside rows of identical doors with boxy air conditioning units under the windows. The room she had been watching was third from the right, near a set of narrow stairs, with the window drapes drawn tight. Room service had delivered a bottle of champagne in a bucket of ice ten minutes after Diane had arrived. She had seen Greg's face clearly when he opened the door, dressed in a robe. He took the champagne and handed out a tip. At that Diane had gripped the steering wheel, twisted her fingers tightly around it, imagining it was Greg's throat she was crushing. While she sat in the car, watching and waiting, she replayed the same scene over and over again in her mind until her head throbbed. Seeing Greg dressed in a robe was the ultimate insult. He was swaying around, drinking champagne like Hugh-fucking-Hefner! While she was broke!

The door of the room opened and two figures emerged, their dark outlines melded into one shape, pausing at the threshold.

Diane slid upright, craned her neck, leaned forward, tilted her head, and looked up through the windshield, observing the ritual. The kiss was long and lingering. Not short like a goodbye, but something more. Much more. Holding hands until the last moment, arms outstretched, then fingers, and finally separation.

Diane felt her insides churn as she watched.

It spoke of a temporary parting of ways…for now, until next time, until the next act of betrayal. Such a display of intimacy revealed the permanency of what she was witnessing. It was not a quick fling. It was enduring.

Diane gripped the steering wheel, her anger white-knuckled and boiling.

The woman strode along the walkway, heels echoing off the cement, guiltless strides, hips and hair swaying. No shame to hide. Brazen as much as she was self-righteous in her sin.

She came down the steps, her heels louder.

Greg rested his hands on the railing and looked down lovingly as he watched the woman walk across the parking lot toward her vehicle. Sidelights blinked twice on a small sedan. The woman opened the door, then paused, turned, and looked back up at Greg.

Then she blew him a kiss.

Aghast, Diane watched as her husband returned the affection, a term of endearment he had never expressed to her—ever in all their years of marriage. It was so out of character...or was it?

Diane felt sick to her stomach. She physically wanted to vomit. Quickly, she took another swig from her spring water.

That was the final transgression, the giant leap beyond the mark, beyond what Diane believed their relationship *ever* had been.

There was something in the way Greg looked down at the woman below, how he returned the kiss, his lingering gaze long after she had pulled out of the parking lot and drove off.

Diane realized she had miscalculated. This was worse, much worse than she'd imagined.

Her husband wasn't having an affair. Her husband was in love with another woman.

The ultimate betrayal.

Chapter 23

The first stop was at a secondhand car dealer the next day.

Greg had come home late last night. Diane was already in bed. He mumbled the obligatory apology. Something about how he had to work late on an account he was pitching. It took every ounce of restraint for Diane to lie next to him in bed. While Greg slid into post-sex-induced snoring, Diane lay wide awake, plans and machinations taking shape in her head.

There was no self-realization left. Just affirmation that the decision she had reached in the cold, dark hours before dawn was the right one. She was going to run, disappear off the face of the earth. Diane Miller would be no more. She would become a new person with a new identity and a new life. Start over. The money gave her that ability.

As soon as the first rays of the new day breached the bedroom drapes, Diane was up and showered while Greg was still asleep. She didn't want to spend a single moment longer in the same room as him, under the same roof as him, such was her revulsion.

She didn't waste any time at the car dealership in town, immediately seeing a white, low-mileage, 2005 Chevrolet Trailblazer SUV for under six grand that would be perfect for her escape. It had enough space in the back for her to fill up with what she intended to take with her, plus off-road capabilities, should she need that.

Diane retrieved the money from the storage unit and returned to the dealership. After reviewing all the paperwork in the tiny office under the salesman's watchful eye, she handed over the cash. The salesman could hardly contain his glee as he counted the wad of notes before placing it in a small safe.

The car was mechanically sound, everything in order, and within thirty minutes of entering the dealership a second time, she was driving out, leaving her own car parked down a side street while she headed to a shopping mall in Grand Island for phase two of her plan.

All the stores she needed were concentrated in one convenient location. At Dressbarn, Diane selected a whole new wardrobe, including underwear, practical tops, sweaters, and pants. No dresses. No skirts. Comfortable flats. No wedges. No heels. She purchased luggage from another store. A large duffel bag, a medium expandable suitcase, and a hard side carry-on spinner. She grabbed durable plastic luggage tags at a display near the checkout, paying cash for the lot. Then, she purchased a prepaid smartphone, with a 25GB unlimited 30-day plan card. In the toiletries section of a superstore, Diane selected a compact travel kit that contained everything she needed, including toothbrush, shampoo, deodorant, and hair brush, all conveniently packed in a TSA-compliant clear plastic tote bag. In the grocery section of the store, she purchased spring water, some dry food snacks, and a box of protein bars, placing everything into the cart, before taking it to the checkout, paying cash, then wheeling it out across the parking lot, where she loaded it up into the back of her SUV.

Cash was the currency of her anonymity.

She went to a full-service gas station, filled up the car because, as expected, the car dealership ran their cars on fumes, leaving the burden of filling the tank to the purchaser. She paid cash and slipped ten bucks to the attendant—a rakish teen with mousy hair that poked out from under an oil-smudged ball cap—for him to double check that all the fluids were topped, including the battery levels. The last thing Diane wanted was to break down in the middle of nowhere, or worse still, a few miles into her escape.

Next, she drove to the twenty-four-hour storage facility where she had left the attaché case. At the gate, she punched in her key code and drove right up to her designated unit at the rear. The place was deserted this time of day. She opened the roller door, backed into the unit, and closed the roller door behind her. Once inside, she flipped on the florescent lights, opened the tailgate, and began organizing her purchases.

She took the tags off all the new clothing, folded them neatly into the suitcase. In the carry-on spinner, she placed a few essential items including her toiletries. She ripped opened the packaged spring water and placed two bottles in the center console up front.

She added luggage tags to everything, writing her new name on the labels.

She gave one final look at everything packed in the rear of the SUV, closed the tailgate, and locked the vehicle. She let herself out of the storage shed, locked the roller door, and walked back along the concrete driveway to the front of the complex, then went out through the side access gate.

Using her new cell phone, she called a cab and rode back to the used car dealership to where she had left her own vehicle.

Once behind the wheel of her old car, and with the doors locked, Diane took a deep breath and ran through a mental checklist, making sure she had ticked off everything that she needed to do today.

For the first time in months, she felt invigorated, had direction, a purpose. She felt in control, making her own decisions, more self-reliant, all the things she had and loved while in the military. Sure she had a team, a support network around her back then. Now she was just a team of one. She felt liberated and also a little anxious at the same time.

Then she remembered there was one last thing that she had forgotten to do.

She drove to the drugstore where she was a few days previously and got a refill of her new medication. She also brought back to the counter the ash blond hair dye she had seen, paying in cash once again.

Back in her car, Diane flipped open the glove box and retrieved the first bottle of pills. She stared at the label. The new meds had given her back her pride, her confidence. She wasn't all the way there yet. But it was a start.

She swallowed two more tablets.

Tiny steps, she told herself as she put the car in gear and backed out of the parking lot.

Chapter 24

It was the third towing company they'd visited, the last of only three operating in Sherman County.

It was located forty miles west of Grand Island.

They sat in their SUV across the street. Vincent with a pair of binoculars to his eyes, Alex next to him.

The place looked like the other two towing and wrecking businesses they had visited earlier. There was the obligatory chain-link fence topped with barbed wire, a dusty dirty parking lot beyond that, and a small portable office to one side. In the background was the yard proper, where hulks of dilapidated vehicles sat rusty and mangled in surprisingly neat rows, some stacked in piles on top of each other. A faded green and orange sign on the front fence said Kramer's Towing, Wrecking & Recovery and promised twenty-four-hour service.

From where they were parked, Vincent couldn't see anything in the yard that resembled the wreckage of the white laundry van. He needed to get inside to take a closer look. He handed Alex the binoculars. "Stay here, and keep an eye on the street. Any problems, text me."

Alex took the binoculars and watched as her brother slid out of the driver's seat, crossed the road, and went through the open gates of the yard like he owned the place. She wasn't happy being left to keep lookout, but it made sense. Two people showing up at the yard would be suspicious, draw attention. Also someone needed to watch the street, provide coverage.

They say that Will Towner liked to run—run a scam that is.

He certainly didn't get paid enough to take real notice of whoever came into the yard to ask questions or poke around the wrecks or pick through the huge pile of scrap metal and auto parts, trying to find something for their own vehicle. Especially with his boss, Bob Kramer, away doing some large recovery job near Grand Island. Kramer had told Towner to mind the yard while he was gone. And like all other days when he had the place all to himself, Towner was going to supplement the measly wage that Kramer paid him in his own enterprising way. His boss wasn't going to miss a fender here or a headlight or door panel there. As long as people gave him a few folds of green that Towner promptly tucked away in the pocket of his grubby overalls, he was happy to turn a blind eye to what was pilfered.

But Towner was not stupid either. He could spot an opportunity to leverage his knowledge and earn more. To trade up from Abe Lincolns to Alexander Hamiltons if possible. Even a few Andy Jacksons if the right opportunity presented itself.

And the right opportunity came in the shape of the slick-looking man who just walked through the front gates of the yard, and into the dank, little site office. All it took was one look at the leather shoes, pleated pants, and quality coat he wore over a crisp white dress shirt, for Towner to lick his bristly lips in anticipation. The man was definitely not local. Which meant Towner's chances of making more than a few dollars grew exponentially.

"I'm looking for wreckage that was brought here a few days ago. A white van." Vincent gave Towner a brief description without providing too much detail of the laundry van. Glancing up, Vincent couldn't see a security camera inside the tiny office. There were none outside in the yard, either; he guessed there was nothing of real value worth stealing in this dump.

"Seen no white van around here," Towner said innocently. For the uninitiated, those unaccustomed to his little side hustle, Towner first resorted to his standard tactic: deny everything until the possibility of money being exchanged for information raised its welcomed head.

Vincent stepped closer. "Are you sure about that, kid?"

It was the way the man had said it. No smile. No frown. No nothing. Just a not-so-subtle hint of violence if you were lying. The man's piercing eyes began to rattle Towner, making him rethink his approach.

Under the counter, Towner had a weapon. A foot of welded, twisted steel, fashioned into the shape of a baseball bat. Capable of cracking skulls and breaking bones. More lethal than any baseball bat you could buy. Yet even the thought of reaching for it seemed like a life-ending option for Towner. Subconsciously, Towner's eyes darted to the man's breast pocket where he saw the telltale bulge of a wallet. Unfortunately for Towner, there were no telltale signs of the two handguns Vincent Romano was also carrying.

"I'd like you to reconsider," Vincent said as he opened the flap of his coat and retrieved his wallet.

Almost as mesmerizing as watching a stripper slowly peel off her panties, Towner watched the man peel off five notes, then lay them out individually on the counter in front of him with the deliberate slowness of a winning hand in Vegas.

Towner licked his lips as he stared at the notes. The five faces of Ulysses S. Grant stared up at him. He could almost hear the whispered words of the eighteenth president of the United States. "Take the money, Will. Take Mary Lou some place special you tight-ass." Mary Lou Hollis was a young woman Towner had only taken on one date. The disastrous evening had ended abruptly when she told him, in no uncertain terms, that there would be no second, third, or even a fourth date if he ever took her to a burger joint for dinner again. She also mentioned that a fourth date with her usually meant sex. But based on his current idea of a date, he had little chance of ever getting to a second date, let alone a fourth date.

Towner reached for the bills, but Vincent grabbed his wrist before he could gather them up. "Where is the van?"

Towner nodded behind him. "Third row on the left, out the back. About fifty yards in. It's been set aside. Towner was tempted to ask the man why he wanted to know about some wrecked van, but that amount of cash bought the "no questions asked" service he was happy to provide. It wasn't like the man could steal it or drive it away. It was just a useless piece of twisted junk.

Vincent nodded, then let go of the man's wrist and walked out.

Towner rubbed his wrist, then greedily snatched up the money. He slid out his cell phone and dialed a number as he smiled lovingly at the bills.

On the third ring, his call was answered, and a big smile spread across his face as he slipped the notes into the pocket of his overalls. "Hey, Mary Lou, whatcha doing tonight?" He listened for a moment, then shook his head. "No, no, no. We ain't going back to no burger place. I promise. I going to take you to someplace special. Real nice. Just you wait," he said, laying on the charm. Some green in the pocket always made him more confident with the ladies.

Then he frowned. "Of course I can afford to. What kind of cheapskate do you take me for?"

Following Towner's directions, Vincent soon located the twisted remains of the laundry van. Someone had wrapped a bright yellow warning tape around it. The wreck was a twisted, dented ball of metal, rubber, plastic and shattered glass. The driver's cab was smashed in, main body collapsed, and one axle had sheered clean off. Next to it sat a pile of loose debris, components from the main body that had been shed as the chassis rolled. Vincent kicked through the pile of loose debris. It was too wishful to expect the case to be there.

Squatting down next to the wreck, Vincent noticed the license plates didn't match his information on the van, confirming the extent of planning behind Anton Wheeler's treachery. Next he examined the underside of the chassis where the compartment was that held the case. The section was completely twisted, buckled, and pried open, with part of the floor plate ripped open, leaving a gaping hole. The case would have certainly come loose during the crash, been thrown clear from the underside of the van. Vincent took his time, checking over the rest of what remained of the van. The case was definitely not there, and from what was left of the van, Vincent wasn't counting on Anton Wheeler waking up anytime soon. He should be dead. He would be if Vincent got his hands on him.

Vincent's cell phone buzzed, and he promptly read the message.

He immediately turned and started walking, deciding not to return the way he had come. He skirted around a wall of crushed cars, making his way in a wide arc around to the entrance of the yard.

Alex looked up from her cell phone and watched as a

Sherman County sheriff's vehicle pulled up to the opposite curb, and a middle-aged woman, a female sheriff, climbed out.

"Damn it." Alex powered up the dark tinted window, and quickly shot off a text to Vincent. She watched as the female sheriff looked around, then spotted the black SUV across the street. For a moment the woman just stood there, her eyes fixed on Alex's vehicle. Even through the dark tinted glass, Alex could feel the woman's eyes boring right into her. Then the woman slowly turned and walked through the gates of the yard.

Moments later there was a thump on the passenger door. Alex released the central locking, and Vincent slid in.

"Drive," he hissed, keeping his eyes on the yard across the street and the figure of the sheriff walking toward the office.

Alex put the SUV into gear and accelerated away while Vincent filled her in on what he had seen of the wreckage.

"Could someone have removed the case after the van crashed?" Alex asked. She glanced in the review mirror certain to see the shape of the sheriff's vehicle tailing them. But the road behind them was clear.

"No chance," Vincent replied. "The entire underside was torn open like a can opener. The case would have been dislodged."

"So someone found the case, or Wheeler removed it first."

"The only lead we have is Wheeler," Vincent replied, clearly agitated. "We need to find out where he was going and who else was involved. I don't believe the money was lost, or someone just found it on the side of the road."

Alex had to agree. The likelihood of that was simply too implausible.

Chapter 25

"It was the same SUV that was at the other two towing businesses."

It was late afternoon and Styles and Charmers were back in the office in Loup City.

"I ran the plates; the SUV is a rental taken a few days ago at the airport in Omaha," Charmers continued. "Couldn't find out much about it except that it was a corporate rental."

"And it was definitely the same SUV that visited the other towing companies?" Styles asked.

Charmers nodded. "There's only three in the entire county, so if someone wanted to find out where the wreckage was being held it wouldn't be too difficult." Charmers had already explained to Styles that she had visited Kramer's Towing in Rockville as a routine follow-up to examine the wrecked van herself.

"Don't get many SUVs like that around here," Charmers said, thinking back. "All black. Tinted windows. So I put two and two together and called on the other two towing businesses. They also mentioned seeing the same vehicle earlier today and the same man." Charmers had taken statements from the owners of the other two towing businesses about the man who had come in and started asking questions about a recent van wreck that may have been towed to their yard.

"So someone else has taken a keen interest in the crashed van," Styles said.

"Looks that way," Charmers replied. "I bet there's more to

that van than just a pile of dirty laundry. But when I took a good look at the wreck, I couldn't see anything." Charmers had already decided to get the truck onto a flatbed and get it over to Grand Island and have the forensic team there pull it apart one rivet at a time.

"Drugs?" Styles offered.

"Maybe. The guy behind the counter said no one had been there asking questions about the van. He was lying. I could tell. When I went back outside again the black SUV across the street was gone. Whoever the man was he must have slipped past me and back out the gates."

"If I see the SUV, do you want me to pull it over?"

Charmers nodded. Then added, "Be careful, though, Mons. Something is not right about that van. I'm going to pay another visit to the laundry business in Grand Island when I get the chance." Charmers then turned her attention to her deputy and asked how her day had progressed.

Styles explained she had done some background checking on the Millers, but it was early days yet. She would give Charmers a full update when she was completed. "I want to call them again, see if I can talk to Diane Miller. I didn't get a chance to go by there again today." Styles was tempted to reveal what she had discovered last night about Diane Miller. But she stopped herself. She needed to gather more facts. At this stage, it was just theory and speculation. Charmers would just throw it back at her, tell her to get something more solid. And yet, deep down, Styles felt there was something deeply disturbing about Greg Miller. Something that went beyond his arrogance and smugness.

The rest of the evening passed with excruciating slowness for Diane Miller as she waited for Greg to return from work.

The thought of confronting him made her feel nauseous as well as enraged. However, he had made it easy for her. Just after 6:00 p.m. he called, telling her he had to work late again and not to wait up. It only fueled her determination, knowing that Greg was probably at another motel with the same women she had seen the night before.

Diane made good use of the solitude. She searched the rest of the house, making sure there was nothing more she could find about Greg's deceitfulness. Knowing what she now knew, she almost expected to find hidden spy cameras. So she walked the house thoroughly, looking in every possible location, from behind picture frames on shelving to ceiling light fittings. However, to her own disappointment, she found nothing.

Then, she sat down at the kitchen counter with pen and paper and mapped out her plans for tomorrow. She compiled a list of everything she had purchased, double-checking if she had missed anything that was essential. She wanted to travel light and decided to pick up anything else she needed while she was on the road.

As she lay awake in bed alone, she knew she would get little sleep. Her mind systematically went back through her plans, mentally ticking off every possible contingency. She felt good as she lay there, knowing that her military thinking was slowly returning. She had missed the discipline, the logical approach to planning every possible scenario well in advance and to leave nothing to blind luck or chance. Slowly her self-confidence was returning. Over the last twelve months, Diane had never viewed herself as a weak person. She knew now that somehow Greg had weakened her through a combination of over-medicating her and pure dishonesty, undermining her financially and as a wife.

She finally drifted off to sleep, wrapped in the warm contentedness of knowing that tomorrow was going to be the first day of her new life.

However, as dawn approached, there was one scenario Diane had underestimated in her carefully thought through plans: The extent to which Greg would react to finding she had left him.

Chapter 26

She waited until he had gone.

Until she heard his car back out of the garage, then drive down the street, the sound slowly fading, the street slowly waking for the day.

Waited for a whole five minutes, lying in bed, staring at the ceiling. With the bedroom door shut, she waited and listened, just to make sure, pretending to be asleep if he suddenly returned.

Time to move.

Diane threw off the bed covers and leaped out of bed.

Taking the hair dye she had bought, she quickly applied it, standing in front of the bathroom mirror, careful not to spill any on the floor. It was difficult to reach fully around the base of her neck at the back, but she did the best she could. Once done, she checked herself in the mirror, packaged up the spent tube and bottle in a plastic grocery bag, and tied it off.

She quickly showered, rinsing out the dye, dried her hair, and changed into comfortable clothes and practical shoes. These would be the only items of clothing she would take with her, to be disposed of later. Everything else she would leave behind. No clues of her intentions.

Glancing in the mirror, seeing her new blond hair, Diane felt a surge of excitement—and a tinge of fear. She was buoyed by the possibility of what the future would bring. She was shedding her skin, being reborn. A new person, glistening, waiting to emerge from beneath the shell of what she had become.

She hurried into the kitchen, dropped the plastic bag on the counter, and grabbed her car keys off the hook, not bothering with food or drink. She wasn't hungry. Nervous excitement and adrenaline was her sustenance. There would be time for food later. She would grab a coffee and a bite to eat on the road. She wanted to leave no residue behind, partake of nothing that would delay her leaving this place a moment longer. The house had become toxic over the last few days. The revelations about Greg had contaminated everything around her. She could no longer breathe, the air noxious, the memories poisonous. She could no longer bear being there another second.

Taking the spare office key she had hidden, Diane went to Greg's study, unlocked the door, and slid open the desk drawer. There it was. His second cell phone. Still sitting there, silent but screaming of his scheming, treachery, lying, and adulterous betrayals. She scooped up the phone and slid it into her pocket. She would have to work out a way to unlock it later. Perhaps pay some kid in an electronics store fifty bucks to do it for her. There had to be a way to unlock it. There was always a way if you were determined enough.

Closing then locking the study door, Diane went back along the hallway and into Ella's room, pausing there for a moment. The space was filled with such pain and bad memories, like everything else in the house that Diane didn't want to take with her. She wanted to leave it intact, untouched—all but the framed photo on the dresser. The photo was taken two years ago, mother and daughter, their cheeks pressed close together, their smiles almost interlocked as one.

Happier times.

But Ella would live on forever in Diane's mind in her new life, not in her old one. Diane turned and gave the room one last final look. Not committing it to memory, but rather trying hard to forget. From now on she would only think happy thoughts of a daughter, cherish fond memories, relive the best moments she had with her, and forget the rest.

Diane left the room and didn't stop, pause to reminisce, or reflect in any other parts of the house. She kept on walking briskly, eyes up, mind focused, through the family room and living room, pausing only in the kitchen to scoop up the plastic bag with the spent hair dye inside.

She climbed into her car where she had parked it on the street the night before, started the engine, and focused on the road in front of her. She turned the wheel, pulled away from the curb, and held her breath, not giving even a sideways glance at the house that had been her home for the last sixteen years.

The new Diane would make a new home elsewhere.

Turning out of the street, Diane let out her breath, wound down the window, and filled her lungs with the fresh, cold morning air. Now was not the time to relax, though, to ease up, to slow down. The finishing line was a long way away, and she still had to get there.

She calculated she would have a good eight-hour start before Greg would return home. Then, maybe another few hours after that, if she could convince him she had another evening session with Dr. Redding. Twelve hours at the most. How far away would she in twelve hours? Six hundred miles? Seven hundred?

She doubted he would follow her. He had no idea where she was going.

She expected him to call her around 9:00 a.m. on her old cell phone. She would take his call. Not doing so would arouse suspicion. She would tell him everything was fine; she hadn't answered the home phone because she was resting in bed. He will call again around 3:00 p.m. She would be far from this place by then. She would lie again, tell him she was in town doing a few errands. Diane had it all worked out, mapped it out like a military operation, in the Army again, fighting an enemy who was cunning, secretive, and manipulative. Unlike the Army, Diane wasn't invading or advancing, taking ground; she was retreating, withdrawing, running. As she thought about that as she drove, she felt a buzz of excitement with each mile she put between her and her old house, between her and her past with Greg. It felt like a victory, a sense of winning, not losing the battle.

That would be the final time she would speak to him, the afternoon call, hear his voice just one more time, then no more.

Diane pressed the gas pedal and the world opened up in front of her. Endless possibilities. She checked herself in the rearview mirror and smiled. She took a deep breath, savoring the clean fresh air as it flowed into her body, cleansing her life. This was the first day of the rest of her life, *her* life, a life that couldn't be taken away, controlled, or dominated by anyone but her.

She wasn't alone, though. She had a companion, someone with her, by her side, always in her heart and in her mind, ever-present. She glanced at the framed photo on the passenger seat next to her.

Now was the time to spend with her daughter, to try and make up for all those years she couldn't be there for her child. Money gave her that: time, freedom, options. No matter where she ended up, Diane was going to build a garden for her daughter—not a shrine. That was too morbid. Just a place she could tend to, nurture, and love. Grow again where things had died before. Sunflowers. She would plant them. Plenty of them. They were Ella's favorite. Big, upturned faces of gold that followed the rays of the sun across the sky. Needing and feeding on the warmth and light.

Arriving at the storage facility, Diane parked at the curb, climbed out, and used her swipe key on the side access gate to enter the facility. She briskly walked to her storage unit, unlocked it, slid up the roller door, and closed it behind her. The SUV was fully loaded. Everything had been triple checked. She climbed behind the wheel and started the engine. After opening the roller door, she drove out, passing through the security gate and parking the SUV along the curb, behind her old car. She got out, taking with her the new set of clothes she had folded and placed on the passenger seat. She climbed back into her old car, drove it into her storage unit, and shut the roller door. Inside, she quickly changed into her new clothes and shoes, peeling off everything, even bra and panties in a ritualistic discarding of the old. Once done, she stood for a moment. Everything smelled and felt new.

Good.

She bundled up her old clothes, and together with the plastic bag of used hair dye, exited through the side door, walked back to the steel dumpster, lifted the lid, threw everything in, and closed the lid.

She took a moment, pausing under the bright sun, her face upturned, and breathed deeply again. She went back out through the side access gate and climbed into the SUV. Adjusting the review mirror one last time, she called up on the GPS her destination she had pre-programmed into it and accelerated away from the curb.

The rent for the storage unit was paid in cash for the next three months. Leaving her old car in there would buy her more time if needed. If she had simply dumped the car, abandoned it or sold it, it would easily be traced within a matter of days not months. They would be looking for a vehicle that was now safely concealed, hidden, collecting dust behind four walls. More time wasted by others looking for something that wasn't on the road.

And when the rent ran out, and overdue notices went ignored, the manager of the storage facility would reluctantly walk—bolt cutters in hand—to the storage unit he had rented to a woman named Marion Crane, whom he had met just once, and whose face he couldn't recall for the police.

Then, and only then, would they find inside the unit another piece of shed skin from a woman who didn't exist anymore.

Chapter 27

Diane's cell phone began to ring. Her old cell phone in the center console. She glanced down at the screen, and her heart froze. *Greg.*

His name, his caller ID displayed clear as day on this screen.

Diane tensed and glanced at the clock on the dash: 10:06 a.m.

She was on the return leg back from Grand Island and was approaching Hazard again to pass the town and continue heading west as planned. The entire round trip, including swapping vehicles had taken just under two hours.

Panic began to rise in her throat.

She had already taken the morning call from Greg an hour ago, told him what she had rehearsed, that she was at home resting. It was like every other phone call from him. Except this time she listened intently, trying to pick up any inflection in his voice, any change in tone that would reveal a hint of concern or distrust by him. But there was none. Diane was cool, calm and monotone, as she had been all those other times when he had called. She had ended the call without even breathing a sigh of relief.

She glanced at the phone again. He never called twice in one morning. Never.

The phone kept ringing.

Eighth ring, ninth ring, tenth ring.

She had to answer it. She needed to pull over to the side of the road and take the call.

Braking hard, she came off the highway and onto the

shoulder in a funnel of dust and grit, tires sliding to a grinding halt.

The phone kept ringing.

She had to compose herself. Not panic. Not sound guilty. Not sound worried as to why he was calling—again.

Diane picked up her old cell phone and answered the call.

"Hi, honey." Greg's cheerful voice came through loud and clear.

Diane inhaled, trying to calm her nerves. "Hi," she said, mustering as much courage as she could, her stomach and intestines churning. "What's up?"

Greg let out an audible sigh of exasperation. "You're not going to believe this. I've left a damn client file at home. On the kitchen counter, I think." Greg sounded like he was almost berating himself.

Diane listened intently.

"Vickers is busting my balls this morning about it. He wants to see the projections I've been working on. There's some stuff in the file I need. Can you check, honey? If it's there in the kitchen, let me know?"

Diane swallowed hard. She couldn't remember seeing a file on the kitchen counter this morning. Mind you she was in too much of a rush to notice as she hurried out the door, eager to leave and get on the road. What could she say to Greg? What could she tell him? If she told him the file was there, on the kitchen counter, what if it wasn't? What if he decided to drive home and collect the file himself, only to discover that she wasn't there? And if she said the file wasn't there, he might come home anyway. Just to check for himself.

"Honey?" Greg said. "Are you still there?"

Diane hesitated. Her mind swirled. Uncertainty gripped her.

"Honey?"

Diane rubbed her forehead. "Sorry. I just woke up. I'm in the bedroom."

"Oh, sorry babe. Sorry to wake you. Can you please just check, honey?"

"Just give me a sec," Diane said. "I'll go and check."

"It's the Jenkins file, honey. It'll have a label on it."

Diane pulled the cell phone away from her ear, held it in front of her, and stared at it in horror. She closed her eyes, feeling sick. It was too soon. She needed more time to get away. It wasn't enough. She couldn't return home again, stand in the kitchen, and look for the file. Call him back, tell him it was a mistake if the file was actually there.

Diane counted slowly to ten, visualizing herself getting slowly out of bed, walking slowly along the hallway, past the living room, and into the kitchen. She imagined herself looking at the kitchen countertops, searching for a file that was invisible to her right now.

When she was done searching in her mind's eye, she brought the phone back to her ear and spoke. "No, honey, there's nothing on the kitchen counter."

There was a pause on the line for a moment, and Diane thought Greg had gone, ended the call.

"Are you sure, babe?" Greg's voice came back. "It should be right there near the phone. I thought I left it there on my way out, next to the kitchen phone."

"Positive," Diane replied. "I'm standing right here in the kitchen. I can't see it."

Greg let out a disappointed sigh.

Diane had an idea to sound more convincing. "Did you leave it in your study? On the desk or somewhere in there?"

There was a pause, then Greg said, "Can you go and check?"

"Hold on."

Diane slowly counted to five, the time it would take her in her drowsy state to walk from the kitchen to the study. "No, the door's locked, Greg. I don't have a key."

"That's okay. Look, I'll tell Vickers he can wait until tomorrow. He didn't pay me a bonus last month anyway. So screw him."

Diane closed her eyes. *Thank God.*

"I'll take a look tonight when I get home, babe," Greg said. "Get some rest. I'll see you tonight. I should be home around six."

Greg ended the call.

Diane breathed a sigh of relief, placing her old cell phone back in the center console. It took her a full minute before her heart finally slowed to a normal beat. She took a deep breath, gripped the steering wheel, looked back in the rearview mirror, and eased the SUV slowly off the shoulder onto the highway.

Her plan had worked. Greg would be home at six. And when he called this afternoon, she would tell him she didn't have time to make dinner because she hadn't been feeling well. He would understand. She would also tell him she had to go out for an evening session with Dr. Redding that she had forgotten to write on the wall calendar.

That would buy her more time.

Everything was going according to plan.

The tiny digital clock on the microwave read 10:15 a.m.

Greg stood in the kitchen. Not the kitchen at work. Not the

kitchen of a friend's house. Not the kitchen in a restaurant or diner.

The house was silent, still, empty. Somewhere outside in a neighbor's yard a dog barked.

Greg walked from the kitchen, past the living room, back along the hallway and stood outside the bedroom, looking in. He saw the bed perfectly made, perfectly tucked-in edges, the covering neatly folded back, pillows plump and equally spaced on top of each other.

Military precision.

He tightened the grip on his cell phone in his hand, his cold eyes focused on the bed.

Then, he walked back along the hallway and stood outside the closed study door. He tried the doorknob, as he had done before calling Diane on her cell. It was locked securely. It was the only truth Diane told him on the call.

She was nowhere to be found. He had already checked every room. Outside in the yard. Had even done a quick walk around the block.

He had spoken to her an hour ago. She had told him she was at home, lying down, having a rest. That she wasn't going out, planned to stay at home all day. Maybe she had planned not to go out. But why lie to him when he called her just now after he discovered the house empty when he had come home to grab the file he needed? He didn't want to wake her again. He was just being considerate. He'd planned to come home, ease open the front door, quietly tip-toe in, and check if the file was there.

Then he decided to check in on her. Go to the bedroom to see if she was fine. When he did, everything changed in that one moment.

He went back to the kitchen, walked right up to the kitchen

wall phone, and smiled. He could easily call her back on the home phone, uncover her dishonesty, and scare the shit out of her. Then listen to her squirm and make excuses as to why she was lying.

He reached for the wall phone then stopped, his hand just a few inches from it. She was probably out somewhere, maybe having a coffee with one of her dumb friends. What was that woman's name whose ugly kid had gone to the same school as Ella?

He liked playing games with Diane. Maybe he would call her again. Tell her he hadn't been home. Greg thought for a moment, plans forming in his head.

But there was no need to panic. She hadn't been in his study. She didn't have a key.

So where was she?

Unless…

Maybe she was having affair, sleeping with another man. Greg frowned. But who would be interested in her? In her present state? Most of the time, she walked around the house in a daze, like a zombie, sniveling and vague, thanks to what he had done with her medication. It was a bonus that the high dosage she was on had made her lose weight, caused her to lose her appetite, and gave her that washed-out, sick look. It gave him more control over her. Her emaciated appearance turned men off, he imagined, a natural contraceptive. It had certainly turned him off; that was for sure.

Greg dismissed the idea that Diane was meeting some other guy behind his back. It seemed too incredible just thinking about it.

No. She was out somewhere, meeting one of her friends. Someone she didn't want him to know about. Probably that

Martha Hendricks cow, Greg thought, recalling the woman's name.

No big deal.

It wasn't like she was leaving him. Where would or could she go?

He had made sure all her friends had abandoned her.

And she had no money. There was only enough in the checking account so she could just get by week-to-week. He'd also made sure of that.

Greg's arm dropped to his side, and he turned away from the wall phone. He would find out soon enough what she was up to.

He scooped up the Jenkins file right where he had left it this morning near the wall phone, walked around the counter, and out the front door, locking it behind him.

Chapter 28

No matter how hard he tried, Greg couldn't stop the niggling feeling he had as he drove back to work.

Passing through town again, Greg slowed and turned into the main street of Hazard, looking side to side, seeing if he could spot Diane's car parked somewhere or see her walking along the footpath or sitting outside a coffee shop. But after ten minutes of driving back and forth, he didn't see her or her car.

Then he passed the drugstore again, pulled up outside the front door, and climbed out of his car. Maybe she had been in, had a prescription filled, and they had seen Diane today.

Inside, Greg waited behind an aisle, pretending he was interested in dental hygiene products, while he kept an eye on the counter. The pharmacist was working behind the raised counter at the back, while the only store assistant, a young woman Greg had never seen before, was serving an old woman. The older woman was taking forever to decide on two different types of headache tablets, like she needed to know what every word on the label meant.

"Christ, hurry up," Greg mumbled under his breath as he watched the woman dither. Finally the old woman made up her mind and the assistant rang up the sale.

Greg immediately strode toward the counter. "Old witch," he whispered out of the corner of his mouth at the old woman as she shuffled past him.

The young assistant smiled as Greg approached. After explaining who he was and describing Diane, he asked the assistant if his wife had been in today.

"Not that I can recall," she said.

Greg made a show of pulling out an old prescription from his wallet and threw a look of concern on his face. "It's just that I usually get her medication for her and was unsure if she had another copy of the prescription filled already."

The assistant picked up the prescription and examined it, read the name, then looked at Greg, thinking, *Don't you guys live together? Talk to each other? Wouldn't you already know?*

"I said I would get it filled for her," Greg continued, "but she's out shopping today, and I just wanted to make sure she hadn't already been in and picked up another—and her cell phone is off," Greg hastily added. Then he described what Diane looked like, hoping the dumb college bitch would remember.

The pharmacist from behind the raised counter looked up and saw Greg. "Hi, Greg."

"Hi, Marty," Greg said. "Just checking if Diane has been in today, that's all."

Marty frowned. "Don't think so. Let me check the computer."

While Marty tapped away, Greg drummed his fingers on the counter. The young assistant was staring at him suspiciously. Maybe he looked agitated, and he was. He gave her an awkward smile, but really felt like reaching across, grabbing her around the back of her head with both hands, and slamming her smug little face into the countertop.

"Here we go," Marty replied, reading off the computer screen. "She came in yesterday, got another prescription filled. Different medication than what she usually gets from us."

"I remember now," the assistant said, her eyes still fixed on Greg. "Thin, dark-haired, attractive. She hasn't been in since, or if she has, I haven't seen her."

Greg looked back at the girl behind the counter. *Observant little thing, aren't you? Perhaps too observant.*

"That's her," Greg replied, a little too anxiously. "You don't happen to recall—" Greg pulled himself up. Would it be too strange if he started asking how his wife seemed? Was she acting strangely? Did she say anything odd, like she was leaving her husband?

The girl looked at Greg, expectantly. "What?"

Greg shook his head. "Nothing. Sorry. It doesn't matter."

"I guess you can have this back then," the assistant said, the smug expression still on her face.

"Thanks," Greg said, taking back the old prescription, his teeth grinding away with frustration. The girl behind the counter was getting deeper under his skin. Reluctantly, Greg turned and began to walk away.

Marty watched Greg leave, then shrugged and went back to the important task of separating pills into smaller batches.

"Oh, she did buy some hair dye."

Halfway down an aisle, Greg stopped in his tracks. He turned around and stared back at the young girl, who was watching him carefully, a wry smile now on her face.

She shrugged. "Said she wanted a change, try a new look."

Greg didn't move. Diane had never altered her hair color in all the years they had been married. Never. Hadn't even mentioned it as a passing thought. Unlike him, vanity wasn't one of her traits.

The assistant then added, "She said she wanted to move on, leave her old self behind. Become a new person."

Outside the drugstore, Greg was furious. He stomped back and forth, then tore up the old prescription and threw it into the gutter. He walked to a quiet corner away from the store front, pulled out his cell phone, then logged in to their online bank account. He scrolled through the transactions for the last few days.

Nothing. No purchases. Not even the drugstore purchase Diane had made yesterday. She hadn't used her card at all. Not that she went out much and spent much anyway. She was very frugal, even when she had her Army job.

Greg searched again, looking for any recent ATM cash withdrawals.

Nothing.

Greg's eyes narrowed as he glared at the screen.

So what was she using for money? Cash? Greg had always kept an eye on any cash withdrawals Diane had made. As far as he could tell, there weren't any over the last month or so. Maybe she had a stash of cash somewhere? Been squirrelling it away for this exact moment—to run, to leave him. But how much did she stash away if that was true? There were no significant ATM withdraws over the last six months. He would have known. Plus, he had kept the account balance deliberately low, just hovering above the thousand dollar mark so he wouldn't get hit with account fees.

Perhaps she had taken a job, something part-time that she had kept secret from him. Gone there to work during the daytime while he was at work.

Bitch!

He went to call her cell phone again but stopped, not wanting to let her know he was looking for her. "Whore!" Greg hissed as he paced around in a circle, cursing to himself, oblivious to the strange looks other shoppers were giving him as they hurried past.

He needed to calm down, to think, get his thoughts in order, have a plan. Where would she go? She had no relatives in town or even in the entire state. He was certain of that. And Diane's friends? He had made sure her ties with them were severed long ago.

Greg stopped pacing. A thought suddenly dawned on him, making him feel sick.

Chapter 29

Tires squealed as Greg tore into the driveway, braked hard, ran up the front porch steps, and nearly broke the front door key in the lock.

He threw the door open and rushed inside, slamming the door shut behind him.

At the study door, he fumbled with the keys, trying to find the right one.

"Come on!" he yelled. Finally, he twisted the key in the lock and burst into the room. Three strides and he was around the other side of the desk and wrenched open the top drawer so fast, it came off its tracks and tipped sideways in his hand, spilling the entire contents out onto the floor.

Greg cursed as he got down on his hands and knees, shuffling through the contents, spreading the mess even more, panic slowly rising in his chest.

It wasn't there. His cell phone. His other cell phone. It was gone.

Greg pulled out the remaining two drawers, upended them both onto the growing pile of mess on the floor, his actions more urgent, more distressed. Getting down onto his hands and knees, he pushed and tossed files and stationery aside like a madman, his eyes wild, panic giving way to anger and frustration.

It had to be there. But the door had been locked. And he had a key—the only key.

Greg got to his feet, one foot catching on the swivel base of the office chair, his ankle twisting. He stumbled backward almost toppling over. In a fit of rage, he lifted the chair and hurled it over the desk. It landed with a crash against the bookshelf on the opposite wall, smashing the shelving. An avalanche of books, framed photos, ornaments, and splintered wood tumbled in a cascading heap.

Greg stood there, teetering on his feet, quivering with rage, trying to comprehend the incomprehensible.

He looked around, panting with exertion, his mind racing.

Diane had been in there. Had to be. She had a key he didn't know about.

The lying bitch.

Greg tried to calm down, but he couldn't.

He emptied the plastic tray on top of the desk onto the floor as well and searched again through the mess.

Nothing.

Next he went to the steel filing cabinet, pulled everything out, tipped each folder out onto the floor. Loose paper zigzagged downward, a blizzard of paperwork adding to the growing slush pile in the room.

He turned and punched the nearest wall, putting his fist through the drywall, leaving a fist-sized hole. He didn't care about the pain or the fact that blood was now dripping from his split knuckles and down his fingers.

Greg looked around, his chest heaving, nostrils flared. Then he paused and thought.

His only saving grace was the fact that his cell phone was locked. A biometrical lock. Facial recognition, Face ID. A pattern of thirty thousand uniquely positioned dots converted into a 3D mathematical facial landscape that was then encrypted. Never backed up. Never stored on any server or cloud. Double failsafe. No one could unlock the cell phone except Greg. It was totally useless in anyone else's hands. That's how he had set it up. That's why he bought that particular model. The latest and greatest the salesperson had told him. He had to make sure no one but him could access it.

The tidal wave of fear, panic, and anger began to slowly recede as Greg clambered and stumbled through the mess, making his way out of the study, and headed to the main bedroom.

He went straight to Diane's drawers, pulling each one open one by one. Her clothes seemed to be there. Panties and bras all neatly folded. Socks and other undergarments. T-shirts and shorts. Next he went into the closet and saw her dresses and pants still on hangers. No gaps, no telltale signs where swathes of clothing had been removed. He looked up to the storage shelf above where luggage and bags were stacked. Nothing seemed to be missing.

He walked back into the bedroom and entered the adjoining bathroom. On the counter near the sink, he found all of Diane's cosmetics: lipsticks, makeup, everything still sitting there. He slid open the cabinet drawers and looked inside. More signs of Diane's presence: tampons, Q-tips, sanitary pads, cotton swabs, razors, eye cream, hand cream, face cream. Her toothbrush still sitting in a plastic tumbler next to the faucet on the sink. Another one in the shower with a curled tube of toothpaste and her shampoos.

Greg pivoted around the bathroom, the tiny room swirling. Everywhere his eyes went, he saw Diane. Not just traces of her, the remnants. But her daily life still living there, occupying the space.

He walked out of the bathroom and sat on the edge of the bed.

Nothing was missing—except his wife and her car.

She had no money, not much anyway. Nothing worthwhile to steal and run, leave him. There was hardly any money in the checking account. And she certainly didn't know about his other accounts where he had siphoned off and hidden the bulk of their cash.

She hadn't gone, left him. He was certain of it.

Unless…she had her own source of money? Had a part-time job during the day, small hours, while he was at work himself. He had dismissed the idea before. Now it was a distinct possibility. However, she would only be getting minimum-wage, maybe slightly more. It certainly wasn't enough to build up any decent cash reserves. Plus it would take forever to build enough that would allow her to leave, to run. He would know. She was never good at keeping things from him.

Greg pulled out his cell phone and hit speed dial for Diane's cell. Then quickly stopped himself, ending the call before it connected.

He sat there for a moment thinking, his thumb poised over the screen, hovering over Diane's name.

Now was not the time to be rash. He needed to establish the facts, then recalibrate, reposition himself so he could deal with her without her knowing.

He breathed heavily and closed his eyes, waiting for the inferno of rage to slowly subside to a harmless smolder.

Greg opened his eyes again.

No, he wouldn't call Diane. He didn't want to give her any advantage. Any forewarning. He was going to find her. And when he did…

He gave a little smile, like a coyote stumbling upon a lame animal.

He had a better idea. Something more cunning. Something she wouldn't see coming. And he *was* going to go after her. He would do whatever it took. Pursue her to the ends of the earth if he had to.

He was going to find her, make it his life's mission to track her down.

And when he cornered her, she would beg.

The front doorbell rang.

Greg snapped back from his torture fantasy.

Diane.

The embers ignited again. Flames of rage, hot and burning leaped up in Greg's brain as he rushed to the front door. He was going to drag her inside by the hair and bounce her around the room. And that was just for starters!

Greg wrenched open the front door, almost pulling it off its hinges, instantly regretting that he had been so forceful.

The front door, once opened, couldn't be closed again—especially when a deputy sheriff was standing on your front porch looking at you as though you were insane.

"Mr. Miller." Monica Styles stood on the porch, a look of surprise on her face. Her eyes narrowed. He was expecting someone else, she could tell.

Greg Miller's face was scrunched, twisted in rage, menace in his eyes, his body posturing for violence.

"Sorry to bother you again. But I would like to have a word with your wife. Is she in at the moment?"

Greg Miller just stood bewildered. He was caught off guard and didn't know what to say, how to respond.

Monica cut her gaze down to Greg Miller's hand. The skin on his knuckles was split with a nasty gash. Ribbons of blood snaked down his fingers, dropping big velvety splashes onto the porch. "Are you okay, Mr. Miller?"

Greg's mind snapped into gear. He brought up his hand and regarded the blood. He gave an uncomfortable laugh. "Oh, this? It's nothing. I was just chopping up some vegetables. I must have cut my hand." Greg quickly put his hand behind his back.

Monica studied Greg Miller's demeanor carefully. She knew the telltale signs of when someone was lying. The fidgeting. The darting eyes. Greg Miller looked uncomfortable, anxious, awkward, his speech stuttering, undecided as to what he was going to say, how to best present the lie so it read like the truth. Monica Styles was not a chef or an expert in knife wounds. But she knew enough to know that anyone chopping vegetables, or anything for that matter, wouldn't slice anywhere near the knuckle line of their own hand. The injury was where you would typically punch something—or someone—with your fist.

Monica took a step forward. "Is Mrs. Miller in?" She tried to look past Greg Miller, into the house.

Greg gave a tight, forced smile, still blocking the doorway with his body. "She's not in at the moment."

Monica waited for more, but that was it. Greg Miller offered no more, just stood there.

Monica nodded. He was definitely hiding something. She changed tactics. "Then I'd like to ask you a few questions. Perhaps I could come inside?" She had insufficient probable cause to demand to enter and search the house. But from the look of the injury on Greg Miller's hand, something violent had recently happened. Monica wanted to go inside, take a look, make sure Diane Miller wasn't cowering in the corner with a black eye or a busted cheek. Again she tried to look past Greg Miller, to see if she could see or hear anything.

Greg Miller seemed to swell in size in the doorway. "Like I

said, she's not here at the moment. And I'm also very busy. I've got to get to work. I'm extremely late."

Monica made a show of checking her watch. "Starting late today?" She knew exactly where Greg Miller worked.

"I had the morning off," Greg replied sourly. "I had a few things to do around the house."

"It will only take a few moments." Monica continued to stare unwaveringly at Greg Miller, expecting the man to fold, to crumble, admit that something was wrong.

"Perhaps some other time," Greg said, knowing full well he didn't have to allow the deputy inside his house.

Then, to Monica's surprise, he slammed the door shut in her face.

Chapter 30

The street was quiet this time of day as most people were either at work or out spending their social security checks on frivolous things.

Monica drove across the street to the opposite block, circled back, and parked down a side street. She went on foot, approaching the Miller house from the east, utilizing crooked yard fences and sidewalk trees to shield her duplicity. Three properties down, and diagonally opposite the Miller property, she found a clump of gnarly bushes that acted as a screen, providing a concealed but clear view of the front door of the Miller house.

Crouching and looking through a gap in the bushes, Monica didn't have to wait long.

Greg Miller came out of the front door, rushed down the porch steps, threw a bag into the trunk of his car, then tore out of the driveway, accelerating away with reckless speed.

She waited five minutes before emerging from behind the bushes, then cut across the street, angling toward the house, scanning the end of the street ahead every few seconds.

She went through an open gate and down the side of the Miller house, and tried the sliding glass patio door at the rear.

Locked.

Cupping her hands against the glass, she could see into the living area. A basic table, six chairs, the kitchen beyond. Everything looked orderly, composed, mundane.

The backyard was fenced on three sides with tall wooden

palings, the rooftops just visible of the adjoining properties that were all single-story, like the Miller house. Next, she tried a door.

Locked too.

There was a wide window on the western side, chest-height, a bedroom Monica guessed. White Venetian blinds hung on the inside, drawn down but angled flat so she could get a good view inside. Monica leaned in, cupped her hands to the glass, her eyes taking a few moments to focus through the glass, past the blinds, and into the room.

"Jesus," she whispered, her breath fogging the glass.

The room was small, a study of some sort that looked like it had been ransacked, as though a human tornado had gone through it. Shelves were smashed, drawers upended. Files, papers, books, strewn across the floor, an upended office chair. Tilting her eyes and head, Monica saw a hole punched in the drywall on the left, then a bloody handprint on the wall near the door. Her eyes shifted focus to the floor. More blood was speckled across parts of the carpet, across piles of paper and files that littered the floor. Her attention returned to the hole in the drywall, wondering if Greg Miller's fist had made it, and that's what had caused the gash across his knuckles.

She circled back to the patio sliding door and banged on it with her fist. "Mrs. Miller! Sheriff's department. Are you home?"

She banged again, setting off barking somewhere over the fence behind her.

Returning to the front door, Monica pressed the doorbell and waited.

Nothing.

Then she checked the garage through a side window. Empty.

Maybe Diane Miller was in fact not home. Monica thought about kicking in the front door, but soon dismissed it. Charmers wouldn't be happy. Styles didn't have enough probable cause. Greg Miller, in some fit of rage had torn up the study and punched a wall. Big deal. Men just acted like boys when they couldn't find their car keys or the TV remote.

As Monica contemplated what to do next, she had a niggling suspicion there was more to it. And why did Diane's husband seem so guilty about something?

Diane Miller seemed like a ghost, a ghost Monica wanted to find.

Greg glanced around as he hunched behind the wheel, his eyes hawkish, a plan starting to come together in his head.

It was a simple case of following the steps, backtracking and eliminating the unlikely possibilities.

His cell phone was safe for the time being. Diane could not unlock it. But that didn't matter. What mattered right now was finding Diane—at whatever cost. Find her and he would find his cell phone. She had taken it. There was no doubt. And when he found her, he was going to show her, long and slow, what the consequences were for betraying him.

The first thing he did was call the office and tell them there was a sudden death in the family. A non-existent aunt in Florida had passed away after suffering a long battle with the heat, constant traffic jams, and being surrounded by too many old people.

He smiled when he told them that lie. There may very well be a death in the family—soon.

He said he'd just need a few days, then would return to work.

Placing his cell phone into the cradle on the dash, he called up the GPS map and waited for an installed app to calibrate and orientate.

He couldn't believe Diane had taken his cell phone. Was she going to the police? If she had, then Little Miss Deputy Bitchface would have said something, come to arrest him. But she hadn't, and he wasn't—arrested.

Could Diane have gotten access to his cell? Somehow unlocked it, taken an image of his face while he slept? Was she really that devious? Cunning? He always kept the key to the study door on a separate ring away from his car and house keys. There was no way Diane could have found it to make a copy. She had been in his study, nosing around. He was certain of that.

She must have a spare key of her own. He had checked and doubled checked her belongings, though. Gone through everything. He should have put a lock on the desk drawer. Too late now.

Greg's cell phone pinged and he glanced at the screen.

Good.

His smile soon vanished. She was heading west? Away from Hazard. There was nothing west.

Greg twisted his neck, hearing the vertebrae crack and pop, loosening himself up for what was to come.

Maybe she was meeting a man. He pictured Diane in a sleazy motel, brown laminate and orange fabric everywhere, an old cheap bed creaking away, Diane underneath some sweaty guy, some no-hoper she had met in a therapy class for losers. *He's caring, considerate. He listens to me, Greg. He understands my feelings. He gets me.*

Christ, give me a break! Greg thought. He could hear it all, Diane's excuses spilling out of her trembling little mouth when he caught up with her. He didn't care about Diane, hadn't for at least three years now. Just pretended he cared. Greg had mastered the art of disingenuous concern, care, and empathy for his wife. He smiled when required. Offered her fake affection and attention, when at times, he just felt like slapping her across the face.

She was weak. Especially after Ella had died. Greg was upset by Ella's death, of course. It was only natural. But no one comforted him or paid him any attention. They all seemed to flock to Diane with moral support and offers of comfort and help. Forget about old Greg. He was just the poor schmuck on the sidelines, in the background. He didn't count. Wasn't important enough.

Greg had gotten over it, moved on, replaced his initial grief with simmering resentment. Resentment of how he always played second fiddle to Diane.

He decided, quite rightly so, that the unfortunate event of his daughter's death wasn't going to drag the rest of his own life down into a dark hole of pitiful depression as it had done with Diane. He was stronger than that. It was his time to shine, not to dwindle into some sniveling, pathetic heap. He had been subservient to his wife ever since she came back from her first deployment. She thought she was so much better than him. Ordered him around like he was on a parade ground. Got paid more than him too. Got smiles, handshakes, pats on the back when out in public. Well done! Proud service to this great nation of ours!

Her—his damn wife! Not him. He deserved the attention, the accolades—not Diane.

So Greg decided to medicate her, dumb her down so to speak. Sure Ella's death had had a devastating impact on Diane. But Greg could not afford for Diane to recover, to get anywhere near her old self again. Then she would be elevated to a new unreachable height. Just think about it. A woman in uniform *and* a mother who had lost her daughter. Greg's star wouldn't just fade, it would implode into a black hole, taking him with it.

The medication had helped. But he needed more, something stronger. Keep her at home, home detention while he did what he did—take back control as men should. Me Too? Christ. What a pile that was. A witch-hunt conducted by a bunch of man-hating, lesbian-looking, two-bit actresses whose best performances were in front of the police complaining that a man had glanced at them oddly.

Greg looked at the cell phone screen, saw the red marker edging along, twenty miles in front of him. He hunched farther behind the wheel, a heinous smile spreading across his face, revealing a row of sharp teeth. He pressed the gas some more, not caring about the speed limit. He needed to make up time and ground if he was going to catch her.

But the opportunity had to be right. He couldn't exactly haul her from her car by the hair in front of people.

Or could he? It was a tantalizing thought, and he did like pulling women by the hair, to rein them in, so to speak. That's why most women had long hair, Greg reasoned. It was God's intent that it be used as a bridle by man. To lead them. To give them direction. To ride them.

No, he would slowly come up behind her, like a predator stalking through long grass.

"I'm coming for you, honey." He grinned, his mind made up. "And, you won't even see me."

Chapter 31

Diane breathed a sigh of relief as she watched the town of Hazard slowly shrink for the final time in the rearview mirror as she drove west on the highway.

With every mile that clicked over on the odometer, increasing the distance between her and her past, Diane felt the tension and anxiety slowly leave her. Her face and shoulders relaxed.

The second phone call from Greg had been troubling, unexpected, a glitch in her plans. However, she had handled it well.

The yellow centerline of the highway stretched to the horizon, and she kept her speed constant. The last thing she wanted was to be pulled over by the police, then questioned as to where she was going and why. Surrounded by the flat, featureless landscape, Diane's mind drifted back to Greg. In the last few days, it had become obvious that he was a stranger, someone she didn't really know despite living with him all these years. In the last twelve months, it seemed more like cohabitation than living together as husband and wife. To his credit, he had never beaten her, abused her, verbally or otherwise, in any way. She wasn't a victim of domestic violence. And if he had raised his hand against her, she would've broken his arm, maybe his jaw as well. Despite her size and weight, Diane's Army days had made her perfectly capable of taking care of herself.

He was, however, someone other than whom she had originally married. They say marriage changes you. Diane had another theory. Marriage slowly unravels you, peels away the layers people tend to cover themselves with to hide under. During the first few years, you only see a tiny sliver of that person. As the years roll on, more is revealed until eventually you see their true design. The real person laid bare. That's when you realized they were not the person you initially married. A stranger had come into your home and taken their place.

Knowing now what she knew, Greg was cunning, deceitful, manipulative, devious, and scheming. The synonyms flowed as Diane let her mind wander. His actions were deliberate, intentional, highly planned. And in Diane's mind, all this made him more dangerous than if he was just a blundering, violent fool. The true Greg had always been there, lurking below the surface, covered in the facade he had created since the day they'd met. Diane believed Greg had never really changed since then, evolved that is. He always just—was. And had done a brilliant job of hiding it from her.

Thirty minutes later, a tall sign tower rose into the cloud-filled sky with red neon, blinking the words, *Gas & Food*. The sign made Diane's stomach rumble as the large gas station came into view. She hadn't eaten at all since rising and wanted to get at least one solid meal into her before she settled in for a long stretch of driving ahead.

She eased her foot off the gas and came off the highway.

The gas station was a low, squat structure with a huge convenience store and diner connected together to form a long rectangular shape. Diane drove across the plaza and parked in a slot in front of the diner section, next to a large, black SUV.

Inside, a waitress greeted Diane with a genuine smile. Her hair was tastefully up in a French rope braid that ran along each side of her head and fashioned into a tight curled knot at the rear. The medieval style brought a smile to Diane's face as she followed behind the waitress and was shown to a booth near the window.

The thick, heavy, ceramic coffee mug came first, the coffee piping hot and aromatic. Unfolding the large menu, Diane browsed the items from the all-day breakfast section and selected a breakfast burrito with a side of French toast. She was ravenous and needed the calorie-dense food to add some mass and size she had lost over the months. Maybe it was the new medication, or just the liberating feeling she now had, that caused her appetite to return.

While she waited for her order, Diane drank coffee and watched the people around her. Some customers sat alone at the counter, reading the newspaper or watching the television perched on the wall above the serving area. Some couples sat at tables, blank expressions on their faces, eyes averted to cell phones in their hands, thumbs scrolling through other people's lives. A rather intense-looking couple sat in a nearby booth, poring over a map unfolded on the table in front of them. Unsure of where they should go next.

Two waitresses worked the floor, order pads in one hand, steaming coffee pots in the other. Through the window, Diane saw another waitress outside on her break, huddled under the awning, head cocked, cell phone pressed to her ear, face scrunched, animated gestures, as though she was pleading, then yelling.

Man problems, Diane thought.

Diane watched as a young mother walked across the plaza after filling up her car. A girl, a child, no more than five years old in a bright sunflower dress, was clasping the mother's hand, skipping along, blond hair and ribbons blowing in the breeze behind her. As Diane watched small skipping strides trying to keep up with the larger adult ones, she felt a pang in her throat and hollowness in her stomach that no amount of food could fill.

Perhaps it wasn't too late. After all she had read stories of women well into their late forties and early fifties having children.

There was still time. Could she go through all that again?

Then it occurred to her that she needed a man for that. But men were the last thing on her mind. And it was definitely the last thing she wanted—to fall into another relationship so soon. No, what Diane wanted was solitude. Right now she craved loneliness, would run gladly toward it, embrace it like it was her new best friend. Not another man. She had made her mind firmly up. No involvement. No commitment. No being tied down again.

She could still have another child, though. There were other ways, medical procedures to become pregnant.

She didn't need a man. Not yet anyway. In the future, the distant future, maybe.

The food came and Diane ate like she hadn't eaten in weeks. She wolfed it down and finished it off with her third cup of coffee. Everything tasted wonderful, like the best thing she had ever tasted, and not just because of the quality of the ingredients or the care taken to prepare the food. There was another, more compelling reason; she had made the right choice. She knew it deep down. She was tasting freedom for the first time in a long time.

The waitress with the French braid returned. "Is there anything else I can get you?" she asked, clearing away the plates but leaving the two coffee mugs and refilling them both.

"No, that'll be all thanks," the woman said.

The waitress placed the check on the table, gave a smile, then swirled away, coffee pot in hand.

Alex Romano placed cash on the check and slid a twenty under the saltshaker. She looked up at her brother sitting across from her in the booth.

With the risk of looking like a tourist, which might not be a bad thing after all, Vincent had unfolded a map he had purchased from a gas station convenience store. This morning they had tracked farther west than the previous day, which they had spent in and around Grand Island, exhausting what little leads they had there. Vincent wanted to reconstruct the route Wheeler was following when he had crashed the van. They had kept well away from the laundry itself, preferring to be notified by cell phone if the sheriff's department returned to ask more questions.

"So what's the plan?" Alex asked.

Vincent let out a deep breath as he studied the map. He liked looking at maps, preferring the feel and touch of paper to pixels on his cell phone or GPS. A proper map allowed him to circle, and cross, and underline. That's what Vincent had done on the map in front of him. Planning out his strategy, his campaign to track down the money. It was no easy task.

One of Vincent's contacts had gone to the hospital earlier and reported that Anton Wheeler was still unconscious and under a police guard. No one could get near him, and Alex and Vincent certainly preferred not to show their faces there either. There was no way to reach him without raising suspicion.

"Wheeler wasn't acting alone," Vincent replied, his eyes searching the map, his mind twisting every which way like a

Rubik's cube. He tapped a spot. "As far as I can determine, this is where the van crashed. Someone must know something. Wheeler was heading somewhere, to meet someone, with the cash."

"An accomplice?" Alex asked.

"Or *accomplices*. I've made a few more calls. Put the word out about who could maybe shift a van like that." Vincent had to be careful, subtle, and indirect. He couldn't directly put the word out that a million in cash was stolen from one of the family's laundry business vans. That meant progress was painstakingly slow.

"So where are we exactly?" Alex leaned closer.

Vincent ran his finger along the highway on the map, running west from Grand Island. "We're about here. Wheeler was heading along this stretch of highway when he crashed, I was told. But I don't know exactly where."

Alex craned her head to get a better look at the map. The area was desolate, empty, just a sprinkle of small towns and communities. She traced the highway farther west, her finger settling on a place. "Broken Bow," she said, thoughtfully. "Strange name for a town. Like the name Hazard."

"There's plenty of strange places out here," Vincent remarked. "Wheeler was heading deeper inland, away from major towns and cities."

"He wouldn't have been going too far either because of the signage on the truck. It would draw attention."

"Exactly," Vincent replied. "We have to think like him, put ourselves in his shoes, and figure out where he was going. Who he was meeting up with. I'm expecting another call with some more information."

More time just sitting around waiting. Alex drank her coffee and watched the other customers. This was a hunting trip, Vincent's specialty, his domain. She would only step in when the prey was cornered. Until then, he had to just get them to the money and the people who had it. The rest she would take care of.

Alex noticed a woman eating alone in a booth not far from them. It was the kind of thing Alex noticed—women by themselves, eating alone. She'd had intimate knowledge of what that was like on many occasions.

Vincent's cell phone rang. He listened intently, said nothing, just nodded. All the time his eyes continued scanning the map, his finger tracing the route relayed to him by the caller. "Good," he said before ending the call.

"There's an auto mechanic shop here." Vincent tapped the map with his finger farther along the same stretch of highway, another ten miles away. "The owner of the shop is a likely suspect. It makes sense to sell the van and switch vehicles. Apparently the shop owner is known around these parts for fencing stolen vehicles. A small-time operator who's about to get a big-time shock." Vincent began folding the map. "Let's pay him a visit."

Chapter 32

Returning to the office, Monica Styles ran another check on Diane Miller to see what else she could find out about the elusive housewife.

She went back into the DMV database, in case she had previously missed something. To her complete surprise, a third vehicle now appeared registered under the name of Diane Abigail Miller. A white 2005 Chevrolet Trailblazer SUV purchased from a local car dealership yesterday. The vehicle had not been previously listed on the DMV database for the simple reason the transfer documentation had taken twenty-four hours to be processed and uploaded.

Monica leaned back in her swivel chair, contemplating this new information. Why would Diane Miller, who already had two vehicles registered under her name, purchase a third vehicle? The couple, whose daughter had died twelve months ago, had no other children but now had three vehicles. Styles went back into the database, brought up the purchase documentation for the Trailblazer. It was purchased from a secondhand dealership. Grabbing her notebook, including driver's license details and the photograph of Diane Miller she had printed off yesterday, Monica headed for the door.

The used-car dealership was on the back blocks of town, crammed in between a gas station on the corner and an abandoned warehouse that had once been a farm machinery parts wholesaler. Everything about the used car lot conveyed a sense of being worn, run-down. From the bleached flag bunting draped across the lot to the sun-faded signage out front that promised easy credit financing with no deposit down. Even the vehicles on display had a tired-looking slump to them, resigned to the fact that their best years were in the rearview mirror.

Monica looked around, assuming not many people came in here in a week to purchase a vehicle that would warrant the salesman having amnesia. It wouldn't be too difficult to remember a customer from the previous day.

The small modular office, which sat at the rear of the lot, looked closed, the window blinds drawn shut. Monica was halfway into the lot when a hand parted the office blinds and a face poked out from behind the sliding glass door. Moments later a young man emerged, slow and unsure of himself, like he was coming out of a cave and into the sunlight for the first time. He held up one hand against the glare, visibly grimaced like a vampire would if caught outside during daylight hours. He was tall, gangly, long limbed, wearing an ill-fitting crumpled suit. He gave Monica an irritable glare; his hair was greasy and disheveled, his face puffy and smudged with yesterday's stubble. As he approached, Styles gave a knowing smile, recognizing the familiar symptoms of a big night out and an even bigger next-day hangover.

She didn't need any introduction. The uniform, gun, and badge said it all. She also didn't give the man a chance to speak, simply held up the DMV photo of Diane Miller in front of his bloodshot eyes. "This woman came in here yesterday and purchased a 2005 Chevy SUV from you, correct?"

The salesman made a face like he was going to throw up, suppressed the sudden urge, then squinted at the license photo of Diane Miller, his brow furrowed in concentration. Then he gave a crooked, dry-lipped smile. "Didn't recognize her for a moment," he said with a raspy voice. "Yeah, she did come in here yesterday. Purchased a vehicle."

"What can you tell me about the woman?" Monica pocketed the photo, took out her notebook, and began drumming it with her pen, expectantly.

The salesman shrugged. "She was in a hurry. Wanted an SUV, something reliable and off-road capable."

Styles made a note. *Diane Miller, cross-country?* Monica looked up. "I don't want to know about the car. I want to know specifically about the woman. How she acted. Her demeanor."

The salesman's shoulders slumped. This was going to take a while. He definitely had drunk too much last night—a celebration for the unexpected cash sale, at full sticker price too. No haggling. It was usually the men, husbands and boyfriends, who came in and haggled. He couldn't even remember how he got back to the office last night or why he decided to crash on the sofa in the early hours of the morning. His head throbbed, the bright sun baking his eyeballs like a sun lamp an inch from his face. "Look, I really need to get some coffee. I don't function well in the morning without it."

Monica stopped tapping her pen on her notebook and took a step forward until she was about six inches from the man's face. He reeked of beer, sweat, and the gaseous aftermath of a chilidog hastily consumed at 2:00 a.m. "You can get coffee later. Tell me about the woman; otherwise I'm going to send a DMV audit team here within the hour to go through all your records."

The salesman's face sagged a little more in defeat. He dragged a hand through his hair more out of frustration than trying to look respectable. "Look, everything I do here is legal. She came in, she saw a white SUV that she liked, and she paid six grand cash."

"She paid in cash? Six thousand dollars?"

"Yeah," the salesman replied, now remembering more clearly the events of the previous day. "Don't really get many people paying cash these days. Usually they need a loan or use a cashier's check."

Monica wrote the details down, then made a side note. *Where did the cash come from?* "Did she trade another vehicle?"

"No. But she drove here in another vehicle when she returned."

"When she returned?"

"Yeah, I thought it was odd. When she agreed to buy the vehicle, she drove off and came back with the cash. Like I said, she seemed in a hurry."

"And she was alone? She didn't come here with anyone?"

"Not that I could tell," he said. "After we did the paperwork and I gave her the keys, she drove out of here with the car. But then she came back in a cab, maybe thirty minutes later. I saw her through the window of my office. She got out and walked around to the side street. Then I saw her pull out in a sedan, a different car, out the front here. It was definitely her."

So Diane Miller had purchased a secondhand SUV. Had driven it away, then had returned to pick up her own car that she had parked down a side street. Monica scribbled furiously in her notebook, her shorthand full of question marks. *Where was Greg? Alone. No friend? Why park down a side street? Secrecy? Where did she go with the SUV?*

"What else can you tell me about how the woman seemed?"

The salesman made a show of thinking, rubbing his stubble, his headache growing worse, almost as bad as his craving for coffee. He just wanted to get this over and done with. "She seemed nervous, kept looking out to the street when she was here, as though she was expecting to see someone."

Monica made another note. *Nervous. Fearful—Greg?*

There was nothing else of value Monica could get from the salesman. She had already downloaded full copies of the purchase documentation and transfer of ownership details.

She closed her notebook, slipped out her Sherman County Sheriff Department card and gave it to the man. "If you see her again, if she comes back in, or if you think of anything else, I want you to call me straight away. Day or night."

The salesman took the card and scrutinized the name and cell phone number on it. His eyes suddenly brightened, he gave Monica an appraising stare. "You mean I can call you any time?"

Styles rolled her eyes. "About the woman, Diane Miller. Not about me, you moron."

Chapter 33

There was a deserted rest area on the side of the highway, a small clearing, hemmed in by high scrub on three sides, with an old worn wooden picnic table and two benches sitting on a cracked slab of cement.

Perfect.

Greg could see the red neon sign of the gas station about two hundred yards farther along the highway. The bright flashing words *Gas* and *Food* like a beacon to weary travelers.

He slowed his car and eased over onto the shoulder of the road, the tires crunching on dirt and gravel, and pulled into the rest area. Turning off the engine, he checked his cell phone again just to be certain. The red marker continued blinking but not moving, positioned two hundred yards farther away from where he was parked.

Diane was at the gas station. There was no doubt. Greg did not want to startle her, pull into the gas station plaza only to see her make a run for it and drive off.

He had a much better idea.

He got out and locked the car, cell phone in hand.

Past the high scrub, the rest area was shielded from the gas station by a narrow tract of woods on one side. It ran like a natural wall inland, perpendicular to and away from the edge of the highway, concealing him and his car perfectly.

It was a simple plan. He would circle around, trek through the woods, approach the perimeter of the gas station complex from the side. Then angle around to see if he could gain access from the rear of the building via a staff or delivery entrance. He smiled at the thought. She wouldn't see him coming. Greg was hoping Diane had stopped for a while and was eating in the diner, not just filling up for gas.

He checked his cell phone again. The red marker was still stationary, had been for the last ten minutes while he was on the highway. No one took ten minutes to fill up for gas. She was in the diner drinking coffee or eating. He was sure of it.

Checking his bearings, Greg struck out through the knee-high scrub before reaching the edge of the woods and vanishing inside.

"Wait up, Vincent," Alex said. They were both walking from the diner toward their car. "I need to go to the bathroom," Alex said.

Vincent gave his sister an impatient look. "We need to get going, Alex. Couldn't you have gone before?"

Alex glared at her brother. "I didn't want to go *before*. Now I do."

"Meet me at the car," Vincent said, exasperated, "and hurry up," he called over his shoulder.

Alex pushed open the diner door and walked back inside. The restrooms were located at the far end, at the rear of the building. Walking past the tables and booths, Alex noticed that the woman she had seen eating alone was gone.

A small placard with an arrow indicating the restrooms was on the edge of a sidewall near the back. Alex turned left and walked down a narrow corridor, past the kitchen, a small staff room, and another room marked *Store Room*. Reaching the women's restroom, she pushed open the door and walked inside.

There were two hand basins and two stalls, one already occupied. A pair of ankles could be clearly seen in the gap between the bottom of the door and the tiled floor.

Why was it that restroom stall doors never went low enough? Alex thought, feeling suddenly very self-conscious. Women's restrooms seemed to be designed specifically by males with a complete lack of privacy or modesty and where the tiniest sound was amplified tenfold. The sound of someone urinating in the occupied cubicle echoed loudly in the small space, confirming Alex's thoughts. She entered the other stall and locked the door behind her. It was remarkably clean inside, and she felt a little more relaxed as she settled down.

She heard the flush from the toilet next door, the rattle of the latch, and the occupant's footsteps moving toward the hand sinks.

Good. Alex had a small sliver of privacy now, the sound of someone washing her hands making her task a lot easier. When she was done, Alex opened the stall door and walked out.

The two sinks were barely shoulder distance apart in the cramped space, making it virtually impossible not to interact with another person if you weren't alone. A large dull mirror hung on the wall above them.

Walking to the spare sink, Alex noticed the woman she had seen before, eating alone in a booth in the diner. But now the woman was wearing a baseball cap. Some people wore ball caps as though they were born with one on their head, like it was part of them, suited them. It worked as a fashion statement. Alex was not one of those people. Neither was the woman who was vigorously washing her hands with hot water at the sink next to her. Her head was down, not so much as a quick look of acknowledgement toward Alex. Pressing the soap dispenser, Alex began washing her hands, watching the woman in the mirror, waiting for her to look up.

But the woman didn't.

When she finished washing her hands, the woman deliberately turned her head away from Alex, kept her head low, and reached for the towel dispenser on the wall. Then she turned back and stared directly at Alex in the mirror.

Their eyes locked.

The woman didn't smile.

But Alex did.

Alex stared down at her hands as she rinsed them off and said, "You missed a spot." She looked up at the woman again in the reflection.

The woman in the mirror stared back, puzzled. "Excuse me?"

Alex gave a knowing smile. "You missed a spot," she repeated. Alex flipped off the faucet, shook off the excess water, circled behind the woman to where the towel dispenser was, tugged out three paper towels in quick succession, and began drying her hands while facing the wall. She turned back toward the woman, who now had her back to the mirror. Alex glanced in the mirror behind the woman, her eyes settling on the back of her neck. Alex balled up the damp paper napkins, tossed them into the trash can, then tugged another one from the dispenser, folded it down into a small square the size of her palm, and went to the soap dispenser again. "On the back of your neck." Alex squirted a small dose of liquid soap onto the folded napkin and moistened it with a few drops of water from the faucet.

Almost in panic, the woman whirled her head around, trying to look over her shoulder into the mirror to the spot Alex indicated.

The woman had made a valiant effort to tuck her hair up

under the ball cap, exposing her neckline. But enough hair still poked out from the sides and back for Alex to know the woman had recently dyed her hair, going from dark to blond. A not-so-subtle leap, done by herself, using an over-the-counter product. Either that or Alex would tell her to go back to the salon and demand her money back for doing such a sloppy job.

The nickel-sized blemish on the back of the woman's neck certainly wasn't a birthmark.

To each to their own, Alex thought. Alex placed a gentle hand on the woman's shoulder, twisting it slightly, making her pivot toward the mirror. "Here, I can do it."

Diane Miller flinched, going rigid at the touch.

"Hey, it's okay," Alex said, holding her hands up defensively. "Let me get it off for you. It's hard to see the spot on your own."

Diane looked at the woman in front of her. She was tall, statuesque. Well-dressed, too well-dressed for these parts. Maybe a traveling businesswoman, passing through to someplace else, someplace better. The woman had a look of understanding that made Diane feel strangely at ease. Not threatened by her.

"It'll just take a second," Alex insisted. "If you leave it there for too long it might leave a permanent mark on your skin."

Diane's little charade had been uncovered. The woman knew Diane had colored her hair, not done a good job of it either. Diane had done the best she could under the circumstances, and appreciated the woman's candor in not mentioning the fact directly, not embarrassing her any further. Diane nodded reluctantly. "Thank you."

Diane faced the mirror and removed her cap. Her new ash blond hair unfurled. She swept it aside and away from the back of her neck with one hand and tilted her head down. Diane felt the woman's touch on her shoulder again, gentle but firm. Then felt the cold wetness of the soapy towel against her skin.

"You did a good job. Much better than what I would've done."

Diane smiled at the compliment, as she tilted her head farther down, her chin touching the top of her chest, knowing very well that it was a lie to ease the embarrassment. The woman didn't have to say it, but she had. It was considerate, respectful.

Alex rubbed the patch of skin on the back of Diane's neck a few more times, stopped to appraise her efforts, then rubbed some more. "There you go. All gone." Alex tossed the soiled towel into the trash can, then faced Diane again, glancing down at the ball cap in her hand. It was a poor attempt at a disguise, almost comical.

"Thanks for doing that. I never would have known."

"No problem," Alex said, holding Diane's gaze. "Who are you running from?" And just like that, it was out there.

Diane frowned. "Excuse me?"

Alex gave a smile that said, *don't treat me like a fool.*

It was her smile, the expression on the woman's face that Diane couldn't ignore. Diane felt compelled to answer truthfully. The woman was smart. Observant as well. Diane took a deep breath. "My husband."

Alex gave a nod, turned back to the mirror and adjusted her hair while she spoke to the reflection of Diane Miller. "Most men are pricks." Alex straightened her jacket, removing a few pieces of lint, dusting here and there. "Don't get me wrong. I do like men." Alex turned and faced Diane. "But the good ones are few and far between."

"Amen," Diane said, smiling without knowing she was until she glanced at her own reflection, her face gaunt and drawn, more flesh needed on the bones. That would come with time.

Alex touched Diane's forearm gently. No flinch this time. "Let me give you some advice."

Diane said nothing. Just stared up at the woman standing in front of her, looking at her properly now for the first time. She certainly was an imposing figure with striking features, high cheek bones, flawless skin, dark, perfectly cut hair. A woman who, when she spoke, commanded attention, especially from men, Diane imagined. She had an air of authority about her. Not arrogant or condescending, thinking she was superior, even though Diane felt the woman certainly was…compared to her.

Alex Romano leaned in and stared Diane Miller directly in the eye. "Stop running," she whispered.

Then Diane saw it, deep in the woman's eyes. A glint of suppressed menace that flashed across the gray of her irises. Water freezing in fast time-lapse, all the warmth gone from them.

"If you keep running, you'll be running for the rest of your life. Stop running. Confront him. Tell him it's over. End it. That's the only way you can move on with your life."

Diane thought about the words that this stranger, this woman, said. They made sense. A lot of sense.

And as quickly as it had appeared, the cold menace from Alex's eyes vanished. Replaced with a calm stare and self-assured smile. "What do you want to ask me?"

Diane gave a confused look. It was as if the woman had read her mind. Diane wanted to ask the obvious question. Everyone tells you that you should confront your fears. Don't run from them. Otherwise you'll just be trapped, scared, constantly running from town to town, place to place, always looking over your shoulder. It was great advice—in a perfect world. Yet most people, especially women, don't experience a perfect world in their lives. "What happens if he's not happy?" Diane finally said. "When I confront him. What if gets angry, turns violent." That was Diane's biggest fear of Greg. And she wasn't prepared to confront that possibility—yet.

Alex just grinned, checked herself one more time in the mirror, and walked past Diane toward the door. Placing one hand on the handle, Alex glanced back at Diane. "That's easy," Alex replied, pulling open the door.

Diane didn't understand.

"I'm not from around here," Alex continued. "But I imagine self-defense is still self-defense."

Diane's eyes narrowed.

"Get yourself a gun, and learn how to use it." And with that, Alex Romano walked out, leaving Diane Miller standing alone in the small room, feeling suddenly very vulnerable.

Chapter 34

Crouching in the woods, just behind the tree line, Greg Miller had a clear view of the gas station plaza.

He glanced at his cell phone. Diane was still there. He looked up again but couldn't see her car anywhere. A few people were milling around at the gas pumps, filling up—SUVs and pickup trucks mainly. Scanning to his left, he could see a large black SUV parked in front of the diner with a smaller white one parked next to it and a few sedans.

But not Diane's car.

Maybe she parked around the back, or on the opposite side of the building, deliberately trying to be inconspicuous.

There was no fence around the property. A flat expanse of dirt dotted with grass stubble stretched away from the edge of the woods toward where the lot started. It was a hundred yards of open ground, where someone in the plaza or in a car driving in off the highway would be able to spot Greg emerging from the woods and wonder what he was doing.

Greg decided to keep moving, circle around to the rear of the property, and approach it from behind like he'd planned. Keeping low, he edged sideways between the trees, keeping his eyes on the side of the building until he was past the back corner. At the rear of the building, he saw a row of dumpsters, plastic crates, and piles of flattened packing boxes. Checking that no one was around, Greg emerged from the tree line and walked briskly straight toward a small concrete loading dock with a set of steps that led to a pair of double doors. He went up the steps two at a time. Ignoring the sign on the doors, *Authorized Personnel Only*, he pushed them open and went inside.

He was in a narrow corridor at the back of the building, male and female restrooms on each side. At the far end, the corridor opened into what looked like the diner. Glancing around the corner, Greg searched the faces of the people sitting at tables and in booths.

No Diane.

He checked his cell phone again. He was almost standing dead center on the red marker on the screen.

Diane had to be here.

Turning left, he followed a passageway that led to the gas station convenience store. He searched the aisles looking for Diane.

Nothing.

He double-checked again. A young man was at the counter paying for gas and an older couple were milling around the row of coffee machines, deciding whether to have decaf or not.

There was no place for Diane to hide.

Greg walked through the automatic glass doors and out into the plaza, scanning each vehicle at the pumps, his frustration growing with every second. Turning left, he circled around to the rear of the building from the opposite side of where he had emerged from the woods, thinking Diane had parked on the other side or maybe around the back where staff parked.

There were rows of white painted lines along a curved concrete curb at the side. He continued, passing rows of propane tanks, more dumpsters, and a few cars parked where staff had parked. Diane's car wasn't there. Maybe someone had taken the phone from Diane, stolen it from her? Maybe she had lost it, and someone else now had it?

Greg swore, then checked his phone again. Still the red marker was telling him she was here. *Right here.*

After a few moments of considering what the woman said, Diane emerged from the women's restroom.

Back in the diner, she could see the same woman standing at the cash register, paying for a takeout cup of coffee. Diane ducked her head and faced away, pulling the ball cap down a little tighter on her head. At the first chance she got, she would find a hair salon, get it done properly, and get her hair cut shorter as well. Wanting to avoid any more embarrassment, Diane turned left, headed along the passageway that linked the diner to the gas station convenience store. She would go through the store and back outside, reach her car that way. While she appreciated the advice from the woman, she didn't want to deal with any more questions. She just wanted to get on the highway again.

"Christ," Greg Miller cursed, glaring at his phone.

He had done a complete circuit of the outside of the building, cell phone in hand, and was now back at the concrete loading dock and steps at the rear. A young waitress was sitting on a crate at the base of the steps, scrolling through her cell phone, on a break. She looked up at him suspiciously.

Greg let out a sigh and walked on. He was out of ideas.

Then it hit him. How could he be so stupid? The restrooms! Diane had to be in there. But all this time?

Greg felt a surge of adrenaline as he hurried toward the front of the diner. He didn't care who else was in the women's restroom. He was going in and would pretend like he'd gone through the wrong door, even though it was clearly marked. He was going to catch the bitch.

Reaching the front of the diner, Greg yanked the door open—and ran straight into a tall woman coming the other way.

"Hey! Watch where you're going!" Greg snapped impatiently at the woman, trying to edge around her. But she didn't move, her body blocking the doorway.

The woman wasn't looking at Greg. She was looking down at the takeout cup in her hand, black hot liquid dripping down the sides and onto the ground, her hand covered with hot coffee.

Greg shuffled side-to-side fervently, agitated by the delay, desperate to get inside the diner.

Slowly the woman's eyes tracked upward, taking in every detail of the idiot standing in front of her, finally meeting his eyes.

"Get out of my—" Greg's words stuck in his throat.

Two glacial eyes bored into him, past his retinas and deep into his soul. Invisible fingers slowly wrapped around his throat. Greg unconsciously took a backward step away from the woman.

Alex Romano stood her ground, appraising the man in front of her. Slowly she retrieved a tissue from her pocket and wiped the coffee off her hand, her eyes never leaving Greg Miller's face.

Greg steeled himself and stepped forward, his courage returning. "Get out of my way."

Alex's eyes flicked to her left, *past* Greg Miller's right shoulder, at the darkness that was swarming in from there.

Greg's body jerked violently sideways, away from the doorway, away from Alex's line of sight and beyond the edge of her periphery.

Jarring pain balled in the top of Greg's shoulder as he was slammed into the brick façade. He spun back, trying to face his attacker, but was spun around violently again, and with shocking ease, his back was slammed into the brickwork. Greg gasped and began to slide slowly down the wall.

Vincent Romano halted Greg Miller's downward slide by clamping one hand around his throat, keeping him upright and pinning his back to the wall. Vincent turned to his sister. "You okay?"

Alex nodded.

Vincent turned back to the man.

Greg Miller tried to move but couldn't. He glared defiantly at the man who was holding him there—one-handed. Saw no smile. No anger. Just the same cold, pitiless expression the woman had given him. Equally as frightening, if not more so.

"You owe the lady an apology."

Greg Miller struggled some more, but it was pointless. The man's grip was incredible, belying his size and stature. Greg struggled again and felt his neck pressed farther up against the solid brick wall, grinding the back of his head into it. Shifting his eyes sideways, Greg looked at the woman. She just stood there, casually sipping her coffee. Greg looked from her back to the man. The pressure around his throat intensified, crushing his windpipe.

"I'm sorry," he croaked.

Vincent cocked his head.

Greg Miller took the hint. "I'm sorry," he wheezed, louder this time. Vincent released him by the throat and stepped back. "You should be more careful who you run into."

Greg Miller said nothing, just gasped for air.

Vincent straightened his jacket, then turned to his sister.

"Let's go. We've wasted enough time here today."

Alex studied Greg Miller for a moment after Vincent departed. A thought entered her head—but she quickly dismissed it, turned, and walked away.

Cursing, Greg Miller finally entered the diner and headed straight for the restrooms. He quickly checked the corridor, looking both ways, making sure he was alone, then pushed open the door and entered.

It was a small tiled room, two empty stalls, two sinks, and a mirror.

Empty.

He felt like screaming, punching the wall with his fist.

He glanced down at his cell phone again, and couldn't understand what was wrong. Diane was meant to be here. The red marker hadn't moved since Greg had seen it halt at this location nearly thirty minutes ago.

Undeterred, he walked back into the diner, contemplating what to do next. He looked left, back toward where he had been in the gas station convenience store, and then right into the main body of the diner.

She must be here. Somewhere.

Through the windows of the diner, Greg could see the man and the woman he had just had the altercation with. They were standing next to a large black SUV, about to get inside. Parked next to the black SUV was the white smaller SUV he had seen from the woods. He didn't want to go back outside again, in case the couple saw him. They were leaving, which was good. He would wait a few moments. Perhaps hang around the gas station convenience store, grab a coffee and a bite to eat while figuring out what to do next.

At the coffee machines in the convenience store, Greg filled up a takeout cup and took it to the cash register. The teenage couple in front of him quickly paid then moved on. "I seemed to have lost my wife," Greg said, sliding out a few bills and placing them on the counter for the coffee.

The old man behind the counter looked at Greg skeptically before offering a broad smile. "Half your luck. I wish I could lose mine that easily."

Greg gave a tight smile as the old man handed him back his change. "She's about this tall," Greg indicated Diane's height with his hand. "Thin, dark-haired."

The old man made a show of thinking. "It's been pretty quiet this morning. I can't recall someone like that coming in."

Greg gave a sigh of exasperation and pulled his cell phone out again. The red marker still had not moved.

"Skinny, did you say?" the old man said.

Greg nodded. Maybe the old bastard's memory wasn't fading after all, Greg thought. "Have you seen her?" Greg pressed forward, not trying to seem overly enthusiastic, painting the picture of the concerned, worried husband. Not the man who wanted to strangle his wife with his own bare hands when he found her.

The old man rubbed his chin. "Come to think of it, there was a skinny woman in here before." He gave a little chuckle. "Not many people skinny these days. That's what made me notice, I guess."

Greg leaned forward over the counter. "And?" he said impatiently.

"But she had blond hair, I'm pretty sure. She had a ball cap on too." The old man gave it some more thought. "No. She was definitely a blonde."

"Dammit," Greg mumbled under his breath. Taking his

coffee, he walked through the automatic doors and out into the plaza.

"You drive," Vincent said, tossing the keys to Alex.

"Suits me."

Vincent walked around the back of the SUV and saw how narrow the space was between it and the white SUV parked alongside. He saw a woman approaching, thin with blond hair poking out from under a red baseball cap. She was obviously the driver of the white SUV. There were no other cars parked in the vicinity.

The woman paused behind her own car, waiting for Vincent to open the door and climb into his vehicle.

Vincent turned to the woman as he opened the car door. "Do you think you could park any closer to me?" he asked sarcastically.

"Vincent!" A loud voice came from inside the SUV. "Get inside."

Vincent glared at the woman standing there one more time before squeezing in and slamming the door behind him.

Alex backed out the SUV, turned, then straightened the wheel. She looked out the window at Diane Miller, who was standing there, and simply rolled her eyes and smiled, apologizing for her brother's rudeness.

Diane gave a slight smile, pressed the car remote unlocking her car, then slid into the driver's seat.

Maybe the app was acting up? Greg thought as he stood in the forecourt in front of the automatic doors.

He decided to restart his phone in case there was a malfunction with the tracking app or the cellular network.

In the distance Greg saw the big black SUV slide out of its parking space, turn, and drive slowly toward him, toward the exit. Quickly, he turned and walked back inside the convenience store, wanting to avoid the couple seeing him standing outside. He stood inside, near the doors, watching with agonizing slowness as the spinning wheel on the cell phone screen turned, waiting for the phone to restart.

Diane Miller backed out of the parking slot and drove slowly across the plaza, past the pumps and out to the on-ramp.

She could see the black SUV slowly shrinking in the distance in front of her as it sped away farther along the highway. Checking her rearview mirror one more time, she accelerated, eased into the passing traffic, and headed in the same direction as the black SUV.

"Come on, come on," Greg said impatiently, waiting for his phone to restart.

Finally the black screen vanished and was replaced by the home screen. He tapped the tracking app icon. It took a few more precious moments for the app to pinpoint his location.

"Did you manage to find your wife?"

Greg looked up at the old man behind the counter. "No, I didn't," he said gruffly.

"Well she couldn't have just vanished." The old man turned his attention to serve another customer at the counter.

Finally the cell phone tracking app came alive.

Greg gaped at the moving red marker on the screen. It took his brain a few more seconds to kick into gear, to dismiss the impossible and grasp what had just happened. The red marker on the screen was moving rapidly away from his location, on the highway, heading west, accelerating. He ran to the automatic doors, banging into the glass before they had completely parted. He squeezed through and burst onto the plaza, his head swiveling wildly in every direction, his eyes finally settling on the parking spot outside the diner.

Both were now gone. The large black SUV and the smaller white one.

The white SUV! Greg's mind screamed.

It had to be. That was the only thing different in the last thirty minutes. Both vehicles were there when he arrived, and now they were both gone.

Throwing caution to the wind, he took off across the plaza, narrowly avoiding a sedan coming off the highway, entering the gas station. A horn blasted. Greg gave the woman behind the wheel the finger and kept on running until he reached the exit of the gas station and the edge of the highway on-ramp. He looked desperately into the distance, then glanced down at his cell phone. The red marker was steadily widening the gap between him and it.

The white SUV. It was Diane. She was escaping. She had another car.

"Bitch!" Greg screamed after her, his voice lost in the backwash of passing traffic that sped past him.

Greg turned and took off, sprinting back across the plaza,

dodging more cars as they entered and exited the complex, and headed straight toward the tree line of the woods. As he ran, he glared at the cell phone, the map bobbing up and down in his vision, the red mark moving even faster now. He hadn't bothered to check the white SUV, had given it only a cursory glance. There was no need. It wasn't Diane's car—or so he had thought.

As he ran, he struggled now to picture it. It was white, but faded to a sickly cream color from being left out in the elements for years. An older model, midsize, rounded edges from that era.

The woods loomed up ahead. Greg ran harder, rage fueling his muscles, vengeance feeding his lungs.

He leaped up onto the stretch of stubble dirt without slowing, then tore headlong into the trees, stumbling and swerving between the trunks, falling, re-gathering, then racing on. Suddenly, his legs felt heavy. He wished he was fitter, his lungs and chest heaving, his face twisted in sweaty anger. It didn't matter how she had eluded him, all that mattered now was to get to his car, give chase.

He sped on, dodging fallen branches and gnarly roots.

He could see the clearing, then vertical segments of his car through the trees, growing in size with each slowing stride. He surged some more, his endurance and energy almost depleted. He conjured up a picture of Diane behind the steering wheel, speeding away, her mocking laugh, looking back in her rearview mirror, gloating at her own cleverness and his own dumbness. Greg found something extra, more rage summoned up from the pit of his gut, burning bright, making his arms and legs pump harder, ignoring the crippling fatigue.

He burst out of the woods and back into the rest area clearing, wrenched open the door, jumped in, and thrust his cell phone into the dash cradle. On the third attempt, it slid into place. After starting the car, he tore out of the rest area in a shower of dirt and stones, the rear of the car fishtailing once, twice, before straightening back onto the side access road.

Greg looked at the cell phone screen, noticing for the first time the small flashing battery cell icon. A pulsing lightning bolt over it, five percent charge left. Thumping the steering wheel with one fist, he gave a spittle-laced scream at the instrument panel before pulling over onto the side of the off-ramp just before the entrance to the gas station. He desperately looked around in the center console, then lifted the lid of the storage section and searched frantically inside for a charging cable for the phone. He couldn't find one. He never charged his phone in the car and couldn't remember keeping a plug-in cable in it. No need—until now. He always charged his phone in the study at home or at his desk at work. He didn't really do long car trips that required him to charge his phone on the go. Obviously the lost phone tracking app was power hungry.

Greg opened the glove box, pulled everything out frantically. Did he have one, just in case? Registration papers, owner handbook, box of tissues, flashlight, everything—ripped it all out and threw it onto the floormat below.

No charging cable.

Then he remembered a carousel display stand with hanging blister packs of cell phone accessories in the gas station convenience store.

Greg kicked the gear into drive, and hit the gas pedal hard. The sedan leaped forward as he tore into the gas station entrance, cutting across the plaza before pulling up with a screech of tires in front of the convenience store. He ran at the glass doors, almost colliding with them a second time before they parted enough for him to shimmy through.

He stopped dead center in the store, his head swiveling back-and-forth as he looked around like a man possessed.

"Back so soon?" the old man behind the counter said.

Greg turned and looked at him wildly. "Cell phone chargers!"

"Back of the store." The old man pointed.

Greg hustled down the aisles, found the rotating carousel stand of phone accessories, and spun it fast. There was every kind of charging cable imaginable. The blister packs swung wildly back-and-forth as he pivoted the stand one way, then the next, packs tumbling to the floor. They didn't have the charger—his charger, the one compatible with his phone. He desperately searched again, more packs tumbling to the floor.

With every passing second, Diane was getting farther and farther away from him.

Customers in the store stopped what they were doing and stared at the frantic man who, seemed to be assaulting the display stand.

"What you looking for?" the old man called out, worried that Greg would break the display stand.

Greg gave up his search, rushed to the counter, held up his phone. "I need a charging cable for this."

The old man peered at the device in Greg's hand. "Looks the size of one of them computer pad things."

Greg was about to give up, when the old man called over his shoulder to the open doorway of a small back room behind the counter. "Darlene! Can you come out here and help this gentleman. He's got a phone like yours."

Greg's heart leaped at the words.

A short, teenage girl with pink hair, thick black-framed glasses and a tattoo of Princess Peach from Mario Kart on the side of her neck sauntered out from the back room. She walked around the counter, said nothing, didn't even look at Greg, just took the phone from his hand. "Lightning cable. Out of stock. Just ordered in a new batch." She looked up at Greg, as if noticing him for the first time, then smiled. *Not bad*, she thought as she stared up at him, blinking her thick lashes, her owlish eyes magnified by the thick lenses of her glasses.

"You have none at all? None in the store room out back?" Greg was desperate.

"Just got mine," Darlene replied, still appraising Greg. "You're welcome to use it, charge your phone. Give it enough to reach the next gas station five miles up the highway. They might have the right cable there for you."

"Fifty bucks."

The girl blinked. "But, I hardly know you."

"Excuse me?" Greg said, not immune to the look Darlene was giving him. He stepped closer, looked deep into Darlene's lenses, feeling slightly dizzy as he did, and flashed his best smile. "I would be forever in your debt—Darlene—if I could buy your charging cable from you. Fifty dollars."

Darlene wiggled her nose, thinking about the offer she had misread. "Hell, they only sell for ten bucks, and a new shipment is coming in tomorrow," Darlene replied, her heart fluttering. "I could survive till then. My cell is fully charged anyway. I'll go get it."

Five minutes later Greg was back on the highway, heading west, his cell phone snug in its cradle, power being fed into it from Darlene's lightning cable plugged into the USB port in the console.

The green blip of his car was moving on the map on the screen in unison with the red marker of Diane's car.

Chapter 35

It was best to get her thoughts organized in her head, then down on paper before Monica Styles made the call to Meredith Charmers, asking her permission to do what she wanted to do.

She laid everything out on her desk, then reviewed her notes, filling in some of the gaps in the facts, in the conversations and observations as best she could without throwing out wild speculation that would just rile her boss. It was more of an exercise in affirming what her instincts were telling her: Greg Miller, the only real suspect in the brutal, callous attack on the homeless man, Miles Burke, had done something to his wife, Diane Miller.

After trying unsuccessfully to call Greg Miller on his cell phone, Monica had gone back to the Miller house again. No one was home. She then went by Greg Miller's place of employment. Had struck out there too. After she had spoken to Greg's boss, Monica calculated—after what the manager had revealed to her—that shortly after she had witnessed Greg Miller tearing out of his driveway that morning, he had called his office to tell them he wasn't coming in. Said he needed a few days off work to tend to a sudden, urgent family matter.

Sudden and urgent, indeed, Styles thought. Perhaps his wife had found out that her husband had indeed assaulted Miles Burke. Perhaps Diane had found blood on her husband's clothes stuffed in the laundry hamper or some other compelling evidence. If so, why hadn't she come forward?

When she finally finished organizing her argument, Monica

relayed all this to Charmers over the phone.

As expected, Charmers listened patiently as her deputy laid out everything she knew. Some of it fact. Most of it supposition, as Charmers had described it.

"It's quite a leap, Monica," Charmers said.

"I have him in the parking lot at the rear of the bank. A clear ID on him and his vehicle at the time Burke was assaulted."

"But you can't place him *in* the alley," Charmers countered. "And there is no physical evidence that the techs could find in the alley nor on Burke that links back to Greg Miller. It may have been just a random act of unpremeditated violence."

"Perpetrated by some heartless, cruel individual," Monica argued.

"Is that your personal or professional assessment of Greg Miller?"

Monica let out an audible sigh of frustration. It was like they were in the boxing ring, trading blow-for-blow. Feeling out each other's argument, looking for an opening, a weakness. Evidential sparring Charmers called it. It was the best way for a junior deputy, or anyone in law enforcement, to learn.

"A clear chain of evidence, combined with motive and opportunity, is the best way to avoid having a DA throw out your case before it even reaches court," Charmers continued.

"Then why would he lie?" Monica countered. "Say that he hadn't parked out back. Insisted that he parked out front of the bank?"

"I don't know," Charmers replied. "People lie."

Monica had already explained about the elusive Diane Miller, and how she had seen blood from a nasty gash on Greg Miller's hand as well as in the trashed room at their home.

"Then there's the daughter, Ella Miller," Monica said. It was the one piece of information she hadn't previously mentioned to Charmers. Felt that it may not be relevant to the case, but it could explain some of the backstory about the couple. Especially the current state of mind of Diane Miller. Monica spent the next few minutes explaining what she had found out about the couple's daughter.

"I can't imagine going through that," Charmers replied after she had time to digest what Monica had told her. "It's unimaginable."

"I know, and I can't find Diane Miller anywhere."

"So what do you want to do, Monica?" Charmers knew the answer to the question her young, determined deputy was about to give. The real purpose of the phone call.

"I want permission to track down Diane Miller. Try and locate her. Maybe she holds the key to her husband's guilt. I certainly fear for her safety after what I witnessed today."

"Why don't you just haul Greg Miller in for further questioning after he returns from this family crisis you mentioned? But this time let's throw him into an interrogation room. Put some pressure on him."

"I think something is happening right now. They both seemed to have vanished. I'm certain Greg Miller, for whatever reason, has gone after his wife."

"And you believe she has taken off? For what reason?"

"I do," Monica replied. "And I'll know what the reasons are for all of this once I catch up with her. He will tell me nothing. It's the wife I need to locate."

Monica could hear her boss let out a sigh on the other end, and gave a faint smile.

"Did you flag their licenses and car registration in the system?"

"Did that ten minutes ago before I called you." Monica had flagged statewide the license and registration details of both Greg and Diane Miller and all three vehicles. If for whatever reason either of them was pulled over, and a check done, Monica would automatically receive a notification on her cell phone as well as on the office computer.

Greg or Diane Miller had no outstanding warrants, so they would not be detained by the police officer or highway patrol running the check. The intervening law enforcement officer would not know they had been flagged in the system. It was a low-level flag to simply notify the originator as to the time and location the subject or vehicle had been stopped.

"I guess you'll just have to sit tight and wait until something happens," Charmers said, knowing full well her deputy wasn't the type to just sit and wait. She was determined and self-motivated. "If something turns up, Monica, be careful."

"I will be," Monica replied.

"I'm serious. Call me. Keep me up to date. And follow proper protocol if you cross into another county. Give the sheriff's department there a heads-up. Some can get pretty territorial about another sheriff or deputy poking around in their neck of the woods."

"I will. I promise," Monica agreed. "Hey, it may be nothing." Even as she said them, Monica didn't believe the words. She had the distinct feeling something was wrong. Diane Miller was in some kind of trouble.

Chapter 36

Brendan Cullum Murphy descended from good Irish stock whose family heritage first took root amongst the grime and crime of the docks and seedy back canals of Dublin, Ireland.

His own direct ancestry could be traced as far back as the first of his family who fled the shores of the Emerald Isle during the Great Irish Famine of the nineteenth century, only to arrive as part of the first wave of immigrants to America. They first settled in Boston, South Boston in particular, with a scattering of distant relatives taking up in Charlestown. In the eighteen hundreds, some of the Murphy clan fought for the Union in the American Civil War. But despite being born and bred under the Stars and Stripes, it was the green, white, and orange that hung inside Brendan Murphy's cavernous machinery shop.

It was said that whenever Murphy—a staunch supporter of the IRA—cut himself on the sheet press or with any number of the shop tools, he bled shamrock green, not red.

He was a tight-fisted, rough and tumble, shrewd and bone-hard Irish-American who had never taken a backward step in his life—and wasn't about to start doing so either.

Especially when he saw a large black SUV slip smoothly into the parking lot outside his business. In these parts, something as shiny and new looked as out of place as an Irish pub in Tokyo. Murphy watched as a man and a woman climbed out of the SUV and strolled with purpose toward the wide entrance of the workshop, bringing with them an air of bad tidings.

Murphy had sent the boys home early, also loyal Irish-

Americans whom he paid cash and who had worked for him for years. But strictly speaking, he wasn't alone in his workshop. He kept a watchful eye on the approaching couple as he continued closing up for the day, getting ready to start the weekend early.

Brendan Murphy didn't believe in luck or fate. He much preferred to make his own luck, control his own fate. What he did believe in, though, was the twelve-gauge shotgun he kept close at hand, loaded and housed in a specially made bracket for quick release behind the counter.

Like his father, and his father's father, and his father before him, the Murphys lived by one simple rule: Trouble is unpredictable. It can come knocking on your door, day or night, without warning. Be ready or be dead.

"Brendan Murphy?"

Murphy turned from wiping his hands on an oily rag and regarded the man and woman standing at the entrance of the workshop. "That's what it says on the sign above the door," Murphy said. He continued wiping his hands, watching the two before tucking the rag into the pocket of his overalls. Definitely not from around these parts, either of them. His initial interest naturally fell on the female of the two. Hard not to. She was tall and lithe, strikingly attractive, regal almost. With hair as dark as Ballingarry coal and piercing eyes that could laser cut sheet metal, he reckoned. She had an air about her, like a stockbroker or Wall Street banker. Someone who enjoyed treading with high heels on the hands of men as they groveled at her feet, clawing at her long, supple legs.

Murphy was ambitious, a climber, a survivor too, and he instantly recognized the same in the woman standing before him.

The man next to her was another matter entirely. He cast an elusive persona, beady-eyed and as slithery-looking as a Munster

Blackwater eel. A thug masquerading as a businessman in expensive clothes and shoes, minus the class and emotional intelligence.

Alex Romano stepped forward. "I'd like to ask you some questions about a stolen van."

Murphy scoffed but said nothing. He watched as the man slowly circled around the workshop to his right, looking at the machinery equipment, touching things that didn't belong to him. Lifting up hand tools, examining them closely, seemingly picturing what they could do to human flesh and bone, before placing them back down again. "Hey, mister, this isn't some store you can just walk in and browse."

Vincent stopped and turned but didn't smile at the remark. He just stared blankly at Brendan Murphy, throwing down the gauntlet to him.

Murphy was familiar with the look, the deadness behind the eyes. They were the eyes of a killer. He had seen them many times as he looked in the mirror before he went to bed each night. He turned back to the woman, thinking about the shotgun behind the counter, visualizing its cold dark shape sitting out of sight and out of reach—for the moment.

"Forgive me," Alex said. "My name is Alex Romano. And this is my brother, Vincent."

"Well, I don't take too kindly to strangers coming into my business and asking me questions." Murphy glanced back at Vincent. "Poking around like they own the place." Brendan Murphy's voice was now less than welcoming, more hostile. As innocently as he could, he began to walk toward the counter.

Vincent resumed his tour, looking at the machinery that hunkered in the semi-darkness, angling around to Murphy's right side, keeping the Irishman in his direct line of sight.

"I'm sorry, Mr. Murphy, if I'm being blunt," Alex continued, disinterested in her brother's movements. "But we are pressed for time. The van belongs to a laundry business in Grand Island. It was stolen a few days ago and we are just following up with anyone who may know about it." Alex was testing the waters, judging Murphy's reaction to see if he was indeed involved before she dropped the name Anton Wheeler.

Murphy had reached the edge of the counter. "Well, I ain't seen no laundry van around here. What makes you think I would have?"

Alex smiled, not liking being played a fool. Several dubious-looking vans and trucks were already parked up along one side of the workshop. "Because, Mr. Murphy, you are known in these parts as a fence. A moving man. Someone who buys stolen property, mainly commercial vans and trucks, and on-sells them for a profit." Alex watched as Murphy's face went distinctly hard.

"Who you been hearing that from?" he grumbled, placing one hand on the counter.

Vincent stopped walking. Something growled from the shadows in the corner of the workshop.

Murphy looked at where Vincent was standing. "You best not get any closer, mister, else you might lose an arm or a leg."

Vincent peered into the shadows. Two yellow canine eyes glared out of the darkness at him. Heavy chains clinked and rattled as a low guttural sound bellowed out from under a huge snout. The darkness distorted, then parted, and two hundred fifty pounds of raw canine menace, bunched muscle, sinew, and curved teeth slid forward as one. The beast was a true junkyard dog. As big as a small horse, with a head the size of an engine block and bared fangs dripping saliva. The dog stayed low, ears pinned back, the black fur along its spine bristled and quivered as the beast watched Vincent standing a mere twenty feet away.

Vincent dismissed the dog with the flick of his head, not bothered by it. He turned toward where Brendan Murphy was, noticing that the Irishman was subtly working his way along the counter.

Murphy stopped moving.

Vincent cocked his head and smiled at Murphy. Then, in a poor rendition of an Irish accent and mimicking Murphy's threat from a moment ago, he said, "You best not take another step, old man, or you'll end up like your dog."

Murphy looked baffled, like a caveman who had been given a knife and fork for Christmas.

Vincent nodded. "That's right."

Murphy glanced down under the counter. He could see the shotgun snug in its bracket, no more than a few inches from his hand. He glanced back at Vincent. Then his stubborn Irish ancestry kicked in.

Murphy went for his gun.

Vincent Romano went for his two. Why carry one when you can carry two?

In a blindingly fast double-draw, Vincent had both of his handguns out, arms extended right and left at right angles, ten o'clock and two o'clock, both leveled at different targets. The right handgun fired, boomed out, the crushing sound magnified by the surrounding tin sheet walls and ceiling. The bullet nicked Murphy's right ear, taking the top off, before smacking into a heavy wooden post behind the counter, tearing into it, releasing a shower of splinters.

Murphy brought his hands up. "Okay, okay!" he screamed, stooping with his hands above his head, a ribbon of blood coiling around the inside of his ear, then down the side of his face.

Vincent hadn't missed. He hit what he had aimed at. With both arms still extended, Vincent indicated with a flick of his right gun for Murphy to move away from the counter, and away from the shotgun hidden behind it.

With his hands still raised, Murphy shuffled out from the counter.

"That's far enough," Vincent said before turning his attention to the gun in his left hand. The dog hadn't moved despite the loud gunshot. Neither had Vincent's left hand, that gun stilled aimed at its target.

He pulled the trigger just once.

Another shot boomed out and echoed around the inside of the shed.

The guard dog collapsed instantly as the bullet hit it right between the eyes, dead-center. Its four thick legs sprawled out from under it in four opposite directions, as its huge torso slammed down onto the floor with a dusty thud.

Chapter 37

Unlike Joe Durango, Alex did not adopt as harsh a strategy with Brendan Murphy.

He wasn't chained upside down to an electrical hoist. Nor did he have a gun thrust into his groin. Alex would go down that path, however, if that's what it took to get answers out of the stubborn Irishman.

Instead, Murphy was simply placed on a chair in the middle of the workshop, unbound and free to move. The only thing keeping him in place was the constant menace he felt from behind—the barrel of Vincent's gun, pressed firmly behind his only remaining good ear.

Alex sat passively in a chair opposite Murphy, leaning slightly forward, her fingers in a steeple. Alex had already told Murphy about the van, given him a full description of it, including gross vehicle mass, license plate, and model details. But Murphy was sticking to his story. After an additional five minutes of rapid questioning, they were getting nowhere. Time was precious if they were going to locate the money.

"What about a man called Anton Wheeler?" Alex asked, mentioning Wheeler's name for the first time. She saw a flicker in Murphy's eyes, a slight rising of the eyelids. He knew the name.

"So you recognize the name?"

Murphy remained tightlipped, shook his head slowly.

Alex gazed past Murphy, to where her brother was standing behind him. She gave Vincent a slight nod.

Vincent struck Murphy across the back of the head, throwing the man forward off the chair and onto the cement floor. Hauling him back up, Vincent thrust Murphy back down on to the chair again, pressing the barrel of the gun harder this time against the man's skull. "You know Wheeler," Vincent hissed in Murphy's ear. Vincent had run out of patience with the Irishman long ago, around the same time he had shot the dog.

Alex tilted her head questioningly at Murphy.

"I don't know anyone call Anton Wheeler," Murphy replied, a trickle of blood running down the back of his head and neck.

Vincent pressed the barrel of the gun some more, forcing Murphy's head almost down between his knees. "Where is the money?"

"I don't know anything about any money, either," Murphy wheezed.

Vincent looked at his sister, his face pleading. *Let me just kill him. Please, right here.*

Murphy twisted his head sideways and looked up at Alex. She was giving the orders even though Vincent seemed the older of the two. She held the power, not her thug brother. She seemed the more reasonable.

Alex stood up, dusted off her pants, then nodded at her brother. "Kill him."

Vincent smiled, then postured, gripping the back of Murphy's collar, steadying the man for the shot, tensing his grip on the gun, squeezing the trigger, his eyes narrowing, his face morphing into the ruthless killer that he was.

"Wait! Wait!" Murphy screamed.

"I am waiting," Alex replied, her face and voice calm. "I'm waiting for you to die."

"No! No! Just wait!" Murphy had his hands up now,

pleading. Gone was his cockiness, his arrogance. The big burly Irishman was reduced to a squealing pig.

Alex held up her hand, halting Vincent. She had called the Irishman's bluff and had won.

"Look lady, I've no idea what you're talking about. I do shift a few stolen vehicles. But I've never seen or touched anything from your laundry business. I tend to take and sell vehicles that are unmarked, not emblazoned with the company name on it like you said."

"I don't believe you," Vincent said, his teeth gritted.

"What about Anton Wheeler?" Alex repeated. "You've heard of him, haven't you?"

Murphy nodded, sniveling. "I just got a call from a guy who wanted to off load a stolen van quickly for cash. No questions asked. But he didn't tell me where it was stolen from. Just that it was from some business in Grand Island."

"So Wheeler had planned it all along with you? Was he bringing the van to you?" Alex asked, stepping forward, frustrated at the time they had wasted.

"I don't know. He was supposed to bring it here. Said his name was Wheeler. I didn't promise him anything. Said I'd take a look at the van first. But he never showed."

"You are in this together with him aren't you?" Vincent asked, his finger still on the trigger. "You were going to split the money with him; he wasn't working alone. You are business partners."

Murphy tried to twist his neck, look behind him. But Vincent pushed the barrel into the side of Murphy's cheek, forcing him to keep his face forward.

"No. I don't know anything about any money. It was just a van I was looking at. That's all. I swear." Murphy was almost close to tears, his life hanging by a thread. He looked at Alex, his eyes pleading with her. "I just sell vans and trucks, lady. That's all. Please."

Alex turned and walked away, giving herself some distance, some space to think. If Murphy was telling the truth and he wasn't part of the plan, then Wheeler was working alone. But why sell the van? Why bother? Why go to all the trouble of driving it out here for a lousy five or maybe ten grand in cash when you already had a million sitting right in your lap?

Unless…

Alex turned back and faced her brother. "He doesn't know."

Murphy shoulders slumped in relief.

Vincent did a double take of his sister. Couldn't believe what she had just said. He twisted Murphy violently by the collar, determined to get the truth out of the man one way or the other. "He's got the money!" Vincent yelled.

"No he hasn't," Alex said. It was her gut feeling, a woman's intuition. This was all wrong. They were on a fool's errand. Anton Wheeler acted alone and certainly didn't know about the money onboard the van either.

"Just give me two minutes with this dirt bag," Vincent begged, shaking Murphy's collar harder. "That's all I need, Alex. Just two minutes and I'll get the truth out of him."

Alex shook her head and stepped forward. Whoever Vincent's source was about Murphy, they had it all wrong. "He doesn't know anything about the money," she said, nodding down at Murphy. "He would've told us by now. He was expecting the van to show up so he could buy it. Nothing more."

Vincent's face turned ashen. His voice almost a snarl as he spoke again. "You're wrong, little sister."

Little sister. That expression again, used when he wanted to exert his authority over her. But Alex had authority on this assignment, not Vincent. "Let him go, Vincent. We've wasted enough time."

Vincent held on to Murphy. The barrel of the gun still pressed hard at the back of the man's head. "No. He knows something, I'm telling you."

Alex's eyes narrowed as she regarded her brother. They stood facing each other, brother and sister, two gunfighters staring each other down from opposite ends of the main street of some old Western town. "Let...him...go," Alex said slowly.

Murphy craned his neck, his eyes swiveling back to look at Vincent behind, then looking forward again to Alex. Her eyes had frosted over. Cold and ruthless as she stared at her brother.

This was good. This was what Brendan Murphy wanted, to get the enemy to turn on themselves. It was the distraction he needed. The woman was again giving her brother orders that he had to follow. The queen giving one of her pawns a command.

"Let's go," Alex said, wearily. "This has been a complete waste of time."

Brendan Murphy lowered his hands.

It was over.

Murphy gave a wry smile but couldn't resist a parting gesture.

He whispered over his shoulder at Vincent Romano. "*Vaffanculo.*"

Vincent stood firm, kept his grip on the Irishman, then inhaled deeply, and held his sister's gaze. Didn't blink. Didn't flinch. Even when he pulled the trigger—twice.

Chapter 38

"You idiot!"

Vincent ignored the comment. He sat hunched behind the wheel, driving fast, leaving behind a trail of dust, fumes, blood, and the dead body of Brendan Murphy in their wake.

"You didn't need to kill him. I gave you a direct order not to."

"I didn't need your permission," Vincent threw back at his sister. He glanced in the rearview mirror, caught his own eyes staring back at him. No regrets. No remorse there. His conscience was always clear whenever he dispatched someone. Vincent stared straight ahead again, feeling a mix of exuberance and adrenaline. It felt good to kill someone, always gave him such a rush, to extinguish the flame God had created. It heightened his senses, made everything crystal clear in his mind, what he had to do—take control.

His lips curled into a subtle sneer as he relived the sensation of pulling the trigger over and over again. The drought had been broken. He had gone too long without killing someone. But killing Brendan Murphy only heightened Vincent's thirst for revenge. He was just getting started. "He should've complied. Told us where the money was. We gave him every chance."

Alex swiveled in her seat. "Let's get one thing straight, Vincent. Right now. You take orders from me in the field, no one else." Alex was fuming. Vincent's actions were not only careless, rash, and with no thought as to the consequences, they were also callous, cold-blooded, self-gratifying.

It would bring unimaginable attention down on them. The local police, the sheriff's department, everyone would now be drawn into this. Alex had no real idea of how law enforcement operated here or what the local crime stats were in the area. Nevertheless, she imagined they didn't see too many execution-style killings in these parts. "Don't you see, Vincent? I wanted to keep this low-key. Not attract any unwanted attention. Now you've gone and killed someone for no reason. Brought the heat down on us."

"I had my reasons," Vincent said, resentful of his sister's condescending tone, spoiling the good mood the killing had put him in. His *little sister*. Reprimanding him like he was a wayward child. She needed to be put in her place.

There was an invisible hierarchy within the Romano family, one privy to those who hustled the streets, fought in the trenches, did the day-to-day grind, the blood and sweat work, with a gun in one hand and a fist in the other. Alex didn't understand. She'd hidden in her office on the top floor behind a computer most of her life. Had no sense of reality of what the family business was really about on the ground floor, dealing with trash and street grime. She might be *Consigliere* of the family, and Luca Romano, their father, the head of the family—for the moment. Yet, in Vincent's world, he was the head of the army, and that was key.

Over the years Vincent had painstakingly built up a loyal and close-knit following of foot soldiers within the business that supported him, his methods, and his ambitions. And, as anyone who studied history knew, he who controls the army didn't need to sit on a throne to be king. Julius Caesar. Napoleon. Francisco Franco. Qaddafi. Idi Amin. Vincent had studied them all. People often made the mistake of viewing Vincent as a hood in a suit. But he was much more than that. Soon they would really see

231

who he was and what he was capable of.

"We were getting nowhere with your approach. I needed to step in."

Alex rolled her eyes, pressed her fingers to her temple. She could feel a migraine coming on, the impending wave of unwanted pain that Vincent was bringing to bear upon them both. "Step in?" she asked incredulously. "You don't 'step in' until I tell you to."

Vincent remained silent, brooding, simmering in his own self-righteousness. "You had no plan. Decisive action was needed," he whispered, struggling to keep his anger in check. He had the sense to pull the hard disk drive from behind the counter that was linked to the exterior security camera they saw on the way in.

"The plan wasn't to fucking kill him!" Alex screamed.

He glanced at Alex in surprise. He had never heard her swear before. That was good. She needed to get riled, get angry, not treat these people as soft as she had. He eased off the gas, glanced in the rearview mirror. The road was narrow and straight, no other traffic in sight, in front or from behind.

Minutes passed in silence. Alex stared out the window at the flat landscape, dimpled with sand dunes here and there. Bland colors, wide prairies ruffled with mixed-grasses and the occasional glimmer of a low-lying lake in the distance. She was content to say nothing, just sit and assemble her thoughts, her plans for what to do next.

Vincent broke the silence. "Why did you tell me to kill him the first time, then?"

Alex shook her head in exasperation. It was a weak excuse from her brother, and he knew it. "It was a ploy, a bluff," she said, talking to the window glass. "That's what we agreed on, wasn't it?" They had spoken in the car before arriving at Brandon Murphy's business. They had a plan, an understanding. If Murphy was not forthcoming, then Alex would brazenly tell Vincent to kill him. It had worked successfully on a number of past occasions when Alex and Costa worked together. Frighten the suspect, give them one last opportunity at redemption. Staring imminent death in the face, most people quickly told the truth, confessed to their sins.

Brendan Murphy had confessed, had admitted to his sins; he was a fence of stolen commercial vehicles, nothing more. And for his penance, Vincent gave the Irishman death. In doing so, they had both, brother and sister, stepped over the line, a line they couldn't step behind again. There was no going back.

"You need to toughen up, Sister," Vincent said.

Alex took a deep breath. "What? And be like you, Vincent? Just randomly kill people because they don't give you the answer you're looking for?"

Vincent shook his head, gave a slight smile. "You need to wake up and see the big wide world around you. It's a bad place full of bad people."

Alex couldn't believe what she was hearing. "So you add to the badness by just killing innocent people."

"No one is innocent."

"He didn't deserve to die."

Vincent tightened his grip on the wheel. "Grow a pair, Alex. You're too soft, spend too much time in your office in New Jersey, behind your desk staring at spreadsheets all day."

Alex turned and glared at her brother. "Those spreadsheets keep the business going," Alex countered. "Keep the money coming in."

"Yeah, but what about the million in cash we are missing?" Vincent retorted, unable to hide the contempt in his voice. "Your little spreadsheets can't tell us where that's gone, can they?"

"Don't lecture me, Vincent."

Vincent nodded at the landscape outside as it slid past. "It's not money that makes the world go around, Sis. You're wrong."

"Then what is it?" Alex replied harshly. "Violence? Is that it?"

"Correct." Finally she was getting it, understanding his perspective of the world. "Think about it, Alex. Harm, violence, aggression, anger, rage, whatever you want to call it. Fear is a trillion-dollar emotion. It's big business—to stop it, to prevent it, to avoid it, to start it. It's been the same since time began. It's fear that keeps the planet spinning. Fear of your neighbor. Fear of another religion, another country, another race, poverty, of dying, running out of food and water."

Vincent was in his pulpit, and Alex didn't like what she was hearing. He was laying down his plans for the future, for when he took over as head of the family. Dark days indeed were coming.

"You need to embrace that fact, Alex. The entire world, and everyone on it, lives in fear about one thing or another." Vincent stared through the windshield as he spoke, not seeing the road, the sparse landscape, or the mountains in the distance. He saw the future, his future, and how he was going to shape it. Fear and mayhem was the focus of his horizon. "You just have to find what it is for a person. What they fear the most, and then…" Vincent gave a knowing smile and whispered, "Exploit it."

"Is that your plan, Vincent?" Alex glared at her brother. "To eventually take over the family when father is gone and rule by fear? Will that be your legacy? To return to the 'old ways' like before?"

That was his intention.

Alex continued. "I've been trying to legitimize the family

business, with father's help. It's his wish before he dies. To pull back from the past, the violence, the crime."

"We all have blood on our hands, Sister, including you," Vincent whispered. "It's a stain you can't just wash off because you get a change of heart. Suddenly feel guilty."

"That was the past, Vincent. Not the future."

"So how do you see the future of the business?"

"Not like what I just witnessed, that's for sure."

"The world is getting uglier, Alex. Out of control. The only way we are going to survive, the family business is going to survive, is to be more…" Vincent searched for the right word.

But Alex found it for him. "Ruthless," she said. "Is that the answer? More crime. More violence. More fear?"

Vincent nodded. "There are enemies everywhere, Alex. More coming out of the jungle each day. You just don't see them. But I do."

Alex shook her head as she regarded her brother. "Oh, I see them."

Chapter 39

It was just after three in the afternoon when Greg called again.

"Hi, honey. How's everything going?"

Diane had chosen the slower lane in anticipation of the call. "Everything's fine," she replied. She felt more confident this time. More self-assured as each mile on the odometer clicked over. She knew exactly what she was going to say, had rehearsed it numerous times in the last hour. "I'm in town at the moment, running a few errands."

There was a pause on the line. Diane glanced in the rearview mirror. The traffic was light.

Greg spoke again. "How are you feeling?" His voice sounded stilted, forced, like he was slightly agitated but felt the need to cover with pleasantries.

Diane switched into caution mode. She glanced around her, then again in the review mirror, her eyes paying more attention this time to the stream of vehicles. "I'm feeling better," she replied, her head swinging left then right, expecting to see a dark, sleek Chrysler 300 shadowing her.

But Greg's car wasn't there.

"I slept some more after we spoke this morning. I think it helped a little."

Then another unnatural pause, a delay as though the call was being rerouted to the moon and back.

Diane waited for Greg to say something else. She shifted uncomfortably in her seat, forcing herself to remain calm. But she couldn't ignore the growing unease she was feeling.

Greg finally spoke. "That's great, honey. I'm glad you're feeling better."

There was something in his voice. It sounded wooden. Hollow.

"When will you be coming home?" Greg asked.

Now it was Diane's turn to pause, to decipher the meaning. *Coming home?* It sounded so strange how Greg had said it. Maybe it was her imagination. Diane stuck to her script. "I forgot. I have a late session with Dr. Redding this evening."

More silence again on the other end.

Diane's anxiety rose a notch.

"Another session?" Greg finally asked.

"Sorry. I forgot to put it on the wall calendar. I received a text reminder from Dr. Redding just before." Diane grimaced at the sound of her own voice. It lacked conviction, sounded unconvincing. As though she was guilty of something. All the composure and confidence she had just moments ago was slowly evaporating.

She could hear some background noise down the line. Greg wasn't in the office. And he usually was when he called her each afternoon. Diane took a chance, decided to play offense. "Look Greg, I'm nearly finished in town," she said, trying to sound more optimistic. "How about I drop by your office and we grab a coffee or something?"

Another long pause on the line. She could tell Greg was thinking.

"Sorry, honey," Greg replied. "Can't do. I'm outside the office at the moment, in the parking lot, about to head off to a client meeting."

Diane smiled with sweet relief. For a moment, for some bizarre reason that she couldn't explain, she thought Greg was actually in his car following behind her.

"It's an important meeting," Greg continued. "Hopefully I'll be able to close a big sale today, earn my bonus for the month."

"That's great," Diane replied, mild panic now replaced by reemerging anger as she pictured in her mind the bank statements and loan statements she had seen. All her life savings gone. The home mortgage maxed out. All the lies, the deceit, the dishonesty from the same man she was now talking to. It took every ounce of effort for Diane not to scream in rage at Greg. Call him out. Tell him he was a thief. A liar. A cheating, double-crossing pig. He deserved to be confronted, to be made accountable for destroying her financially.

However, as tempting as it was, Diane refrained. Otherwise all her plans for the future would also be destroyed.

There was another pause.

"Greg?" Diane wondered if he was still on the line or if the call had dropped out.

"Yes." Greg's voice came back flat, robotic.

"Are you okay? You sound like something is wrong."

"Sorry," he replied, sounding a little downtrodden now. "I'm just under pressure at work. Need to close this sale today."

"Look, I don't think I'll have time to make dinner tonight, Greg. I'd like to have another rest before I see Dr. Redding."

"That's fine, honey," Greg replied. "You get as much rest as you need."

"I should be home by nine tonight."

"I'll have dinner ready and waiting for you," Greg replied.

Diane ended the call and stared at her cell phone screen for a moment. Suddenly, she felt slightly uneasy again about the phone call. And it wasn't her imagination.

She placed the cell phone back in the center console, then

took a long hard look in her rearview mirror, an unsettling feeling beginning to grow in the pit of her stomach. She searched the traffic behind and around her, looking for Greg's car. But like before, she saw nothing.

Maybe she should come off the highway, take the back roads, the road less traveled. It was difficult to tell if he was hiding amongst the back traffic, tucked in behind a truck or van, watching her right now.

She accelerated slightly, switching lanes, watching closely the cars behind her to see if any mimicked her moves.

Then it struck Diane—about Greg's voice. Not his tone or what he said. It was something else, something she didn't realize until now. Despite the distance, the miles she had put between herself and home, and how he was calling from outside his office, from the parking lot.

Greg just sounded—closer.

Chapter 40

They were heading back along the road they had come when a small rest area appeared.

"Pull over," Alex said.

"Why?"

"Just pull over. I need some air."

Begrudgingly, Vincent slowed, came off the road and pulled into a small dirt lot.

Alex exited the SUV and walked away. She continued past an empty picnic bench and stood on the edge of a gentle rise, the wide, empty landscape stretching away in front of her. The air was cold, bracing, and necessary to clear her mind. Then the atmosphere changed abruptly, and she sensed Vincent behind her. "Anton Wheeler didn't know about the money," she said without turning. A slight breeze ruffled her hair across her face. "He had no idea about it." Her anger had abated. The moments of silent driving and the cold beauty of the surrounding landscape had helped.

Vincent settled at her shoulder, his searching eyes taking in the same natural vista, his mind focused on something entirely different. The money was out there somewhere. He could feel it, almost touch it, and yet it was beyond his grasp. He checked his phone again, his eyes narrowed, then his thumbs worked the screen feverishly, a digital rendition of the same landscape in front of him in the palm of his hand, sliding and expanding.

Alex could sense her brother—as usual—was preoccupied with his phone, so she answered the question before he could ask it. "Because he planned to sell the van, not dump it, not switch vehicles and take the money." She glanced sideways at Vincent. His head was down, eyes engrossed on the screen like he wasn't listening.

"Who are you talking to?" Alex asked, a little more than annoyed that he hadn't heard a word she had just spoken.

"No one."

"The van *was* the money for Wheeler," Alex continued, wondering why Vincent kept checking his phone so often. Was he in constant communication with their father? Giving him hourly updates?

Vincent shook his phone as though it wasn't working properly, then panned it around.

"How hard is it to find the compartment where the money case was?" Alex asked.

Vincent finally turned his attention to her. "Unless you knew what to look for, you would never know it was there. Purposely built into the underframe, part of the floor plate, seamless, invisible joints. Even if the van was placed on a hoist and lifted up, a mechanic would miss it…think it's part of the floor."

"So, the money case was removed before the van crashed? Someone knew about the hidden compartment."

Vincent nodded. "Like I've been saying all along, Wheeler was not acting alone. He passed the money on to someone else before he crashed the van." Vincent cursed at his phone, saw Alex watching him. "Poor signal," he muttered.

Alex continued staring into the distance. It didn't make sense what her brother was suggesting. She was adamant Anton Wheeler had no idea about the true nature of their business, about how the vans were being used to courier large quantities of cleaned cash. There was another, albeit far-fetched possibility that Alex didn't share with her brother. And that was someone had chanced across the crash site before the authorities arrived, saw the money case that had somehow become dislodged from the van's chassis during the crash, and simply took it.

Vincent continued to be preoccupied with his cell phone, as though it held all the answers to their woes.

"You need to control your anger, Vincent," she said. Her own anger had now been replaced with real fear. Fear that Vincent was slowly unraveling. She was afraid of what he might do next—to whom. She couldn't control him.

Vincent ignored the comment.

Alex bowed her head wearily. She didn't want this—any of this. She wanted to go home. But how safe would home really be as long as Vincent was around? Being with her brother was taking its toll on her. An hour with him felt like a day. A day felt like a month. He was quickly draining her energy, sapping what strength she had to control him. He was unstable, would swing between bouts of pure focus and fits of lethal rage. Killing came so easily for him. Almost on a whim. That's how little he valued another human's life. Like it was a commodity, to be bought, sold, or disposed of.

Maybe that's what happened when you grew up on the streets as a foot soldier like Vincent had. You become sanitized to the crimes, the killings. How easy it is to take a life to solve a problem or to extend your threatening influence, or to enhance your formidable reputation. After a while, that's all you know. It becomes the only solution you can offer.

The success or failure of this assignment rested with Alex. She knew if they failed, Vincent would throw her under the bus, report back to their father that the blame lay squarely with her. Another black mark to add to the list she was certain Vincent was already compiling about her. And if they were successful, Alex had no doubt Vincent would take full credit, steal the glory for him alone.

"So what now?" Alex asked, facing her brother.

"Just got a message from one of my contacts," he replied. "North Platte."

"Where is that?"

Vincent started walking back to the SUV, scrolling through his cell phone as he went, Alex following behind. "Eighty miles west of here," he replied, almost jogging now.

"What's there? What did they say?" Alex asked, trying to keep up, uncertain as to how this new information suddenly came to light.

He waved her off. "It's a city, maybe a ninety-minute drive from here. We need to get there fast." Vincent wanted Alex to drive while he navigated with his cell phone instead of using the onboard GPS.

As she climbed behind the wheel, Alex wondered about Vincent's network of contacts and the sudden anonymous tip-off that had just come through. "Can you at least tell me what this person said? How the money found its way there?"

"No other information. They are following up on a lead there. Will get back to me with more information once we arrive."

As they pulled back onto the road, Alex looked at her brother out of the corner of her eye, skeptical not as to what he was telling her—but what he wasn't telling her.

Chapter 41

"Ma'am, can I see your driver's license and proof of registration, please?"

Diane Miller looked up at the Nebraska State Patrol trooper. His sterile expression loomed large through the side window, devoid of any emotion, dark sunglasses hiding any empathy. A sleek, black Dodge Charger hunkered behind where Diane had pulled over. Its big 5.7 liter HEMI V8 engine purring, light bar on the roof radiating flecks of iridescent blue and red in the low light across Diane's SUV. Dusk was fast approaching.

"Sure. No problem."

The trooper was leaning down, invading her space.

Diane opened the center console, retrieved her purse, slipped out her driver's license, then found the registration paperwork. She handed both to him. "Is there a problem?"

The trooper didn't smile.

She had crossed into Lincoln County, approaching the city of North Platte from the north.

"I noticed you driving erratically a few miles back."

Diane frowned. It had been a long day. Too many stop-starts. Not enough miles covered. Perhaps she had been driving longer than she thought. Thinking about it now certainly made her feel tired.

"You're from Sherman County?" the trooper asked, looking at her again.

"That's correct," Diane replied, dwelling on the trooper's comment. She didn't think she was driving erratically at all.

The trooper glanced in again, noticing several empty paper coffee cups stacked inside one another in the center console. Without another word, he turned and walked back to his cruiser.

More psychology, Diane thought as she watched him in the side mirror. He slid behind the wheel and began tapping away on the dash-mounted computer. Diane wasn't concerned. At some point in the future, she would get a new driver's license, get someone to do a proper forgery with the new name she had chosen. She had the money.

On the inside, her new identity was slowly taking shape. She could picture the woman, like she was observing her from the outside. Not a stranger. She wasn't pretending to be another person. She was *becoming* another person. Someone more independent, liberated, forthright. It gave her immense satisfaction knowing the evolution had started. She liked her new name too. Had practiced introducing her new self to her old self in the rearview mirror as she drove. However, until she organized her new formal identity, she was still Diane Abigail Miller, resident of Hazard, Sherman County, Nebraska.

After checking if there were any outstanding warrants for Diane Miller, the trooper returned and handed back her driver's license and registration papers. "Where are you heading?"

"Colorado."

The trooper nodded. "That's a good six, maybe seven hours away."

"I know," Diane said. "But I feel fine, honestly. I have relatives there, and they are expecting me."

The trooper leaned in, placed one elbow on the windowsill. "May I make a suggestion, ma'am?"

"Sure."

The trooper glanced toward the darkening sky in the distance.

Diane followed his gaze through the windshield. It was difficult to judge distance but she saw a large black smudge on the horizon in the direction she was heading. A storm was building, slowly spreading across the calm, clear sky like an amoeba.

"I suggest, ma'am, that you stop driving for a while. Take shelter. Get some rest for a couple of hours. Either that or find a motel for the night." The trooper pointed toward the widening, rotating blackness. "We get some pretty bad storms through here this time of year. And it looks like there's a bad one coming this way."

In the few minutes Diane had been watching, the black smudge had formed into a strange, rotating pancake stack shape, like a flying saucer mother ship shrouded in cloud and mist. She had no idea if it was three miles or thirty miles away. Then a large drop splattered on her windshield.

"That one over there, ma'am, in the distance, is a super cell. They can come out of nowhere. Temperature drops really quick, and it whips up a vortex of rain and wind and violence." The trooper turned back to Diane. "My advice is for you to get off the highway, wait out the storm. Get a good night's sleep. Leave early tomorrow. Get to your relatives in Colorado in one piece."

Diane understood. Thinking about it now, maybe she should stop for the night. Her shoulders slumped, and she suddenly felt exhausted. Physically, as well as mentally. The stress of the last few days was catching up with her. But her mind was still on edge, taxing her energy. She was still thinking about Greg, how he had sounded during the afternoon phone call. She couldn't get it out of her mind. There was something in his voice, he seemed different, as though he was watching her from afar while he spoke to her. Watching her every move. She knew it was ridiculous.

Suddenly, Diane craved a hot shower. To feel the jets of scalding hot water wash away the buildup of grime and anxiety.

As if reading her mind, the trooper spoke again. "There are plenty of motel chains in town. Good rates and facilities."

"Thanks for the advice," Diane said.

"Or if you want something low-key, take the third exit from here and follow the road inland for about a mile or two. There is a nice motel along the back road there. Quieter, if you prefer that kind of thing."

Low-key. Diane thought for a moment. Something less conspicuous suited her.

"Thanks again," Diane said, forcing a smile, thinking about the attaché case of cash in the trunk. "I will take your advice. Rest for the night."

"Safe travels, ma'am, and enjoy the rest of your trip." The trooper turned and began walking back to his vehicle.

Diane put the car in gear, waited for a break in the traffic, then pulled back onto the highway. She noticed the police cruiser followed her into the same break in the traffic and was now tucked in behind her. Not too close, but close enough for her to see him back there, a featureless silhouette propped up behind the wheel. The trooper followed her for another mile before eventually peeling off and vanishing down an exit ramp.

As Diane drove on, it was becoming darker by the minute. In the distance the outskirts of the town started to form. Grid lines and dots of light and neon shimmered off the underside on the clouds overhead.

Diane hadn't intended to stop for the night until she reached Colorado. Now it seemed like a good idea to pull over, wait out the storm, sleep for the night. She was tired and hungry after putting in a decent amount of miles between her and Hazard.

Big bright neon signs appeared to one side of the highway. Best Western. Hampton Inn. She wanted something less conspicuous, a hotel or motel not on the main drag. She remembered the trooper's advice, to take the exit that she had already passed.

Damn.

She took the next exit, backtracked until she was on a service road heading back in the direction she had come, parallel to the highway. She glanced at the map on her cell phone. Several small house icons sprouted up in unison on the screen, motels nearby. The closest was two miles away, along a road that ran inland away from the highway. Sixty bucks a night. That would do.

She passed several eating places as she drove on. She would check-in, take a shower, then get something to eat. Tomorrow she would hit the road again, drive straight on through to Colorado without stopping.

Chapter 42

Within the space of five minutes, Monica Styles received both good news and devastating news.

First, an alert landed on her cell phone. Registration and license details matching an SUV, driven by Diane Miller, had been flagged on the outskirts of North Platte, a city in Lincoln County, one hundred twenty miles east of Loup City where Styles was standing. A state trooper had pulled over Diane Miller in a white, 2005 Chevy Trailblazer on I-83 West, three miles from the city limits. She was given a caution for reckless driving and let off with a warning. Nothing more.

Monica checked her watch. If she hurried, she could make it there in under two hours. As she was about to call Charmers and let her know, Charmers beat her to the punch.

"Miles Burke died twenty minutes ago." Charmers sounded bitter.

Monica turned cold. "I thought when he came out of surgery again, it all went well. That he was stable."

"The surgeon just called me. Unexpected complications. There was a clot on the brain. He flatlined and they couldn't bring him back."

Both women said nothing for a moment, each lamenting the other's mix of sadness and simmering anger. Both knew what this meant. The serious bodily assault had been elevated to homicide.

Monica then relayed to Charmers the notification that Diane Miller had been pulled over in Lincoln County.

"Go," Charmers said without hesitation. "Find both of them.

I'll contact the police department in North Platte as well as the Lincoln County Sheriff's Department. Give them both a heads-up that you're coming. Get co-operation from them."

Monica could hear the seething in her boss's voice, picturing her on the other end of the call, lips drawn back, teeth gritted into the mouthpiece.

"Thanks, boss."

"Be careful, Monica."

Monica paused. "I will."

"The only reason I'm letting you go, and not going myself, is that Miles Burke was—is, your case. You've followed this theory from the beginning about Greg Miller. By all rights I should step in, but I won't."

Monica understood. "If Diane Miller is running, then judging by her husband's reaction when I last saw him, he's giving chase. I've had no notification about him or his vehicle."

"Find her and you might find him."

"That's what I'm thinking."

"But don't get in over your head, Mons. At the first sign of trouble, call in local law enforcement. The sheriff as well—and keep me up to date."

Monica agreed.

"I don't want to hand this over to Lincoln County. This homicide happened on our turf."

"Understood," Monica said before ending the call.

Greg Miller was the only suspect they had. They had nothing else to go on. Diane Miller might hold the key, and something in her gut was telling Styles that if she found Diane Miller, Greg Miller wouldn't be too far behind.

As she quickly gathered her equipment together, she wondered where the road would take her.

Chapter 43

It was closer to four miles off the main road than two.

The glow of the highway and town soon dropped away behind her, and Diane found herself driving along a narrow undulating road, the beams of the headlights cutting through the darkness, nothingness beyond the edges.

The place seemed to be in the middle of nowhere, definitely off the beaten track. Diane felt hemmed by the ghostly outlines of low scrub, tall trees, the occasional glimpse of faraway lights. The porch light of a distant farmhouse or barn, Diane guessed. The landscape seemed more wooded and hilly than the typical rural flatness of grassland and prairie. More than once she thought about turning around, heading back to the bright lights of the city.

Then a glow appeared up ahead, quickly growing into the shape of a low cinderblock building outlined with lights. It was a diner with a few pickups in the parking lot, people sitting behind big windows in the bright interior. Diane drove on, deciding she would return there, go where the locals go, have a bite to eat before calling it a night.

Finally the motel came into view. A small, squat structure with a floodlit sign out front. There were two other cars parked in the lot adjacent to rooms near the front, close to the small office.

A heavy-set woman named Mildred shuffled out from the parlor behind the counter. Thick glasses, gray hair, with a posture crafted from years of constantly getting up from in front of the television, tending to guests, then sitting back down to resume watching her favorite show. Mildred didn't bat an eyelid when Diane requested the end room, Number fifteen, the farthest from the office and other guests. Cash and a name were exchanged for a key and Wi-Fi passcode.

The room was neat and tidy. The bathroom small but functional. The towels fresh and soft. The bed old but firm. Diane brought her spinner case inside. It contained her essentials for one night. She left the attaché case and the large suitcase in the trunk of the SUV, which was parked directly out front, back end in for ease of access—or speed of departure.

Despite being tired, Diane was hungry. Apart from a late breakfast this morning, she had survived on the road on a diet of protein bars and coffee. She needed a solid meal inside her.

At the diner, she sat in a booth near the window, ordered more calorie dense food than she could possibly finish, and stared off into the darkness outside, focusing on nothing but the next few days. She'd always planned one day to visit Colorado, to see its raw wilderness, go trekking in the national parks, experience the natural, rugged beauty of the place. Utah too. She had toyed with the idea of renting a cabin, away from everyone, go off-grid for a period of time, to decompress, dismantle, then reassemble her mind and body while being surrounded by peace and tranquility. Something up in the mountains, not too far from a small town, perhaps. Nothing fancy or filled with too many creature comforts. But not a monastic existence either. She would stock the cabin full of food—local produce, organic if she could find it. Then spend her days thinking and planning. Go on daily hikes. Build her strength and endurance back up the natural way. Clean air, a clean mind and body.

She unscrewed her pill bottle and swallowed another two

with her iced tea. Eventually, she would run out of the medication. But by then she wouldn't need them anymore. She was slowly returning to full alertness and awareness.

The attaché case full of money was still in the back of her car, hidden not too well under an old blanket. Diane didn't know what she was going to do with it yet, how she was going to eventually hide it. If she deposited it into a bank account, it would definitely draw the attention of the authorities. She couldn't keep driving around with it in the back of her car. She ran the risk of someone stopping her again. A police officer or another state trooper, pulling her over, then taking a look in the back, would wonder what was in the damaged case.

Lightning flashed across the night sky, strobing the tree line across the road, momentarily.

She flinched, saw something—someone, a figure, standing among the trees at the edge of the woods across the road. The woods plunged back into darkness.

Diane leaned forward, her face and background of the diner reflecting back at her in the glass as she squinted.

Nothing. Gone. Just a wall of darkness now.

Diane rubbed her eyes and looked again but couldn't see anyone. Then another burst of lightning, this time longer. Light raked the woods again, but the person was gone.

She looked around the brightly lit diner, realizing how exposed she was, a fish in a bowl, the laws of optics coming into play. In the brightly lit diner, she couldn't see clearly into the darkness outside. But someone standing outside in the darkness could clearly see someone brightly illuminated inside the diner.

Chapter 44

As time was critical, they had taken the direct route: a straight line, passing endless fields of crop irrigation circles, feed yards, and wide, open prairies dotted with the occasional farm building or barn.

They headed west along I-92 before cutting south. Then it was a twenty-four mile diagonal run, approaching North Platte from the north.

On the highway, Alex kept to the middle lane. Driving not too fast, not too slow. Maintaining the speed limit, happy to let the big semis blast past her, and the other impatient drivers. She kept a watchful eye in the rearview and side mirrors. The only police vehicle she saw was crouching in the shadows of an underpass where they had pulled over a vehicle.

Vincent sat in silence, keeping a watchful eye on his cell phone. Sometimes his brow would furrow in disapproval. Other times he would offer a cunning little smile as though recalling a dirty little secret that only he knew about. But mainly his eyes were slits, glued to the screen of his phone, a predator closing in on its prey. His shoulders were hunched, his head down, neck protruding, getting ready for an imminent kill.

Alex assumed he was getting regular updates on his cell phone from his contact. Vincent gave her very little information other than they were getting closer.

With each passing mile, Alex felt as though she was being pulled toward another bout of her brother's violence. It seemed unavoidable. This time, however, they had had words, Alex insisting there would be no more killing unless she authorized it. And she would only give that order under extreme circumstances. Unless their lives were threatened. Then Vincent was free to do what he did best: destroy everything and everyone.

She didn't want a repeat of what happened with Brendan Murphy, and she had made that very clear to Vincent. And yet, as he nodded in agreement, she somehow felt it made no difference. He was a force that couldn't be controlled, couldn't be reasoned with.

Dark clouds began to build and so did the traffic around them as they sped on, getting closer to where Vincent was directing them. They made no stops for food or for comfort. As the darkening landscape slid past, Alex wondered if Vincent had passed through here before. And if he had, what bodies had he buried in these fields?

They skirted the edge of the city, avoiding the building snarls of traffic and headed south. Vincent's directions became more frequent. They were getting close. Yet, he remained tight-lipped, only giving her directions and not a final destination.

Soon they found themselves off the main artery and heading inland, leaving behind the neon blaze and twinkling lights of the city.

The landscape opened up again into farmland. The lights became fewer and the encroaching darkness pressed closer around them as they drove on. There was the occasional light of a distant farmhouse or machinery shed. Apart from that, they were driving toward desolation.

Eighty miles farther east, Monica Styles was making good time. With her lights flashing but siren off, she had the fast lane all to herself as other vehicles peeled away, leaving a clear run for her. After leaving Loup City, instead of heading due west, she drove due south to Hazard to check on the Miller home one more time and see if Diane or Greg Miller had returned. The place was as she had last seen it: deserted and in darkness. She pressed on south, slicing through the town of Kearney, in Buffalo County, before merging on to I-80 west. From there it was all lights blazing, and her foot down to the floor.

When she reached North Platte, she had no real plan. Charmers had already called ahead, paving the way for any contact she was going to make in the county. Hopefully, either Diane or Greg Miller would resurface. In a city of close to thirty thousand people, Monica knew the chances were slim.

But she was willing to take that chance.

Chapter 45

After drawing the drapes, locking the door, and applying the security chain, Diane turned the television off. She went into the bathroom, stripped, then bundled her clothes into a plastic bag.

A ghostly shape skirted the periphery of her vision. She paused and glanced around. Cautiously, she edged into the frame of the reflection in the wall mirror above the sink.

She stood there for a moment, front on, naked under the harsh fluorescent glow. She turned one way then the other, sorrow not admiration in her eyes—eyes that began to slowly fill with tears as she looked at herself properly for the first time in months, perhaps even in years. She saw a human canvas stained with pain and misery. Her face was drawn and pale, sunken cheeks, hollow jaw. Her skin, cavernous around collarbones. Thin, elongated limbs. She looked like a living, breathing anatomical chart.

Taking a deep breath, she watched as her translucent skin slithered up the steeple of her ribcage, before settling back down when she exhaled.

A tear rolled down one cheek, which she angrily rubbed away, vowing to never allow herself to fall into such a state ever again. She was unrecognizable. Someone else. A stranger. Yet, this was how she now looked, everything laid bare. Nowhere to hide. She had endured so much already. Looking at herself in the mirror only made her more determined to go on, to finish what she had started, to build a new life. To fix what had been broken. She owed it to herself. To the loving memory of her daughter. She had made a start, but she needed to finish the race. So, in front of the mirror, commitments were made, judgments not given.

Diane stepped into the shower and stood under the hot jets of water, allowing all the tension and stress to slowly seep from her body. Steam billowed out into the small room, the flimsy shower curtain hazing over with condensation. She closed her eyes and gave in to the heat and comfort of the swirling steam.

She drifted off—then her eyes sprang open. She felt odd, a change in the atmosphere, the hot water suddenly feeling slightly colder. She peered through the shower curtain and saw the dark smudge of the open bathroom door, everything else blurred. Holding her breath, she strained to listen. Water cascaded off her, making gurgling sounds as it coiled into the drain at her feet. Gripping the shower curtain, she pulled it slightly aside and looked out. The clouds of steam shifted inside the room. She could hear the faint murmur of the television in the bedroom beyond the open door.

Nothing.

Just her imagination. She had to relax. Mild hallucinations were one of the side effects of the new medication, Dr. Redding had explained. In time, they would pass. Greg hadn't sounded suspicious on the cell phone when he had called her. There was no one following her on the highway. And there certainly hadn't been someone watching her from the woods across the road from the diner before. There was nothing to worry about, Diane told herself as she slid the plastic shower curtain across again and held her face under the stream of water. She was in a small motel in the middle of nowhere. No one knew she was here. No one knew where she was.

Her skin had begun to wrinkle. She turned off the faucet, stepped out onto the mat, and toweled herself off as steam swirled around her. She wrapped a towel around her body and combed her damp hair, the mirror too foggy to see herself again, thankfully. Absentmindedly, she found herself humming to the tune of a commercial that was playing on the television in the bedroom.

She took a few moments to dry her hair with the hairdryer she found in the small cupboard under the sink. The first thing she was going to do when she arrived in Colorado was find a decent hair salon to get her hair properly dyed blond.

She walked out of the bathroom, took three steps into the bedroom—and stopped.

Muddy footprints on the carpet ran from the door toward her before suddenly veering to her right.

Diane spun her head to the right just as powerful arms wrapped around her from behind. She felt herself being lifted, then flying through the air across the room before hitting the opposite wall.

Blinding white exploded behind her eyes. She tumbled to the carpet, gasping for air from the sudden impact. Dazed and with her head throbbing, she tried to push herself upright with one arm. Slowly her vision began to clear, the room gradually coming back into focus.

A man, a stranger, was standing over her. His clothing— soaked dark, mud-stained, and dirty—clung to him. His hair was plastered to his skull. His face, glistened, beaded with water. Demented eyes, cold, dark, and pitiless peered down at her. One cheek was cut, a line of blood from where a branch had lashed him across the face in the woods.

The man looked around the room, then his eyes settled on the cell phone Diane had left on the bed. He picked it up, turning it over in his hand as he regarded it for a moment. He brought the screen closer to his face, then straightened his hair with his other hand and turned his head as though using the screen as mirror. It was a bizarre gesture, as though his outward appearance suddenly mattered to him, despite looking like a drenched rat from having spent the last two hours standing outside in the dark woods, suffering in silence…the driving wind and freezing rain unable to dampen the raging heat inside him.

The cell phone unlocked. The home screen appeared.

Without so much as a smile, he gave a slight nod of satisfaction, then slipped the phone into his pocket.

Diane shook her head, blinked hard, trying to comprehend and dispel the vagaries of the concussion she had just experienced. The man's face came into crystal clear focus, and her stomach plummeted through the floor beneath her.

"Hello, Diane."

Shocked, sickened, and repulsed, Diane felt all three emotions collide at once in her head, gut, and limbs.

Her heels kicked along the carpet, pushing herself away from her husband, her back pressing farther against the wall. She was jammed in between the side of the bed and a set of drawers. She glanced at the closed motel room door and saw the flimsy safety chain hanging limply, no apparent damage to the lock or door frame. The mere fifteen feet between her and freedom looked more like fifty feet. All the previously insignificant and unmemorable details of the room suddenly became vitally important to Diane.

The bedside lamp? Dim bulb, thin white cable. Precious seconds would be lost unplugging it to utilize it as a weapon. Chair? Out of reach. Alarm clock radio? Pointless. Then it dawned on Diane that she was naked, cornered like an animal, no choice but to fight for her life. The towel she had worn had unwrapped, torn away when she was violently hurled across the room.

She could feel Greg's eyes scraping over her nakedness, like claws of a wire rake. Her skin, her body violated. A slow, heinous smile spread across his face as he watched her.

Seeing Diane's own cell phone and car keys on a side table, he picked them up too and slid them into his pocket. He turned to a small, black backpack that sat on the bed, the top open. He had come prepared.

Diane looked on in horror as Greg reached inside and, with meticulous care, laid out on the threadbare bedspread the items he had brought from home. Cable ties. A ball gag. Riding crop. Alligator clamps.

Greg Miller took his time as he laid everything out on the bed, savoring the anticipation building inside him, the suffering he was about to inflict on his wife. She deserved it. The implements from the backpack had been used on several of his past female acquaintances. Taught them the delicacies of pleasure derived from exquisite pain. Opened their unwilling minds to another world. Now he had all the time in the world to introduce his wife to the same. His soon-to-be-dead wife.

After he was done, Greg planned to strangle her, watch the life leave her eyes right in front of him. Then take her body to some remote location and dump her. The storm would wash away any trace of evidence. He would drive home and resume a normal life, saying his wife had left him. Saying he had come home to find the house empty and Diane gone. Thousands of people go missing each year. Diane was going to add to that tally.

Greg checked that he had everything. Satisfied, he turned back to Diane. He smelled her fear before he saw it, the damp patch of carpet under her that wasn't water.

He smiled at the sight.

Good. This was going to be so good.

The room door burst open. A torrent of wind, rain, and leaves swept in, bringing with it a man with a gun.

"Well, well, well. What do we have here? A lovers' tiff?"

Greg Miller spun around to see Vincent Romano standing in the doorway. The barrel of a gun angled up at Greg's head. Behind Vincent stood Alex Romano. A mortified look on her face.

Chapter 46

Four sets of eyes exchanged looks.

Then came the slow recognition.

"You!" Vincent hissed, as he focused on Greg Miller's face. Vincent never forgot a face. Especially one he had been so up close and personal to recently.

Vincent and Alex stepped inside, closing the door behind them. Both looked around, assessing the situation. It was as though they had accidentally stumbled into a scene on a theater stage, two actors playing out a disturbing confrontation. But this was no act.

The space was tight, not designed to accommodate four grown adults, let alone the expanding animosity, bewilderment, and anger that made the small room feel extremely claustrophobic.

Greg Miller hadn't moved. He just stood with cable ties in one hand, staring at Alex and Vincent Romano.

Diane Miller lay huddled on the floor, pale limbs drawn tightly around her protectively.

Alex Romano looked at Diane, her mind having a difficult time trying to process the scene in front of her. Her eyes then shifted to the items laid out neatly on the bed.

Vincent hadn't seen them. He was too preoccupied with how he was going to kill Greg Miller. Head shot or gut shot? Quick kill or slow and painful one? And he was going to kill him, and the woman too. There was no doubt, regardless of what he had told Alex before.

"Where is the money?" Vincent asked.

Greg Miller look baffled.

Vincent shook his head in disbelief, the amusement of the situation barely keeping his anger in check. "A couple of thieves. Partners. A modern-day Bonnie and Clyde." He glanced at Alex. "We had you. Both of you. You were right there in our hands, and we let you slip through." Vincent gestured toward Greg with the gun but addressed Diane "Who is he? Your lover? Friend—"

"Husband," Greg cut in.

"Married thieves?" Vincent smirked as he regarded Diane Miller's nakedness, before turning his attention back to Greg Miller, all humor gone from his face, replaced with a cold loathing. "Where is the money?" Vincent repeated.

"I have no idea what you're talking about," Greg Miller replied.

"Sure you do," Vincent countered. "Empty your pockets. Now!"

Greg Miller emptied his pockets onto the bed. Three cell phones. Two sets of car keys, the room key he had taken, and a small compact handgun.

"You did come prepared," Vincent said with mocking disapproval.

Vincent picked up the gun and passed it to Alex. "Cover him. If he moves, shoot him."

Alex checked the action and took aim at Greg Miller.

Vincent slid his own gun away and gathered up the rest of the items from Greg Miller's pockets, noticing the Chrysler keychain. "Where did you park the other vehicle?" He held up the keychain. "It's not outside in the parking lot."

Greg thought about not answering or just lying. But there was no point now. "About a mile from here. On the other side of the woods at the back of the motel."

Vincent thought nothing of it. He already knew the money

must be in the back of the Chevy Trailblazer that was parked directly outside.

While still covering Greg Miller with the gun, Alex picked up the towel from the floor and tossed it to Diane. "Get dressed."

Diane took it gratefully, wrapped it around herself, then got to her feet, grabbed some clothing out of her case, and went to the bathroom.

"And leave the door open," Vincent called after her.

Moments later she came out fully dressed. While in the bathroom, she had contemplated trying to escape. But the window above the toilet was too small, even for her. And it had bars.

Vincent patted down Greg Miller but found nothing else. Taking the cable ties, he bound both Greg and Diane's hands behind their backs, leaving their feet so they could walk. "I don't know who the hell you both are," Vincent said, checking that the ties were securely in place. "But we're going to get answers, one way or another." He picked up the ball gag off the bed, glanced at Greg Miller and smiled. "Perfect."

Greg Miller recoiled. "Get that thing away from me!" he snarled.

The reaction was swift and brutal. Vincent punched Greg hard in the face, knocking him to the floor. Vincent got behind him, wrestled him upright, thrust the ball into his mouth, jerked his head back violently, and cinched the thick strap around his head, securing the heavy buckle. Using his foot, he shoved Greg Miller squarely in the back, pushing him down to the floor again.

He removed a pillowcase from a pillow on the bed, twisted it, placed it between Diane's teeth, and knotted it behind her head.

He took out his gun again. "Move!"

"What's going on, Vincent?" Alex asked, lowering her gun.

Vincent turned to his sister. "I'll tell you what's going on. We had these two in our grasp. The money was right under our noses back at that gas station. They were hiding in plain sight, and we let them both go. That's what's going on." Vincent turned back to Greg and Diane Miller and gave a flick with his gun. "We're going for a little ride. Move."

Vincent pushed Greg and Diane toward the door. He gave them one more instruction before Alex opened the door. "You run, you die."

Outside the wind had mellowed and the rain had petered out to a light drizzle.

Vincent opened the back of Diane's Trailblazer and looked inside. There, pushed into the back corner, was the aluminum attaché case. "Bingo," he said, turning to his sister.

"How did you know to come specifically here?" Alex had no idea what had led them to this particular location in the middle of nowhere. It was too accurate. And she had her suspicions that her brother's so-called 'contacts' hadn't directed them here either.

Vincent checked his phone but said nothing. He bundled both Diane and Greg into the back of the Trailblazer, then tossed the keys to Alex. "You drive. Just follow me and stay close." Vincent walked to where they had parked the Suburban.

Alex looked down at Diane. She felt no compassion for the woman who had deceived her.

Dread-filled eyes swiveled and looked back at Alex.

Alex leaned in. "You lied to me," she hissed. "You told me you were running from your husband. The disguise, the hair, everything was a lie. You're nothing but a common thief on the run."

Diane struggled against the cable tie, giving a muffled protest from behind the gag.

"It was a convincing act," Alex said, stepping back. "But, understand this. What happens next to the pair of you, you both brought upon yourselves."

With that, she slammed the tailgate shut.

Chapter 47

Monica Styles was saved from the tedium of driving around North Platte, aimlessly looking for Diane or Greg Miller's vehicles, as well as the awkwardness of having to pay a visit to the county sheriff's department.

A call had come in from the police department. Diane Miller's SUV had been identified and involved in an incident at a local motel four miles south of the city. The details were scant at best as Monica listened to the call, jotting down the address before entering it in her GPS.

She felt a slim glimmer of hope as she headed toward the location. It would be a simple case of just talking to Diane Miller. Ask the woman about her husband and Miles Burke. Find out if her husband was after her and, if so, why? There was a connection with either one or both of the Millers to Miles Burke; Monica was certain of it.

Twenty minutes later, Monica pulled into the parking lot of a small, secluded motel on the rural outskirts. A North Platte police cruiser sat parked next to an EMT truck, its doors open, a heavy-set woman inside being tended to by a paramedic.

Only two rooms had vehicles parked out front, and Monica saw partial faces through the gaps in the drapes of both rooms as she walked past.

The police officer on the call was young, long-limbed, and gangly with red hair and freckles making him look like he should still be in high school. He introduced himself as Officer Swift. And as Styles was about to find out, he was anything but.

Swift opened his notebook and began relaying what he knew so far to Monica. Obviously he'd been told to co-operate with the young deputy from Sherman County, even though this was out of her jurisdiction. Charmers had made the right calls, paving the way for her. Reading from his notebook, the manager of the motel, a woman named Mildred Wilkins, had been knocked unconscious by an adult male who was not a guest. Wilkins had given Swift a description of her attacker. It sounded like the young police officer was describing Greg Miller. "When Wilkins came to, she called the police immediately. Nothing had been stolen, just the spare key to room fifteen."

"And she's positive nothing else was stolen?" Monica asked, wanting to make sure this wasn't just a robbery. Swift checked his notebook again. "Nothing. The man just wanted to know the name of the person in room fifteen. She refused to give him any information."

"Who is in room fifteen?" Monica asked impatiently, wondering if it was going to take twenty questions to get a single answer she wanted.

Swift slowly ran his pen down his notes, searching for a name he should have memorized. "Crane," he finally said. "Marion Crane."

Monica felt her heart sink. Maybe there was a mix up with the license plate details in the system. Diane Miller hadn't been here. It was all a misunderstanding. The name sounded familiar, though. But Monica couldn't place it.

Swift explained that he had already knocked on the door of room fifteen. There was no answer, but he hadn't gone inside. "So when the man couldn't get any more information out of the manager, he struck her, knocked her unconscious, and I assume took the spare room key off the hook in the office."

"So why did I get the call?" Monica asked.

Swift looked up from his notebook. "Beats me," he replied. "I'm just following procedure. The manager told me she records the license plate of each guest in case they abscond without paying. But the woman in room fifteen paid in cash." Swift had the sense to run the plates on the woman's vehicle that was now gone, and that's when Monica's flag in the system came up. "So I checked the plates, and you got the call."

Monica rolled her eyes and felt like slapping herself in the forehead with the heel of her hand—then thought otherwise in front of this junior officer. It suddenly all made sense. The name, Marion Crane…almost as if Diane Miller was leaving a satirical clue. She was the woman in room fifteen, and she was running. Greg had found her. "So the woman's name," Monica asked, "that the car is registered to is Diane Miller?"

Swift nodded.

"Why didn't you tell me that in the first place?" Monica now felt like slapping the young police officer in the forehead. Getting relevant information out of him quickly was like pulling teeth.

"I was getting to that if you just give me a chance," Swift said defensively, not taking too kindly to being harassed by some young deputy sheriff from another county—a woman too.

"And the car the man drove? Where is that?" Monica snapped impatiently.

Swift looked guilty all of a sudden. "I didn't ask the manager about that vehicle."

Monica bit her tongue, as tempting as it was to be critical. This was not her patch of ground, as Charmers had reminded her. She didn't want to be seen telling local law enforcement how they should conduct themselves. "I want to talk to her, the manager, Wilkins. I'll ask her."

"No problem." Swift closed his notebook but just stood there, unsure what to do next.

"Have you spoken to the other guests?" Monica asked.

Swift shook his head. "Not yet. But they could be asleep."

Monica doubted it with all this commotion outside.

"Officer Swift."

Swift smiled, stood a little straighter upon hearing his title. Most people back at the station just yelled his surname when they wanted him to do something.

Styles stepped closer to the young officer and put on her best smile. "Go and wake them up—please. While I talk to the manager. See if anyone heard or saw anything."

Swift gave a nod, then slowly trudged off.

"Ms. Wilkins?"

Thick glasses glinted and turned toward Monica as she approached the open back of the EMT truck. Mildred Wilkins sat perched on the end of the ambulance cot. Monica exchanged a nod with the paramedic who was finishing off securing a dressing on Mildred's forehead.

Monica noticed the woman frowning at her uniform. "I'm from Sherman County," she explained, taking out her notebook. "I'm following up on a lead, a person of interest who may be here in North Platte."

"I told everything I know to the nice young police officer," Mildred replied. "I hadn't seen the man before. And he wasn't a guest. Just rude and nasty-like."

Monica took out a picture of Greg Miller and held it up for the woman. "Is this the man who attacked you?"

Mildred leaned forward, her face pinched. Then her eyes went wide. "Yes," she said with certainty. "That's him. The man who hit me. Had eyes like the devil, he did."

Monica felt a sudden surge of adrenaline, the woman confirming that it was indeed Greg Miller. "Like the devil?" Monica queried.

Mildred nodded her head vehemently, then winced in pain, forgetting about her injury. "He said he wanted to know if his wife was here. He told me her name was Diane Miller."

Styles wrote faster. Another huge detail that Swift should have brought to Monica's immediate attention.

"That wasn't the name the woman registered under, though," Mildred replied. "But I didn't tell that to him. The man got kind of angry when I told him about guest privacy, and the like. I said I couldn't tell him any guest details. But he was very insistent. There was something about him. Something threatening."

"What can you tell me about the woman in room fifteen?" Monica asked, not looking up for her notebook as she scribbled away. "Marion Crane."

Mildred gave a slow nod. "I knew from the moment I laid eyes on her that something wasn't right," Mildred replied, her voice full of foreboding, like she had had a premonition. "She acted nervous. Like guilty of something. She paid in cash and wanted the room at the far end, away from everyone else. Room fifteen."

Monica slipped out the photo of Diane Miller and held it up. This time Mildred took longer. She squinted at the picture, tilting her head, like she couldn't make up her mind. "I think that's her. She looks thinner, though. But she doesn't have dark hair. Like in the photo. She has blond hair."

Blond hair? Monica wrote down, circling the words several times.

"And the woman's vehicle? You told Officer Swift that you wrote down the license plate number."

"I got suspicious of her. When she came back from the diner, I noted her license plate number. A white Chevy Trailblazer."

Mildred Wilkins had been very helpful. Despite her thick glasses, she had a fine eye for detail. Most managers in small motels like these didn't pay much attention to those who came and went. Didn't even bat an eyelid if something was out of the ordinary. As long as the guest paid, they didn't care.

But Mildred had taken a keen interest, and Monica was thankful for that.

"Did you see another car?" Monica asked. "A black Chrysler? Sleek-looking?" She told Mildred the license plate number for Greg Miller's vehicle. But the woman shook her head slowly this time. Said that she was probably unconscious behind the counter, and by the time she had woken up, Diane Miller's car was gone. She hadn't seen any other vehicle during that time. That wasn't to say that Greg Miller's vehicle hadn't been in the parking lot during that time. "I turned around for just a second at the counter. The next thing you know, I woke up on the floor. And the spare key for number fifteen I keep on a pegboard in the office was gone."

"Do you have another key to the room? Monica asked. "I'd like to take a look inside."

Mildred rummaged in a side pocket, then pulled out a master key. She handed it to Monica. "Don't lose it."

"I'll bring it right back when I'm done. I promise." Monica reached out and squeezed Mildred's hand. "You've been very helpful."

Mildred beamed. What a lovely, nice, young woman, she thought as she watched Monica head toward the room at the end of the property.

The room had definitely been occupied recently. The lights

had been left on, the drapes drawn tight. Monica donned a pair of latex gloves, then unlocked the door. A trail of muddy footprints on the carpet led from the front door to the open bathroom door on the other side of the room.

Styles closed the door behind her. This was her domain, and she didn't want the young police officer in here until she was done. The television had been left on, and the bed had been moved slightly at an angle, away from the wall. A spinner case sat open on a chair. But what caught her attention was the open backpack that lay on the bed. Next to it someone had laid out cable ties, some kind of whip, and alligator clamps. Inside the backpack Monica found something long and thick, made of silicone, and from its size and length was anatomically impossible. The tools were either for bondage or torture, and Monica had the distinct feeling which it was.

She caught a whiff of something…a smell—sour, rank. Following her nose, she walked to the space between the bed and a set of drawers. The smell was stronger there. Crouching down she noticed a damp patch on the carpet. Someone had urinated on the carpet. Baffled, she stood and went to the spinner case. Inside were neatly folded piles of women's clothing. She picked up a T-shirt, brought it to her nose.

New.

She smelled another. All the clothing was new, unworn, the tags removed. There was a small vanity pack inside that was also new, the seals on the plastic bottles unbroken.

In the bathroom, she found a few toiletries on the sink and a soap wrapper in the small trash can. The plastic shower curtain was beaded with water. Water pooled in the tub. The towel on the ring was still damp. Monica felt the hair dryer that hung from a hook next to the towel ring.

Warm.

Diane Miller had been here recently, maybe not more than an hour ago at the most. She had taken a shower, dried her hair. But her car was gone.

Monica turned and headed back to the bedroom, then paused in the bathroom doorway. She stepped back and swung the bathroom door slowly away from the wall stopper.

There, scrawled in lipstick on the back of the bathroom door was a message.

Help me...and a cell phone number.

Chapter 48

There was no bad to come first.

It was all bad.

Both were taken to a cold, dark place long since abandoned, then their feet were also bound.

Greg Miller, bloodied and bruised, was forced to kneel on the cold, hard floor, facing his wife in silent judgment. Diane Miller leaned awkwardly to one side on an old milking stool opposite him. Her side ached from where she had hit the motel room wall, but she swallowed the pain.

The tin walls and roof sheeting of the old barn around them shuddered and rattled, the storm picking up again. The framework of hewn wood and iron nails had endured a hundred years of beating rain, snow, and blistering heat, and would endure another hundred years or more. Any screams or cries that might escape through the gaps in the timbers would be swallowed up by the roar of the wind outside.

It was another four hours until dawn. Plenty of time for Vincent to extract the truth and the names of the others involved. He wanted to know everything. He had everything he needed in the bag he had also brought from his car into the barn. However long it was going to take, whatever needed to be done, no one was leaving until he was satisfied.

Alex stood partially hidden in the shadows, observing the proceedings. This was Vincent's domain.

In the middle of the floor between the two captives, Vincent had placed the battered aluminum attaché case. Kneeling down, he opened the lid, and quickly transferred the bricks of cash into the empty duffel bag he had taken from the back of Diane's vehicle. The process of taking back the money was important to Vincent. He wanted both of them to watch. To understand that what they had taken wasn't theirs to take. Some, like Joe Durango, thought it was their right to steal from the Romano family, that they had earned it. Vincent was about to correct the Millers on that misconception.

Greg Miller looked on in astonishment as he saw the bricks of cash. He glanced at Diane, looking for answers, but she averted her eyes.

When the case was empty, Vincent ran his fingers along the inside lining, to where it was buckled and split. He began pulling and bending and prying until he finally came away with a small object in his hand, a tiny rectangular box with a blinking light. He looked at it for a moment, then smiled an evil little smile.

From the shadows, Alex's breath caught in her throat when she saw the object in her brother's hand, realizing now it had all been a lie, realizing the depth of his deceit. It was a homing device, a way to track whoever had taken the case and the money inside it, provided the money was kept inside the case. Despite seething with the anger of not being told about the homing device, Alex held her ground in silence. It would be a discussion she would have with her brother later, when they were alone.

Unfortunately for Diane Miller, she had left the money inside the case. Ignorance was ultimately her downfall.

Vincent pocketed the homing device and turned his attention to the couple in front of him. Slipping out his handgun, he first approached Diane, ripped down her gag, and pressed the barrel to her forehead. "I'm going to give you just one chance to tell the truth. One chance only."

Diane gritted her teeth and swallowed the pain she felt. The race was over. She had lost.

"I found the money," Diane said.

"I don't believe you," Vincent replied, pressing the barrel of the gun harder, forcing Diane's head back at an acute angle.

Alex continued to watch from the shadows.

A muffled groan came from Greg Miller through the gag. His eyes were wide with confusion as he watched his wife.

"Was it his idea to steal it? Your husband?"

Another groan came from Greg Miller.

Diane Miller shook her head. "It was my idea. I found the money in the case on the side of the highway." She then went on to explain in intricate detail how she happened upon the battered attaché case when she was returning from town. How she had then hidden it, leaving out the details of the location of the storage unit with her old car inside.

"Who are you?" Vincent demanded, not believing a word she said.

"My name is Diane Miller. I'm a mother, a housewife from Hazard, Nebraska."

Vincent stared at Diane Miller incredulously. *A housewife?* She was lying. She had to be. There was more to it than just some random housewife stumbling across a case full of money on the side of the highway. "You're lying. You know Anton Wheeler. He was working with you both."

Tears started to run down Diane's face. The searing pain in her side getting too much to bear. "That's all I can say," she pleaded. "I'm not lying. I don't know any Anton Wheeler. I'm running from my husband. I wanted a new life. I found the case, saw what was inside, and took it."

Vincent watched Diane for a moment, undecided if he

should just shoot them both and be done. He left Diane, walked to where Greg knelt, and pulled down his gag. "Maybe you can tell me the truth."

Greg Miller glared at his wife. "I had no idea about the money," he said in desperation. "I had no idea she had stolen anything. You must believe me. It's her fault not mine. I'm innocent," Greg squealed like a cornered hog. His words gushing out with a spray of blood and spittle.

Vincent threw his head back at the ceiling and laughed. Everyone was lying to him. He looked back at Greg Miller. "Then how come we found the both of you together? With the money?" Vincent pointed his gun directly at Greg Miller's head. "You are either going to tell me the truth, or I'm going to kill you both in the next ten seconds."

"Diane?" Greg pleaded, his face stricken. "Tell them the truth. I had nothing to do with this. I had no idea about the money."

Diane looked up at Greg but said nothing. She turned and looked at where Alex stood, in the shadows, then replied. "I took the money. Not him. He has nothing to do with this," she finally conceded.

Alex eased herself out of the darkness and stood between the couple. First she looked at Greg Miller, then turned to face Diane Miller, searching the woman's eyes for the truth. Was she telling the truth? Had she really just happened across the case? Maybe the case was thrown free when the van had crashed. Alex was not so convinced now that they were a couple, working together to steal the money.

"Let's just get this over and done with," Vincent said impatiently to his sister. "They're not worth the time. Let's just kill them both right here, take the money, and leave."

Alex said nothing for a moment. She was interested in knowing more. Especially how this woman, a housewife from Nebraska, who had confided in her that she was fleeing from her husband, fearful of her life, ended up being the one who had stolen the money. The motive was clear. Diane Miller had revealed that much to her when their paths had unexpectedly crossed. She was going to start a new life, change her identity. Money gave her that ability. Her metamorphosis had already begun with the blond hair. Or, she could be just a clever little liar.

However, there was something else there, Alex could feel it in her gut. There was more to this.

She addressed Greg Miller first. "Why are you chasing your wife halfway across the state? What was so important?"

Greg took a deep breath and stared directly at Alex Romano defiantly. "She's my wife," he said. "She was leaving me. Running from our marriage."

"So? Move on." It seemed strange to Alex that Diane's husband would so vehemently pursue his wife. It was almost as if she had stolen the money from *him*, not from the Romano family. He wasn't telling the truth—or not all of it.

Alex turned to Diane. "Did he beat you?"

Vincent hung his head in frustration.

Alex ignored the look her brother was giving her. She focused instead on Diane Miller. "Look at me," Alex demanded of Diane, determined to get the truth out of the woman.

Diane Miller looked up and straight into Alex Romano's eyes.

"Did he beat you?" Alex repeated the question. "Did he abuse you at all?"

Diane's gaze shifted to her husband.

"I didn't lay a finger on her." Greg sneered at his wife with contempt, as though now he wished he had.

Alex nodded at her brother.

The retribution was swift and lethal. Enough to throw Greg Miller to the floor with one vicious punch. Vincent stood over the dazed, moaning form of Greg Miller. Then grabbed him by the scruff and hauled him up to his knees again.

"Shut your mouth, little man," Vincent hissed.

Alex turned her attention back to Diane, looking at her questioningly.

Diane shook her head. *No.*

"Let's just kill them and get it over with," Vincent pleaded again impatiently. "We've wasted enough time. We've got the money. That's all that's important."

Alex silenced her brother with a wave of her hand. She could see Vincent's anger turning on her, his eyes smoldering with disdain that she had intervened. But she didn't care. She would deal with her brother later. Her instincts were telling her that Diane Miller was telling the truth. But Greg Miller wasn't. Alex slowly walked to where Greg Miller knelt, her brother Vincent next to him, the gun pointed at the side of his head. She looked down at Greg Miller, remembering how panic-stricken he was to get past her and into the diner at the gas station. Their worlds had all nearly collided at that one moment. Paths of trajectory almost aligned. But somehow, each of them was slightly out of orbit, avoiding a momentous collision—until now. Now everything lined up and their paths had all intersected at the same moment in time and space.

But in Alex's mind, there was still a misalignment somewhere. And that misalignment was Greg Miller.

Stolen. Alex thought about the word she had considered when thinking about the reason Greg Miller was almost manic about finding his wife. Had his wife taken something from him? Something vital? This whole turn of events was about the stolen money. Yet, something was out of kilter. There was another missing piece.

"Did you plan to kill her?" Alex demanded of Greg. "When you caught up with her? Did you plan to kill her? Find her, bury her somewhere, and leave her for dead? But we interrupted your plans. Is that it?"

The side of Greg Miller's face ached, and his teeth rattled. But he pushed aside the pain. "You have to let me go," he croaked. "I know nothing about the money. I was not part of this. I just wanted to find my wife. Bring her home."

Alex look down at the man and smiled. The words that spewed from his mouth belied the hatred she saw behind the veil of his eyes. He didn't come after his wife to reason with her. To plead. He hunted his wife so that he could catch her and hurt her. Maybe even kill her. Alex now accepted that she was wrong. There was no missing piece. Diane Miller had acted alone, was running from her husband. Greg Miller was just a vengeful, murderous husband that couldn't bear the thought that his wife had left him.

"I took his cell phone."

Alex and Vincent turned in unison toward Diane Miller. It was just a whisper, barely audible above the pelting rain hammering off the tin roof and the howling wind.

Water dripped from a leak above. A section of tin sheeting above their heads rattled, threatening to peel open.

Greg, however, had heard clearly what Diane had said. He began to squirm against his bindings around his wrists, ignoring the cutting pain.

"What did you say?" Alex asked.

Diane Miller eyes never left her husband as she spoke. "He chased me because I took his cell phone. A secret cell phone he kept hidden from me. That's how he found me. I was stupid. Forgot that he could track me with it. I should have known. I used to fly drones in the army for heaven's sake." Diane felt sick. The oversight was going to cost her her life.

"Let me go," Greg pleaded again, more urgent this time. "Take the money. She stole it. I won't tell anyone. Won't say a word."

Alex cocked her head, urging Diane to go on, to explain.

Diane jeered at her husband. "He's been unfaithful. I caught him having an affair. So I took his cell phone. To see if there's proof on it. I'm sure there is. Texts and photos. If I can unlock it."

Vincent tapped his gun against his thigh. "So who cares if your husband is cheating?" Vincent turned to his sister. "Let's just kill them. Move on."

Alex dismissed Vincent again with her hand. "So where is this *secret* cell phone?"

"There's nothing on it," Greg Miller said frantically. "She's a lying bitch. I'm not having an affair. She's just jealous. She's to blame for our failed marriage, not me!" He turned to Vincent, pleading his case, begging for his life. "It's your money. I had no idea it existed. My wife is a thief. Let me go. You can have her. Do whatever you want with her. I don't care. I swear, I'll tell no one."

Diane glared at her husband. It was so pitiful to watch him grovel. *Do whatever you want with her?* Her husband's only concern now was his own self-preservation.

Greg Miller was relentless. His head swung back-and-forth between Vincent and Alex, trying to plead his case to anyone who would listen. Greg's eyes suddenly lit up. "I have money!" he gibbered enthusiastically. "Lots of money. You can have that too!"

Diane's eyes narrowed at the words Greg had just said.

"She's to blame for the marriage failing. She's to blame for our daughter killing herself. She's failed as a wife and as a mother."

Diane closed her eyes. The agony she now felt went beyond anything physical. She didn't want to admit to it. But, now maybe it was true after hearing Greg's words. Maybe Ella would have been alive now if Diane had been there for her daughter.

Alex shot a quick look at Greg Miller, then turned back to Diane Miller. "Your daughter committed suicide?"

Diane began to cry. It was too much. No amount of medication or how many times you tried to convince yourself you were getting stronger made any difference now. Her fragile self-belief began to unravel.

"My daughter, Ella," Diane sobbed, "killed herself twelve months ago."

Alex felt her chest constrict, the vessels around her heart involuntarily tighten as she watched a mother's grief slowly consume her.

Chapter 49

Monica called Charmers.

Got her out of bed. The request was above Monica's pay grade, but not her boss's.

Within sixty seconds, Monica brought her up to date with what had happened at the motel and the message Diane Miller had scrawled on the back of the bathroom door.

"Something has gone wrong," Monica explained. "She's in trouble. Her husband has taken her. Her car is gone, the room is empty, but some of her possessions are still there."

"Kidnapped?"

"Snatched more like it," Monica replied. "She definitely didn't go out for a late-night stroll with her husband. Greg Miller gained access to the room by stealth. He wasn't about to knock on the door and announce his arrival or his intentions to his wife."

"Why leave behind the backpack and the bondage toys?"

"I have no idea," Monica replied. That part didn't make sense. "Maybe Greg Miller was interrupted. Maybe he—"

"Already killed her?" Charmers completed the thought Monica didn't want to admit.

"But there was no blood. No sign of a struggle."

"And the motel manager? How's she faring?" Charmer's listened intently. Her young deputy would not have woken her at such an ungodly hour if it was not important, critical. The urgency in her deputy's tone was obvious.

"Head wound. Mild concussion. She's en route to the ER

now for observation." On the end of the line, Monica could hear her boss rummaging around, then a door closing.

"I need to pinpoint her cell phone," Monica said. "If I call it, chances are Greg Miller will answer and he'll know. And it's a new number…what she wrote on the bathroom door. It all fits with my theory of her fleeing from him. New cell phone. A different car. The blond hair. She's running for her life."

Monica gave Charmers the cell phone number that was scrawled on the bathroom door. Charmers told her she would call her back in two minutes. Monica sat inside her cruiser in the motel parking lot, tapping the steering wheel with her fingers, glaring at her cell phone, willing it to ring. A light drizzle was falling and the wind increased. Officer Swift had completed his door-to-door with the other two guests. None of them saw or heard anything. Swift decided to wait in the office for the owner of the motel who had been notified. Monica still held on to the master key for safekeeping. She would hand it over to local police once she had found Diane Miller.

Monica's cell phone buzzed.

"They managed to triangulate the signal. Took a bit longer than I hoped," Charmers said. "It appears to be stationary, which is a big help for you." The sudden gust of wind buffeted the side of the vehicle and leaves and stray branches tumbled into the parking lot. "It's off a road, literally a mile away from the motel where you are. Isolated, looks like the middle of a field. No fixed street address." Charmers sent through the location details. Seconds later, Monica's cell phone buzzed as the information landed. She opened up the map, rotated it on the screen, and zoomed out. "Got it."

"Monica," Charmers said, just before Monica hung up.

"What?"

"Get the local law enforcement involved. Call in some back-up."

"I will if it escalates. If it turns out he's grabbed her. I just want to make sure she is safe. It could be just a domestic between the two of them," Monica lied. She knew there was a lot more to it. But she wanted to collar Greg Miller without any local help.

"You get help if you need it," Charmers insisted.

"I promise."

"I mean it, Mons. Call me as soon as you know anything. Otherwise, I'll be calling North Platte PD and the sheriff's department myself."

"I understand." Monica ended the call and propped her cell phone up in the center console, checking the spot on the map. The location was in the middle of nowhere, no signs of buildings or key points of interest at all on the map. It was under a mile away from where she was. She wasn't going to notify the local police. This was a matter she had to follow up on.

No flashing lights. No siren. If Greg Miller had kidnapped his wife, Monica didn't want to spook him into doing something rash.

Through the windshield she could see Officer Swift walking across the windblown parking lot, making a gesture with his hand to her, as though twisting a key in a lock.

Ignoring him, Styles put her car in gear and roared out of the parking lot.

Chapter 50

"Where is this *secret* cell phone?" Alex asked again, keeping her eyes on Greg Miller, noticing how his head swiveled around in mild panic at the mention of his cell phone.

"You should know," Diane replied, looking at Vincent. "You took everything."

Alex gestured to her brother.

Reluctantly, Vincent slid out what he had taken from Greg Miller. The three cell phones.

Alex took the cell phones and held them up.

Diane nodded to the more expensive looking of the three. "The screen is locked." She nodded toward her husband. "It requires his face to unlock it."

"Which one is yours?"

Diane told her.

Alex pocketed Diane's cell phone, then handed one phone to her brother, the one Diane had taken from Greg's study drawer. "Get him to unlock it." She promptly stripped apart Greg's other cell, letting the pieces fall to the floor.

Vincent gave an exasperated look. "What difference does this make, Alex? We've wasted enough time."

"Now!" Alex said, more forcefully.

Begrudgingly, Vincent took the phone, stood in front of Greg Miller and pushed the screen toward his face, trying to capture the man's facial image.

Stubbornly, Greg Miller twisted his head every which way, his teeth clenched.

Vincent grabbed a handful of Greg Miller's hair, yanked his head back violently, then brought the phone toward his face. "Hold your damn head still," he snarled.

Alex called over to Greg. "Unlock the phone, or I will order my brother to shoot you in the head, right now."

Greg Miller stopped resisting and glared at Diane. Pure hatred burned in his eyes.

Vincent pushed the cell phone closer, within inches of Greg Miller's face. "Look directly at the screen," Vincent ordered.

Greg tensed, stared at the screen, then watched as dots danced, swarmed and converged, capturing his facial geometry, comparing it to the thirty thousand dots that comprised the unique facial image that was stored on the phone.

The phone unlocked. The home screen appeared. Vincent pushed Greg Miller away.

Alex held her hand out expectantly, and Vincent handed her the phone. She rapidly entered a new password, overriding the old one, then disabled all biometric locks. Now only she could access the cell phone. Alex walked away from the others, back into the shadows, thumbing the screen as she went.

Opening the phone's camera app and scrolling back, Alex saw dozens of tiny movie file thumbnails grouped chronologically. But, the most recent date was over twelve months ago. *Strange*, she thought, as she scrolled further back in time. Maybe Diane had imagined that her husband was recently fooling around. Either that, or he had broken off the affair soon after their daughter had died.

Alex had miscalculated. There were hundreds, not just dozens of movie files, each one time stamped with their duration in minuscule white digits in the bottom right hand corner of each thumbnail. Most of them appeared to be around thirty minutes long. Alex could see what looked like a tangle of limbs, arms and legs, in most of the tiny thumbnails. Too small however, to clearly see the people.

Alex glanced over her shoulder again to where Greg Miller was kneeling, then turned back to the phone, located the volume buttons on the side, and muted the sound. She went back two years, then selected a movie to watch.

Distressed, Greg Miller anxiously tried to see what Alex Romano was doing with his cell phone in the darkness. He turned back to Vincent. "Please." He was practically begging now. "Just let me go. I'm innocent in all of this."

Vincent ignored the man and walked toward his sister, then paused. She was just a few feet away, but the darkness that surrounded her was total. Vincent could just see the detached, ghostly glow of her head and shoulders, the bright screen of the cell phone inches from her face.

As he watched, he saw her tense suddenly. Then he saw her facial expression abruptly harden. Her eyes suddenly widen. Her facial muscles tighten. Her jaw muscles bunching. The clenching of her teeth.

Two minutes later, Alex had seen enough, and she strode out of the darkness a different person than what she had been two minutes prior. Her face was cast in stone, her eyes lacking any signs of life, her chin jutting outward. What she had seen could not be unseen. She would go to her grave knowing the truth— what really had happened to Ella Miller.

But Diane Miller wouldn't be allowed to know the truth. Alex would make certain of that. The poor woman had suffered enough. The death of her daughter had nearly destroyed her. And the footage on the cell phone, the small sample that Alex had just viewed—raw, homemade, but clear enough to see a young, distraught girl, with her father slithering over her in his own nakedness—would surely kill the housewife from Hazard, Nebraska.

Three sets of eyes followed Alex as she transitioned from the darkness back out into the light again.

Alex didn't meet any of their eyes. Saw none of them. Her eyes were staring straight ahead as she walked past all of them. Her mind was too preoccupied, trying to reconstruct the image, the face of Ella Miller in a happier light. Alex tried to imagine what the beautiful, young twelve-year-old girl would have been like. Before her innocence, wonder, and joy for life was so brutally and systematically blackened. The darkness had engulfed the young girl so completely that there was no possibility of light, not even a glimmer. Just an endless, bleak, wilting existence, from which her only escape was to take her own life. Ella's saving grace was to not leave a note, a clue as to why she had done what she had done. One parent knew why. The other was saved an eternity of pure self-guilt.

Alex finally met Diane's gaze, and saw there, in a mother's face, her daughter's eyes staring back at her from the grave. If Diane Miller knew what Alex Romano had seen, it would be a simple act of kindness just to shoot the woman here and now. Put her out of more eternal misery and bottomless despair that already was her life. There would be no possibility of healing for her if the truth was known.

But Diane Miller wasn't to blame. The blame fell squarely on one person.

Alex turned and faced a man whose eyes could not meet hers—Greg Miller.

Alex took a deep breath. Some good had to come from this.

"What was on the cell phone?" Vincent asked.

Alex said nothing. She went to where the duffle bag of cash sat in the corner and returned with it and dumped it on the floor next to Greg Miller.

"What are you doing?" Vincent asked. Perplexed by his sister's actions.

Ignoring her brother, Alex turned and addressed Diane Miller. Her voice cold and detached. "You have a simple choice: the money or your husband."

Despite his feet being bound, Greg Miller tried to rise. "Please—" he said before Vincent pushed him back down again.

Alex saw confusion in Diane's eyes. "Either you take the money, leave here, and never look back. Or you take your husband, you both leave, and the money stays."

Diane Miller's eyes swiveled to the bag of cash, then to her husband. She had two choices: Greg or the bag of money next to him. One. Not both.

"Either way," Alex continued, sliding the cell phone into her pocket, "the phone stays with me."

"Alex!" Vincent shouted, peeling away from Greg Miller's side, walking up to his sister, the gun wavering in his hand, uncertain as to who to point it at.

Alex held up a hand and shot him a glare that Vincent had never experienced before from anyone, halting him in his tracks. Alex checked her wristwatch, then casually folded her arms across her chest. "I'm going to give you thirty seconds to make a choice. Or, I will order my brother to kill you both."

Chapter 51

The windshield looked like it was molten glass, warped and distorted under the torrent of water lashing at it, the wiper blades useless under the deluge that seemed to have come out of nowhere.

Monica, hunkered behind the wheel, pressed on regardless, driving as if she were underwater, driving up stream, fighting the current that was determined to push her back.

The car crawled along the back road, the wind slamming into it in waves. Several times she thought something huge had hit the side of the vehicle, that something massive had loomed out of the eternal black and rammed into her, shunting the vehicle sideways.

But it was just the wind as the storm seemed to be reaching its peak.

Monica glanced at the map on her phone. She was less than half a mile away, but her progress was slow, almost walking pace. With such low visibility, she had to be careful or she would be pulled right off the road and end up in a ditch.

With dogged determination, Monica pressed the gas a little more.

She was nearly there.

Chapter 52

He was already a dead man.

"What's on the cell phone, Greg?" Diane asked.

Greg looked at Alex.

She just stood there, dead eyes affixed on him.

With his hands tied behind his back and his ankles bound, Greg Miller began to shuffle on his knees toward his wife, away from the bag of money. "Please, Diane," he begged. "Let's just go, the two of us. Put all this behind us. Make a new start."

Diane tilted her chin downward, her eyes narrowed, then emphasizing each word separately, she repeated, "What is on the cell phone?"

"What the hell are you doing, Alex?" Vincent growled. In one hand he still held his gun. His other hand was balled into a tight fist of building rage. "Why are you doing this? Why are you giving her the money? She stole it from us in the first place!"

Alex said nothing, just continued watching what was unfolding before her, between husband and wife. She already knew the choice Diane would make. Alex glanced at her watch again. "Ten seconds."

"Please! I beg you, Diane," Greg screamed. "Everything will be better. I promise. I'll give you whatever you want. I've got money."

Diane watched as her husband slowly collapsed into a blubbering, whining, excuse of a man. He kept edging forward on his knees toward her, tears streaming down his face. Despite all this, he refused to answer the one question Diane wanted answered. She shook her head slowly, anger boiling up her throat, threatening to choke her. She was right. She had been right all along. Her husband didn't just have one affair. He had many. The proof was on the hidden cell phone she had discovered.

"You bastard!" Diane spat at her husband, hitting his face, her saliva mixing with his tears.

Alex stepped forward. "Time's up."

Greg shook his head vehemently. "I promise, anything you want. I'll do whatever you want." Greg looked at his wife, then at the gun in Vincent Romano's hand.

It was a puzzle, with two solutions—both bad. He was going to die regardless.

Diane smiled, turned, and looked Alex squarely in the eye. "I'll take the money."

"No!" Greg Miller lurched forward—then fell face first into the cold cement.

Vincent brought the gun up. But instead of pointing it at Greg Miller or his wife, he pointed it directly at his sister.

Vincent's fingers tightened around the grip, his finger resting on the trigger. "She isn't taking the money, Alex."

Alex looked at her brother pointing the gun at her. His face twisted. His mouth and lips curled in a snarl. His eyes black, full of hatred and contempt. He began to squeeze the trigger. At this range he couldn't miss.

"This is my decision, Vincent. Not yours. I will take full responsibility." Alex turned her back on Vincent and went to Diane. She gently lifted the woman and undid her bindings.

Diane was unsteady on her feet. Alex held her by the arm as she handed Diane her cell phone and her car keys. With her back still turned, Alex produced something else from under the folds of her coat and pressed it into Diane's palm. "You should have listened to me before," Alex whispered.

Diane looked down at the gun in her hand, her husband's gun Alex had kept from the motel room. She looked up at Alex, gave a nod of mutual respect and understanding. No words were needed.

"Go," Alex commanded.

Diane stumbled forward, reached down, then hefted up the duffel bag and walked slowly toward the door, not looking back.

"You're finished," Vincent said, watching as Diane Miller and a million in cash disappeared again for the second time. He turned back to Alex. "The family will disown you. I'll make sure father knows about this. You will be cast out, expelled from the family."

Alex sighed wearily. She had had enough. Enough of the killing, the deceit, the dishonesty, the lies. All of it. Her last act was to do something good for someone who had experienced nothing but bad.

Alex slid out the cell phone, entered the code, and offered it up to Vincent. "Take a look."

Vincent stared at the phone clutched in his sister's extended hand. He faltered. The gun wavered. Finally, Vincent slowly lowered his gun and took the cell phone from her.

"Take your pick," she said, suddenly feeling very tired. "There's hundreds of them, and they're all the same."

Vincent watched dumbstruck as Alex turned and walked away.

As her heels swept past Greg Miller, who lay whimpering on the floor, she didn't bother looking down. She opened the side door of the barn and vanished into the swirling darkness beyond.

Chapter 53

Diane was drenched and racked in pain.

Her teeth chattered and her entire body shivered with a bone-numbing ache. She could easily just collapse, slip to the ground, and let exhaustion and the bitter cold wash over her. Despite all that, Diane pushed herself beyond the limits of what she thought she was capable of.

Hunched behind the wheel of her SUV, she fought to control the vehicle as it pitched and skidded along. She was driving away from the barn as fast as she could, leaving everything behind, all memories of Greg. His fate was his own doing.

She was driving too fast and she knew it. But she needed to escape, get away in case minds changed and they came after her. Or worse still, Greg somehow managed to escape and pursue her again.

Glancing in the review mirror, Diane saw nothing but black.

It was almost impossible to keep the vehicle straight. Everything around her was swaying violently back and forth. She didn't know if she was driving in the right direction to get to a main road or highway. She could be driving deeper into the remoteness for all she knew.

Wind and rain lashed at the vehicle, pushing it sideways at one point before Diane managed to correct the slide, turning the wheel, steadying the sway. She squinted through the sheets of water and whipped-up debris, the headlights providing a diffused dull glow, barely reaching a few feet ahead of the hood of the vehicle. There were no points of reference, no outlines, nothing to judge distance or direction.

The dirt road was gone, replaced with a brown, oily torrent filled with a myriad of fallen debris, branches sheared from their trunks. Small tree trunks ripped from the earth then hurled. A section of fence wire, ripped, twisted, and torn from its post. Diane concentrated furiously as she navigated through the debris field and the constant blizzard of airborne vegetation that rolled across the windshield and headlights.

The wiper blades thrashed violently, pushing solid walls of water aside.

Diane couldn't feel her lips. Her cheeks were numb. Her ankles and wrists sore from where she had been bound, and her side burned in pain from the effort of hauling the duffle bag into the back of her SUV. Her hair was soaked, plastered to her head and face. She went to rub her eyes, then grimaced as her fingers came away in a watery red dribble. She touched her forehead, felt a deep laceration, the edge of torn skin, followed by the inevitable sting of raw pain. She knew something had struck her as she stumbled away from the barn. A flying object, a piece of debris, a tree branch, perhaps. Thought nothing of it. Just had to escape.

More blood dribbled into her eyes, and she wiped it away with her sleeve. Her medical kit was in the back, too far to reach. Too insane to try. She would patch herself up later—and there would be a later. A point in time in the near future when she would feel safe again. She was determined to. Alex Romano had given her a second chance, and Diane wasn't going to be content to die trying.

Lightning burst all around her, followed by exploding thunder, like a nuclear bomb detonating overhead. The roof and side panels shuddered and vibrated.

The terrain dipped and began to slope downward. Diane eased off the gas a fraction. The steering wheel went sluggish in her hands as she felt the sensation of the rear end beginning to swing around behind her. The hood dipped some more. She tried to brake but couldn't halt the vehicle angling sideways. The SUV continued its slew through the mud, churning and plowing as it went, burrowing deeper, until it finally came to rest.

Glancing down at the gears, Diane cursed. In her haste to leave the barn, to escape, to run, she forgot to put the vehicle into four-wheel-drive. She was driving on two-wheel traction.

She changed gears and gunned the engine. The tires squealed and the rear of the SUV lifted as the tires skidded in the soggy ground. The vehicle lunged, faltered, then slid back again. Diane screamed and pummeled the steering wheel with both fists. She took her foot off the gas. She needed to calm down, assess the situation, problem-solve it but not panic.

She undid her seatbelt and pushed the door open. Outside she was assaulted by the pummeling wind. Rain pelted her face; her feet sank into the thick, muddy quagmire. Her feet made sucking noises as she pulled them free and wrestled around to the rear of the vehicle.

The taillights gave off some illumination. Diane pulled out her flashlight. One wheel was almost completely submerged in the mud, the SUV tilting down in one corner. As Diane looked hopelessly at the buried wheel, her hopes sank a little further too. She needed to get out of there. She couldn't walk. All her gear was in the vehicle. And there was no way she could carry the duffel bag full of cash more than ten feet in this weather.

She panned the flashlight around and spied a broken log a few feet away. She staggered toward it, the wind pushing and jostling her back like a defensive tackle. She fought on, determined not to die in some mud-festering hole.

Reaching the log, Diane dragged it back to her vehicle, ignoring the searing pain in her side. She dropped it next to the front of the tire, then wedged it hard against the tread, stomping it down with her foot into the watery mud, cursing with each stomp, until the log could move no more.

Lightning pulsed across the sky. Seconds later the boom of rolling thunder crushed down on her, rattling her chest, numbing her ears. Delirious with the pain in her side, Diane fought her way back along the side of the vehicle.

Then a wide blade of light hit her from behind.

Diane turned to see headlights coming at her.

Another vehicle. It was Greg. They had let him go. Panic gripped her and her mind wavered.

The vehicle pulled up behind Diane. She raised her arm, to cover her eyes from the blinding glare, struggling to see the driver.

A person climbed out, their shape distorted by the headlights and deluge of rain.

Diane wasn't going back, back to her old life with Greg. She teetered on the brink of consciousness.

Then another burst of brilliant white raked across the sky followed by an immense crack of thunder, closer this time.

"Diane!"

Her name.

It was Greg. He would kill her for sure. Diane began to shake uncontrollably, hypothermia and fear racing each other through her body. Water invaded her eyes. She couldn't see straight. Couldn't think straight. The figure was getting closer. It was Greg looming out of the darkness toward her.

Desperation took over. The will to live not to die. Diane

would join Ella one day, someday, but not today.

A flashlight cut across the darkness, painting Diane's face white, blinding her momentarily. Her training kicked-in. She fumbled into a side pocket, her fingers searching, finding, then closing around cold steel.

Her mind screamed. It had to end. It had to end now. The woman was right, when she had given Diane advice.

Self-Defense.

Diane had to stop running.

"Diane!" Greg yelled.

Diane brought the gun out and up. The front sight wavered back-and-forth over the center mass of Greg as he moved toward her. He stopped. "Dian—"

Another crack of thunder, then a small burst of lightning.

Monica Styles couldn't breathe. Water filled her eyes, her nose, her mouth, even her ears. Ahead she could see the vehicle in front of her, caught in the twin glare of her police cruiser. The license plate clearly illuminated. It was Diane Miller's SUV. The white Trailblazer.

"Diane!" Monica hollered.

There she was, Diane Miller, standing next to the SUV, her face deathly pale, colorless. Blond hair plastered to her skull, gaunt features, skittish eyes, wide with fear.

Grim-faced, Styles pressed forward, chin down, leaning into the wind that threatened to topple her. *Thank God*, Monica thought. *I've found her.*

The wind surged, pushing the rain sideways, smacking Monica in the face, momentarily blurring everything in front of her. A wave of horizontal water swept past, the air cleared for a moment between surges. Monica brought her flashlight up and shined it directly at Diane Miller's face. She had to make certain it was her.

She yelled again, "Diane!" The words were ripped away as soon as they had left her blue lips, the sound reconfigured amongst the torrent of wind and rain. A woman's pitch lowered to a man's deeper tone.

Monica watched as Diane Miller brought her hand out of her pocket, bringing her arm up to acknowledge her. To wave?

No!

Imminent danger swamped Monica's mind. She watched in horror, the seconds unfolding fast, too fast. Nothing was in slow motion as she had been led to believe in moments like this—when death came speeding toward you. When you needed to react first, not last.

Her hand went to her hip, to her gun. The response automatic. No thought process. Just the primal urge to stop a threat. To save her own life, and the life of another.

Too late.

Another burst of lightning. Not from above, but from in front of Monica. Then the sound of a dull crack traveling behind the flash of light.

Monica felt something hit her, ram into her stomach, a tight fist of pain. Her legs went from under her. She collapsed, her knees smacking, then sinking, into the mud. She knelt there, upright, her head down, staring at the watery mud, wondering why it was turning red. She lifted her head and saw Diane Miller turn away.

The swirling world around Monica slowly turned opaque, black edges drawing in toward the center of her vision, all light shrinking to a pin prick. Just before total darkness finally closed in front of her face, Monica felt something die inside her.

She toppled forward, face-first into the mud.

Chapter 54

From underneath the shelter of the awning outside the barn, Alex stood next to the SUV and looked up at the threatening sky.

Clouds spun and boiled overhead, a glowing, conical mass of silvery-gray. The storm was moving away, clearing from the east, breaking up as it slowly twisted itself to the west. The air was brittle with cold, thick with dampness, buzzing with electricity.

Three gunshots echoed out from inside the barn.

Alex didn't flinch, didn't turn toward the sound.

The side door of the barn opened, and Vincent stepped out. Grim-faced and staring straight ahead, he avoided Alex's eyes, walked past her, climbed into the SUV, and started the engine.

After ten minutes of driving in silence, Vincent finally spoke. "It changes nothing," his voice restrained. "What I saw on that cell phone changes nothing. You shouldn't have given the woman the money. *Our* money."

"You lied to me," Alex retorted. "You knew all along about the homing device inside the case, and yet you chose to keep it from me."

Vincent remained silent.

Alex knew Greg Miller was going to die regardless of what Diane Miller's choice was. Despite all other sins, the Romano family had a strict moral code: no harm to children and swift retribution to those who did. Deliberately, Alex had handed Diane Miller a *Morton's fork*, a false dilemma. If her husband had revealed to his wife what was on the cell phone, she would most certainly have chosen the money, left her husband behind to suffer the consequences. But he refused to tell Diane, which left her no option but to take the money and leave her husband anyway. Either way, the outcome was the same for Greg Miller. He was offered the chance of short-lived redemption, though. Alex was keen to see if he would take it, if there was a glimmer of remorse in his black heart. Being the person he was, however, he preferred, even then, not to reveal his vile, heinous acts to his wife.

Vincent was going to kill Greg Miller anyway. The fact that he was consistently abusing his own twelve-year-old daughter made the task just that more enjoyable. The act, however, did not quell the burning contempt Vincent felt for his sister by allowing Diane Miller to walk with the family money. "I'm going to speak to father as soon as I can, in person when we return home. Tell him what you did. Tell him I found the money, had it in my very hands, in my possession, then you decided to give it away to some woman who had stolen it from us in the first place."

Alex sat with her head pressed up against the window glass, her eyes shut, her mind elsewhere. She expected nothing less from Vincent. To go running to their father at the first opportunity and tell him what had happened.

"I couldn't get a signal from it." Vincent looked at his sister, attempting to justify his secrecy. "I was going to tell you when it started working. It must have been damaged, the transmitter. When I was absolutely certain that the signal was correct, and it was reliable, I would have told you. Until then, I was just as much in the dark as you, Alex."

In the dark. Alex doubted that. Her brother had deliberately misled her. Kept her out of the loop. Withheld vital information from her about this assignment that made her feel somehow hamstrung from the very outset. A passenger just to appease her father.

The revelation left Alex wondering about what else Vincent hadn't told her. Operational information about the business. Countermeasures. His alliances. His channels of communication. His allies and his enemies, both inside and outside the family business.

"I tried to get it to work," Vincent went on to explain. "Believe me. But the signal wasn't reliable. It was intermittent. I tried as soon as I had been notified that one of our vans was missing, that the money on board had potentially been stolen." Vincent continued to stare out of the windshield as he drove. "I got nothing. The transmitter was either malfunctioning or damaged." He glanced at his sister. Her face was full of resentment. "I even tried that evening in your room. Before you returned."

Alex believed not a word that came out of her brother's mouth. This wasn't sibling rivalry. It was pure treachery.

Was this his plan? Alex thought. Was this a sign of things to come? To slowly push her aside, out of the business once their father died? To be drip-fed information only on a need-to-know-basis. On the assumption that Alex, as *Consigliere*, didn't need to know everything in order to function properly in her role within the family?

"You should've told me, Vincent. Instead you kept it from me. I could've helped. Wasn't my opinion, my input, important to you on this task?"

"Like I said, there was no point in telling you anything unless I was certain where we were going. The transmitter must have been damaged," Vincent repeated. "That's all I can put it down to. The van had crashed. You saw the condition of the case."

"When did you have them installed?" Alex asked.

"Do you honestly think I would let that amount of money be driven around without keeping track of where the vans were at all times?"

Alex shook her head in disbelief.

"It would've been implausible for you to think like that. To believe each case inside each van didn't also have its own tracker. Too much money is involved." Vincent gave a self-congratulatory nod. "And, as this whole event has proven, I was right."

Not for the first time on this trip had Alex made a critical tactical error when it came to her brother. She should have known better. Should have learned. This assignment was as much about getting a glimpse into the future of the Romano family, under the governance of Vincent Romano, as it was about recovering the stolen money.

As they drove on, distancing them from yet another violent aftermath, Alex felt like Abel being led down the path by Cain—an unsavory outcome awaited her at the end of this journey.

She was a realist, not an optimist. Her father had at best only two more years to live. What he hadn't confided about his medical condition, she had found out on her own from his doctors and medical specialists. The diagnosis was not good. The prognosis—her prediction about the future, her future and that of the family—was even worse: blood and violence under the mantle of her brother.

The last few days had been but a sample, a taste of the reign of terror that was coming when Vincent stepped off the path to pursue his own ends rather than follow in their father's footsteps. Footsteps that Alex had so tiresomely counseled her father to take in recent months, to alter course, to shift the family direction. Away from the dark history of spilled blood and unfettered brutality toward a more legitimate, bloodless existence.

Alex watched her brother. It was now all in vain—her subtle, and less than subtle, efforts over the years to change course. She would have no influence, no say in the course her brother was so eager to take when he took the helm.

"Who else knew about the homing devices?" Alex asked.

"No one except me, and father of course."

So even her own father had kept that vital piece of information from her.

"We didn't trust any of the others in the laundry business."

We? The word excluded her. She had been passed over, circumvented. "So who do you trust, Vincent?"

Vincent gave a sly smile as he focused on the road ahead. "I trust myself." He turned to his sister. "I'm comfortable with who I am. How I am. That's all that matters."

Anger flared in Alex's eyes. Her jaw tight, teeth clenched. "I should have been told about the transmitters."

"Well, father didn't seem to think you needed to know. And I concurred with him."

It felt like a slap in the face to Alex. A double betrayal. Father and brother.

"I am *Consigliere* of this family, Vincent. Not you."

Not for long, Vincent thought. Plans were already in motion. Upon returning to New Jersey, his sister would be stripped of her role and power within their hierarchy. Vincent Romano was an impatient man. Not the kind to wait for his father's worsening health to finally claim him. Luca Romano was a weak man already. The time to act was now. Others were waiting in the wings. Over the past months, Vincent had stacked the ranks, key positions both inside and outside the family, with his loyalists. Ready to take up arms if required. A purge would be initiated.

Alex would be the first casualty of that purge. Collateral damage.

"I know you are Consigliere," Vincent replied, his words sounding hollow. Unconvincing.

Thinking back, it all made sense to Alex. Vincent's obsession with his cell phone, how he kept referring to it constantly. He was trying to get the transmitter to work, infuriated by the intermittent signal. And yet he still didn't confide in her.

"Double overage," Vincent continued, rather proud of himself. "That's what the transmitters were. Always have a backup plan, little sister. You should know that about me by now. It's a pity you haven't learned anything in these last few days."

Little sister. Alex turned and watched her brother carefully. Thinking about what he had just said.

"Always have a backup plan," he repeated thoughtfully, reflecting on the phrase. "And never tell anyone or trust anyone with that plan."

Alex watched another cold, raw dawn. Another killing. Another tainted departure. She felt dirty, stained, like she hadn't washed in weeks. Grit and dirt on her skin, under her nails, her hands soiled. What filled her nostrils and coated her eyes wasn't a smell, however. It was an existence, her life so far.

Good things or bad things happened under the cold, murky veil before dawn. Before the sun rose to chase away the darkness and bring color and light into the world. Alex, however, only saw a bleak dawn.

Despite what her brother had said, she had learned a lot during the last few days—especially about him. And no lesson was as important as how something so benign, so innocent as a child, could grow into something so cancerous and malevolent.

Chapter 55

"Diane Miller has vanished," Meredith Charmers said, looking across at her deputy.

"So has her vehicle. State Patrol as well as the Lincoln County Sheriff's Department are out searching for both. She could be anywhere by now."

Light spilled in through the window as Monica Styles sat propped up in the bed. Charmers went silent when a nurse entered the room and took Monica's vitals again, recording the information on the chart clipped to the bed, before drifting out again.

It had been a week since Monica had been rushed into surgery, and she had only been fully conscious for the last few days. Charmers had been busily coordinating a cross-county hunt for Diane Miller but so far, the woman seemed to have eluded everyone.

"Are you sure it was Diane who shot you?"

Since waking, Monica had been asking herself the same question. For hours she lay gazing out the window, thinking about that fateful night, trying to piece together her fragmented memory of what had happened. She remembered getting out of her own vehicle during the height of the storm, seeing Diane Miller's SUV stuck in the mud on the side of the road with someone standing next to it. The rest was a blur.

"I can't be certain," Monica replied. "My memory is still patchy." Monica glanced at the flowers Charmers had brought her. A bright bunch of sunflowers sat in a tall vase on the window ledge. Charmers hated hospitals and wanted to bring something bright and colorful to cheer up the otherwise sterile room.

Monica had relived every moment, every drop of rain, every gust of wind that night, and yet the face of the person who shot her still eluded her. She shifted in annoyance, trying to get comfortable, then resting her hand subconsciously on her stomach, tears reaching the edges of her eyes.

Charmers squeezed her arm. "Don't worry about it. We know for certain that Greg Miller is dead."

"Tell me what you found," Monica said.

"He was executed as far as we could tell, in a barn maybe half a mile from where you were found. His hands and feet bound. It looked like a drug deal gone wrong. There was an empty attaché case next to him, the kind you use to carry cash in. That's when the Feds stepped in. They believe he was involved with organized crime. It's rumored they are following up a lead to a crime family from New Jersey."

Monica nodded and closed her eyes for a moment.

"There was obviously more to Greg Miller than we thought," Charmers said.

"He was hiding plenty of dirty secrets," Monica whispered, her voice drifting.

"And get this," Charmers continued.

Monica opened her eyes and continued to listen, feeling slightly drowsy from the painkillers. The surgeon said once the stitches were removed, she would just have a tiny scar. Nothing more. There was a much larger scar in her mind, though, one that would never vanish.

"The odd thing is, we found Diane Miller's therapist, a Dr. Amelia Redding. She was gagged and bound in the trunk of her car for at least two days."

"You're kidding me."

Charmers shook her head. "Found her in the underground garage of the building where she was working. She wasn't Diane's regular therapist. He was on a leave of absence, and Dr. Redding was just standing in for him while he was away."

"Poor woman. Do you have any leads on what happened?"

"She's okay now. A little dehydrated, but apart from that, she'll recover. She didn't get a good look at her assailant. Apparently he wore a mask and didn't say much, just threatened her with a knife and told her not to scream. More like a warning than a mugging."

"It doesn't sound like some random attack. It seems all connected. I get the distinct feeling Greg Miller was involved."

Charmers agreed. "I'm working with local police. We're talking to Dr. Farrell, her previous therapist. There seems to be some connection there with Greg Miller. I think Diane's husband was a control freak. Exerted undue influence over his wife and anyone she associated with."

"Men," Styles uttered as she began to drift off again, her eyelids getting heavier. "There's a common thread running through all this."

Charmers went on to explain how they had also discovered a similar execution-style killing just outside the town of Broken Bow, west of Hazard. "A petty criminal who traded in stolen commercial vehicles. Had all the same trademarks as the Greg Miller killing." Charmers glanced at the food tray that sat untouched on the trolley table next to the bed. "You going to eat that?" she asked, eyeing the bagel and jelly.

Monica smiled, then waved her hand. "Go for it. The thought of food makes me want to puke."

"Thanks," Charmers said gratefully, reaching for the bagel.

"I've been running on just coffee for the last twenty-four hours. It's been a nightmare trying to keep up with this. Multiple county jurisdictions. Local police, and now the Feds."

"The Broken Bow killing supports the theory that Greg Miller was involved in something nasty. Keeping it from his wife." Monica said. "Maybe she found out about the criminal activity he was caught up in, so he threatened her to keep quiet and she fled."

Charmers nodded between mouthfuls. "So he goes after her, without realizing he's also being hunted." Charmers finished eating and dusted herself off. "Now, do you want some good news?"

"Is there any?" Monica replied skeptically. It had been nothing but bad news since she'd regained consciousness. She would make a full recovery, she had been told. That was something positive at least.

Charmers tilted her hand up and down. "Yes and no. We found a pair of men's shoes in the closet at the Miller house. There were traces of blood and tissue on the soles and on the heels that matched the DNA of Miles Burke. Looks like Greg Miller tried to clean the shoes but made poor work of it."

Monica breathed a sigh of relief. That was good news. She was right after all. In a weird twist of fate, even though they hadn't actually caught Greg Miller, he was a brutal murderer who ended up being murdered himself. The irony was not lost on the two women. Who said there was no justice?

"Anton Wheeler came out of his coma as well."

"And you spoke to him?"

Charmers nodded. "Apparently he just stole the truck so he could sell it for cash, chasing some piece of ass in Vegas. He was going to meet up with her, but I ruined his plans."

Monica moved again, trying to get comfortable. ""Broken Bow?"

"I thought so too. Seems where Wheeler was heading, to meet the guy who was also killed."

"It's all connected."

Charmers let out a long sigh. "Seems like it." Then she went uncharacteristically somber. "I also went to his funeral, Miles Burke, a few days ago," she said, a hint of sadness in her voice. "I was the only one in attendance—except for the priest and the undertaker, who was keen to fill in the grave."

That was sad, Monica thought. To die alone. Unclaimed.

"Couldn't find any next of kin," Charmers said.

"Makes you realize how lucky you really are," Monica whispered. Her voice removed, detached. She slowly rubbed her stomach, the stitches itchy.

The two women sat in silence for a few minutes, each alone with their own thoughts. Monica thought about Miles Burke. The poor man had been brutally murdered for no reason. Brought into the world, loved and raised as a son, maybe even as a brother to others, only to die alone, no one there to mourn the loss. Both women knew it happened a lot, was the harsh reality. But it still left them wondering what had happened along the way that he ended up homeless and destitute, living off the streets. What had gone so horribly wrong?

Charmers brightened up and forced a smile, determined to lift the mood in the room. "There's plenty of time, Monica."

Monica smiled. She regarded Charmers not as her boss, but as an older sister, or perhaps even a surrogate mother.

"You're young." Charmers eyes twinkled, moist with her own gathering tears. "Healthy, and you'll make a great mother." She squeezed Monica's arm again.

Monica could no longer resist the pull of the drugs and gave in to their warm, sleepy caress. Her eyelids closed as she finally drifted off, but not before her lips moved and she mumbled, "Someday."

Charmers stood up, bent across and kissed Monica on the forehead. She then stood back and tilted her head, looking down affectionately at her deputy. "Someday."

Chapter 56

The phone call would last only two minutes.

Unbeknownst to the caller, however, it would cost him ten thousand dollars. Cheap compared to the million-dollar alternative and the likelihood of the recipient of the call stopping a bullet with their skull if they failed to answer the phone when it rang or strayed from the carefully crafted and rehearsed script that had been placed in front of them less than an hour ago.

For Jasper Collins, the New Jersey bookie in question, it was a simple choice that Gabriel Costa, a man of few words, had laid out for Collins on his desk: a loaded silenced Beretta or a plain envelope stuffed with fifty-dollar bills. By the time the call was over, Jasper Collins was going to get one or the other. As to which one would be entirely up to how he conducted himself during the next two minutes.

Some would have called it fortuitous that when Jasper Collins's cell phone began to ring, the device—sitting inert between the gun and the money—happened to vibrate its way across the desk toward the envelope stuffed full of cash.

A sure sign, indeed.

As instructed, Collins waited until the fifth ring before answering the call. He looked up at Costa, who was perched casually on one corner of the desk.

Costa nodded.

Collins brought the cell phone to his ear. "Mr. Romano, I've been expecting your call." Collins listened for a few moments, his eyes shifting back and forth between the two alternatives on the desk in front of him. It wasn't a huge amount of money, the cash in the envelope. More of a token gesture of appreciation for two minutes of his time. However, the huge disincentive the alternate choice represented motivated Collins to pick the one he much preferred.

"I understand, Mr. Romano," Collins said. "Let me just say that it was a private matter between your son and myself. I can assure you that—"

Collins was cut off as Luca Romano continued to castigate the bookie. Collins nodded. "I agree. Under normal circumstances As a policy, I do not extend that much credit to my clients. But your son"—Collins paused for effect rather than being lost for words—"was very insistent that he was good for the amount." Collins paused again as another probing question was asked of him. "It was close to one million dollars that he owed me. It had built up over a six-month period. Lady Luck, it would seem, was not on your son's side."

Collins fielded another question. "That's right. The debt was repaid in full by your son, directly into my bank account. The matter is now closed."

Collins listened intently for another moment. The next claim by Luca Romano had been anticipated and brought a mere shrug of the shoulders. "I can only speculate, given the size of the debt owed by your son, Mr. Romano, that he *would* deny all knowledge of such things, including me, to save face so to speak."

Collins's facial expression relaxed slightly. "Absolute confidentiality is assured, Mr. Romano. As it is with all my clients, no one will ever know." Collins's eyes shifted to the envelope of cash and he licked his lips, almost tasting the wads of cotton fiber paper. "Thank you, Mr. Romano. I fully understand. We will never speak of this matter again." Collins ended the call.

The transaction was complete. The deceit absolute.

Costa retrieved his handgun, and Collins slid the envelope of cash into the top drawer of his desk, not before dabbing the sweat from his brow with a red paisley pocket square he had taken from his jacket.

At the doorway, Costa, a man of few words, spoke. "Alex Romano is grateful for your co-operation and for your discretion."

"And what of her brother, Vincent?" It was one thing to lie to Luca Romano. It was another matter entirely to make that lie about his son. "What if he finds out? Decides to come after me for lying to his father?"

Costa looked around the small office, then selected his next words appropriately. "The odds of that happening are nil." And with that cryptic answer, Costa was gone, leaving Jasper Collins pondering what the man of few words had meant.

Chapter 57

Bursts of blood-reds and coral-pinks floated, suspended in the air. Azaleas in full bloom hung from overhead baskets and spilled from terracotta pots.

It was mid-morning, and the encroaching sun had just breached the stone steps of the sheltered terrace that overlooked the expanse of lawn and ornate gardens.

Black coffee and toast were the order of the day. Alex Romano folded and placed aside the newspaper she had just finished reading and smiled. It was still front-page news.

Ordinarily, she wouldn't welcome such attention for her family, being splashed all over the front page of the newspapers and the online news sites. However, that was a necessary consequence.

The story originally broke three days ago and was still getting mileage. Maybe it was a slow news cycle, nothing else more interesting to broadcast.

Alex had weathered the storm, as she had planned. So had the family. But it had taken every skill, every subtle, and not so subtle, psychological tool and trick in her extensive arsenal to appease her father. To convince, persuade, then eventually assure him the family was well-protected and completely insulated from any fallout. Only after he had calmed down, could Alex broach the subject of what needed to happen next. *He who hesitates loses*, Alex had told herself during those darkest, lonely hours when she was putting the finishing touches to her ascension.

Now was the time for bold moves. So, Alex carefully

counseled her father that life had to continue as normal, especially within the family structure. A united front had to be presented to the public, to say that what had happened in Nebraska was unfortunate and to display genuine empathy for all involved—especially the dead and their families. For the benefit of her father—himself an avid gardener despite having an army of household staff on hand—Alex drew the analogy of a tree, where one branch had suddenly become infected with a disease. The course of action she then prescribed, so as to protect the rest of the tree—the family tree in this instance—was to cut off the branch immediately, stop the contamination from spreading, and then discard the rotten limb.

Not surprisingly, it was a relatively easy argument for Alex to win. Luca Romano always put the needs of the family as a whole before the needs of any individual family member. Even if that family member was your only son, the heir apparent.

Luca Romano took Alex's sage advice, telling her that she was correct—as always. However, the said branch of the tree in question would never be completely discarded as her analogy suggested. Alex agreed. She would always have a brother and her father would always have a son. However, it was unlikely, after speaking at length to the family lawyers, that anyone would be seeing Vincent Romano anytime soon unless they were willing to undertake the six-hour drive, three hundred fifty miles west to the Attica Correctional Facility, a maximum security prison in the town of Attica, near Buffalo.

Alex certainly had no intention of ever making the trip but did not share this with her father.

Breaking with tradition, Alex then advised her father that she would, unlike him, not require the services of a *Consigliere* of her own. As a woman, she was more than capable of making her own decisions. She had made some significant decisions already just to move to this point. She quelled her father's concerns by telling him she would defer to him from time to time for advice, if she saw fit, and if his ailing health permitted.

He was pleased knowing this.

And then it was done. Her father's blessing was given, and everything else was, as they say—history.

Alex took a deep breath, savoring the rich earthy smell that surrounded her: newly turned soil, freshly cut grass, and pruned foliage. She instructed the gardeners to be brutal…to cut and hack and clear away the dead and the decaying. But new growth was coming. New shoots were emerging already, and she was curious to see how her designs would take shape in the coming months.

She glanced at the newspaper again, wondering who the anonymous person was who had tipped off the police and the FBI that led to Vincent Romano being arrested for a double homicide in Nebraska. Apparently the authorities had in their possession a gun with Vincent's prints and DNA on it, as well as a ballistic match to the two execution-style killings.

The evidence was as condemning as it was irrefutable.

Alex gave another smile as a man clad in a white-buttoned jacket appeared silently next to her and carefully topped up her cup from a silver gooseneck coffee pot.

"Thank you," Alex said, when he finished pouring.

"Domina." The man bowed slightly before retreating.

Chapter 58

The local children called her, *La mujer triste*. The sad woman.

For they had never seen her smile in the six months since she first stepped off the small launch from the mainland. She had stood on the tiny dock, her physique pale and thin, her eyes hidden by dark glasses, her face obscured by a wide, practical sun hat, a few strands of red showing from underneath.

She watched the colorful fishing boats bobbing up and down in the sheltered harbor for a moment, as though contemplating if it was a mistake to have come there.

Then as the days became weeks, and the weeks stretched into months, she began to transform, both inside and out. Her skin toughened, her frame thickened, her limbs and mind strengthened as she went from a milky alabaster to honey gold, then to the sun-drenched molasses she was now.

Some of the locals, who were up at dawn, often saw the *sad woman* hiking along the cliffs amongst the thistle and rocky outcrops that ringed the town and harbor below. She moved with purpose, with newfound vigor and determination, as though she was constantly being followed or chased.

Then there were times, when the heat of the day began to subside and the warm land wind reversed into a cooling afternoon sea breeze, she could be seen out at the lighthouse on the edge of the seawall. She cut a lonely figure, her red hair billowing, her gaze turned outward toward the endless blue waters as though searching for something on the horizon.

She was generous, though, and loved the children who

followed her around the market place, always sparing a few coins to drop into their tiny hands when they pointed out to her the freshest fish or the sweetest and most succulent fruit to buy.

At dusk, when the sky and the ocean were melding into one smoldering haze of burnt orange, and the first of the evening lights began to wink along the coastline, she wandered down from the small villa she rented high up among the rocky pinnacles and sat in a lounge chair on a secluded shingle beach, where she read and watched the sun gently sink into the Pacific Ocean.

In the evening she vanished like a ghost. She did not frequent the many outdoor restaurants and numerous bars that dotted the waterfront. She much preferred to retreat to the safety and seclusion behind the walls of her villa and sit out on a small, stone terrace under the stars, drinking red wine and watching the lights of the cruise ships anchored farther out in the bay.

No longer did she look so emancipated and hollow. She had put on weight, thanks to a diet of local fresh fish, caught daily and sold off the back of the fishing boats in the harbor, and locally-sourced produce she bought from the market in the town square.

She had tried to forget that fateful night when she was caught up in the wind and the rain, surrounded by ghostly faces and fragmented voices. It was behind her, gone, and so was the woman she had once been.

Most days, she could be found in the small walled garden at the rear of the villa. It was a place of solitude and quiet reflection she had carved out of the dirt and rock with her own bare hands, bringing in bags of nutrient-rich soil sourced from a local farmers market. The plants she had propagated from seed then loved and nurtured, now stood as tall and as strong as her. Big golden florets the size of dinner plates, circled by thick, broad petals of neon yellow, lifted their upturned faces, tracking the sun as it arced across the sky.

A single stemmed sunflower always sat in a glass vase next to her bed. It was the first thing she saw upon rising and the last thing she saw when she closed her eyes at night. That and the framed picture that sat next to the sunflower.

The two things of radiant joy and beauty in her life. One would eventually wither and die. The other—the memories—would live on forever in her heart.

THE END.

If You Enjoyed This Book

Thank you for investing your time and money in me. I hope you enjoyed my book and it allowed you to escape from your world for a few minutes, for a few hours or even for a few days.

I would really appreciate it if you could post an honest review on any of the publishing platforms that you use. It would mean a lot to me personally, as I read every review that I get and you would be helping me become a better author. By posting a review, it will also allow other readers to discover me, and the worlds that I build. Hopefully they too can escape from their reality for just a few moments each day.

For news about me, new books and exclusive material then please:

- Follow me on Facebook
- Follow me on Instagram
- Subscribe to my Youtube Channel
- Follow me on Goodreads
- Visit my Website: www.jkellem.com

About The Author

JK Ellem was born in London and spent his formative years preferring to read books and comics rather than doing his homework.

He is the innovative author of cutting-edge popular adult thriller fiction. He likes writing thrillers that are unpredictable, have multiple layers and sub-plots that tend to lead his readers down the wrong path with twists and turns that they cannot see coming. He writes in the genres of crime, mystery, suspense and psychological thrillers.

JK is obsessed with improving his craft and loves honest feedback from his fans. His idea of success is to be stopped in the street by a supermodel in a remote European village where no one speaks English and asked to autograph one of his books and to take a quick selfie.

He has a fantastic dry sense of humor that tends to get him into trouble a lot with his wife and three children.

He splits his time between the US, the UK and Australia.

Printed in Great Britain
by Amazon